HITCHHIKERS TO EARTH

LINDA NOVAK

Continental
RIGHTS LLC

Hitchhikers to Earth
Copyright © 2025 by Linda Novak

Library of Congress Control Number: 2025916524

ISBN
978-1-967804-20-7 (Paperback)
978-1-967804-21-4 (eBook)
978-1-967804-19-1 (Hardcover)

Hitchhikers to Earth

1

EARTH

Normal was difficult for Jane. It was a normal day in a normal high school in a normal little Ontario town, and Jane was trying to act normal. Unfortunately, her Asperger's made normal *almost* impossible.

Jane looked just as normal as anyone. She was of average height for a ninth grade girl. She had brown chinlength straight hair. She was thin, but not skinny. She had a nice face with a little nose. There was nothing really remarkable about Jane, except that she was unsure of how to react and interact with others.

Hallowe'en was coming and the schoolhalls were decorated with skeletons, pumpkins and ghosts. As Jane headed to her first class, she saw her science teacher, Mr. Busby round a corner. Busby taught biology and bore a striking resemblance to the Cro- Magnon man on the front of their textbook. Jane was thinking about the fact that his resemblance to a cave man was one of those obvious things that everybody probably noticed, but no one dared say aloud.

"I see poor little Plain Jane looks confused as usual." Bart and two other boys came up beside her, looking at her with bogus pity. She had known these guys since kindergarten. Individually, they weren't bad people, but when they got together, they were a major pain.

I hate being called 'plain Jane.' I'm not plain. It's so unfair that just because there were two Janes in kindergarten, they decided to call me 'plain Jane.' The other Jane, Jane Andrews, was blonde and really beautiful. Nobody could deny that.

Jane straightened up and stretched to her full height to show the boys she was a bit taller than any of them. She thought about ignoring them and walking away like she usually did, but this was high school and she wanted things to be different. So she fluffed her hair, turned her head in their direction, looking over their heads at the wall behind them and said, "Funny how I manage to consistently make better grades than you three. The only thing that perplexes me is the fact that you three have the acumen to walk and masticate gum at the same time." At this point, she had intended to walk past them with her head held high, but she stumbled on her own feet and had to grab the arm of passing student to keep from falling. As she looked into the face that belonged to the arm she was holding, she realized she wasn't holding onto the arm of just anybody. She was clinging to the arm of the football-playing, debate-winning idol of the entire school, Hooper Dickson. *Oh, no! That's Hoop! Everyone calls him Hoop. Well, everyone who is anyone. And I'm not anyone. I'm sure that he doesn't know that I exist.*

"Oh, sorry." She quickly released his arm and shuffled down the hall looking at her feet. *Yikes! That was so embarrassing. And why did it have to be him? Mr. Perfect.*

As she rushed away from the scene of the crime, she heard Hoop yell, "Are you all right?"

She called over her shoulder, "I'm good." And quickly rounded the next corner, trying to disappear into the crowd.

Jane had spent most of her school years as a loner. She had only one real friend, Ava. But she was determined to make new friends this year. She took a deep breath before she stepped across the doorway into her next class. *I will find someone who looks relatively friendly, and I will smile and compliment them about something. Not sure what. I'll just comment on something. Then I'll wait for a response.*

As she glanced over at the desk on her left, she saw a blonde girl who had been in junior high school with her. Something about her looked a bit different. She had a new hairstyle today. The girl's eyes scanned her. Jane smiled and remarked, "Nice hair."

The girl glared at her and slammed her hand down on her desk in anger. Jane jumped at the sound and froze. The blonde snarled at her in almost a whisper, "Listen, bitch. I know I look awful. This stupid haircut was my mother's idea and I hate it. I'm going to try to fix it when I get home. You… "

From the front came the teacher's voice saying, "Is there a problem?"

The blonde cooed, "No problem, Ms. Harold. I just dropped a book."

Jane turned her eyes toward the front of the room and concentrated on not looking right or left for the rest of the class. When the bell rang, she slowly put her stuff away so that she would be one of the last ones out of the classroom. For the rest of the day, Jane avoided any interactions and kept her eyes focused on either the floor or her desk. When school let out, she met Ava at their usual bench.

"How's things?" Ava asked as she plopped down on the old wooden bench.

"Not good. I tried to make a new friend and… "

"You got shot down."

"I was annihilated, crushed, pulverized, and kicked to the curb."

"And who was the perpetrator of this dastardly deed?" Ava inquired.

"You know the blonde medium height girl who sat two seats to our left in sixth grade math class?"

"Yeah. Cindy something."

Jane starred down at the sparse bits of brown grass by her feet. "I smiled and complimented her hair. Her hair was different today."

"Oh, hair. That can be a touchy subject. Especially a new hairstyle."

"Yeah. Now you tell me." Jane traced circles in the dirt with her right foot.

Ava nudged her. "So exactly what did you say?"

"Two words. Just two words and she flew into a rage. I said, 'Nice hair.'"

"Okay, here's one problem with what you said. That could easily have been taken as sarcastic. You know, like you were insulting her hair. She doesn't know you, so she took it the wrong way. There's a science to complimenting people. If possible, be specific, like 'That style accents the shape of your face.'" Generalizations can be taken the wrong way. And… I hear that Cindy's family has suddenly become a one-parent family because her dad moved in with his secretary. So she's probably living with one mad mother. I think you can relate to that."

Jane stood up. "Now that you've shared this insight, I feel much better. And I can easily envision what life is like living with an angry parent since I also live with one of those. Now, I must go so that I don't incur the wrath of my mad mom. I'll look up the science of compliments later today, so I can get it right next time." Jane's face lit up. "If I can quickly zip through my homework, I should have time to go into the park to continue my oak tree study this afternoon. I always feel welcome and calm when I'm alone among the trees."

Ava scowled at her. It had been two years since Ava had moved into Jane's neighborhood. Ava had been hit by a drunk driver a week after the move and had spent four months laid up at home. Because Jane was a whiz at all her classes, the principal asked Jane to visit Ava regularly to help with her classwork. It was an awkward beginning to what became a close friendship.

"I know. I said the T-word twice. You know… *tree*. That was a joke. I'm not good at jokes either, am I? Sorry. And, thank you. Sometimes I need your worldview to balance my Asperger's version of the world."

Ava shoved Jane's shoulder. "So go. I hear your oaks calling your name."

Jane smiled and flew off down the side walk toward home.

2

ICE MOUNTAINS

On a planet far away from earth, two small fur-covered creatures stood nose to nose. Anyone seeing their animated gestures could see they were not getting along. It was a sunny day with a few white clouds slowly gliding across a gray sky. Mera and her father stood toe to toe on the front lawn of their house, their brown fur blowing in the wind. One could see by the depressions in the green springy ground cover that they had been moving around each other like boxers in a ring. Vehicles zipped by on the stone road behind them. A flying machine could be heard buzzing in the distance.

"We must have weapons of mass destruction." Mera yelled at her father. "Without them, we are helpless. If... not, if." She paused and snorted, "It's not an if anymore. When..." She glared at him. "When the Palalans discover that we're here, they could just stomp us into oblivion. It's going to happen and we have to be ready." Mera glared at her father.

"So you are certain that, after all these years, centuries, in fact, of keeping our existence hidden from the Palalans, somehow they are going to find us and come kill us all? Is that what your rabble rouser friends are telling you?"

"Not exactly. It's just logical that two civilizations can't live on one planet and never be aware of each other. And, some Palalans wearing heavy heated suits were seen in the edge of our ice mountains four rotations ago. So maybe we have another twenty-five or fifty rotations before they find us. Or... maybe they will be at our door tomorrow. We need to be ready. We need to find or make a weapon so we aren't helpless when it happens."

Mera's father sighed and stared up at the clouds that drifted by. Jolocko-lo was taking a second to calm down so he wouldn't say things he would later regret. He looked at his daughter and pointed toward the door. "Inside. We are not having this discussion on the front lawn, and no child of mine is going to a WMD rally. It's undignified to stand in a public park and shout slogans. There are better ways to achieve what you want."

Mera looked down at the gray stones of the walkway that led to front door of their square white house, but she didn't move. Putting her hand to her forehead, she combed her fingers through her fur and raised her head to catch his eye. "But, I have my birth anniversary soon. I'll be an adult and then I can do whatever I want." *I can't wait until then. My name will change from Mera to Mera-lo and everyone will know that I am an adult. Then, finally, they will leave me alone to make my own decisions.* "Why? I don't understand why I can't go today?"

"Because I am hoping that between now and the coming of age ceremony, you come to a more balanced view of how the world works. Probably not going to happen, but I can hope."

"But… I was going to meet friends there."

"You'll see them later." Her dad looked thoughtful for a tick and then smiled. "How about you grab our coats and we go to the sled run?"

Mera did a double take, then paused in silence, surprised at what she heard. Her father had never been a ray of sunshine. He was cautious; he was methodical. He always seemed to find the downside of everything. And, since the death of her mom last year, her father had become gruffer than ever. So Mera was relieved to see him finally smile and suggest something fun. Even if he was a bit crusty, she knew he loved her. She hated to give in. She felt like she was being bought off, but it was so good to see that smile again. She beamed back at him. "Sure, I'd like that. I'll get our coats." Her rich brown fur went flying as she turned and ran toward the door.

As Mera ran inside, Jolocko-lo's smile faded. *She is right to be worried about the future of her people.* He looked down their street at the rows of square white houses with their black domed roofs. Many were hidden behind lush green bushes. It was a pretty neighbourhood. He could see the city in the distance; the tall black buildings of Athebus gleamed in the afternoon sun. Behind the city, ice-covered mountains sliced up into the sky. In the distance, to the right of the city, steam rose from the geothermal lake that made all this possible. Their city was an oasis in a frozen land.

The Ume race could never have evolved in such a cold place without the geothermal springs. Around them lay barren wasteland covered with sheets of grey-white ice. But the springs provided a lush, warm haven for the Ume. Jolocko-lo's thoughts wander back over to the topic that was on everyone's' minds these days. *What will the Palalans do when they discover us?*

The Palalans live in a hot jungle around the equator.

Because the planet is not tilted on an axis, there are no seasons. The jungle is always hot, allowing the cold blooded Palalans to live there. And the mountains, where the warm blooded Ume live in the hot-spring-fed valleys, are always cold. A dry sterile desert lay between the jungle and the ice mountains. It divided their planet into two very different worlds.

Mera returned with her arms full of coats and boots. "I thought we'd need boots too."

"Good idea." Jolocko-lo took two steps toward their little three wheeled car, then stopped and turned to Mera. "Would you like to drive?"

Mera's face lit up. *Finally... finally, he's realizing that I'm almost a grown-up.* "Uh... Yeah, I'd love to."

As Jolocko-lo mockingly bowed and handed her the keys, his communicator buzzed. He straightened up and took it out of his vest pocket. "Jolocko-lo here. Greetings, Senoa-lo"

Mera stood there frowning as he turned his back to her and talked in hushed tones.

As he closed up the communicator, he turned back toward her, wearing his serious face. He put the communicator away and ran his hands up the side of his face, ruffling his fur. He always did that when he was nervous or upset. It was a reliable tell.

"We must talk."

CHAPTER

3

ICE MOUNTAINS

The sun was edging down toward the white mountaintops as Toboo-lo hopped down the road. Each hop of his strong legs sent his little ears flapping, his fur fluttering, and his red vest flying up. He was so happy to be out of his botany lab and free to go putter in his garden that he didn't care how he looked. Dignity had never been his forté. As he neared his garden, he slowed down and started to walk. The clean cool air drifted in off the surrounding icy peaks. He inhaled deeply; he was so glad to be back home in the frozen north. He so hated the stuffy, warm air of the tropics. *I'd never travel there ever, ever again if I have my way.* It was hot. It was damp. But the worst part was having to act like a dumb primitive that couldn't speak. For centuries, the Ume had hopped around in the jungle inhabited by the Palalans under the guise of being cute, furry, non- sentient, grass-nibbling animals. This ploy had made it possible for them to gain valuable knowledge in engineering, construction, and so many things. The whole concept of being a spy bothered him; it was just his nature to be open and honest. All he wanted to do was stay in Risus and experiment with his plants. *But, that's not going to happen now that I'm part of the committee charged with finding a weapon that can defeat the Palalans. Some call it a WMD. I don't like that term. The words 'mass destruction' give me chills.*

Just as Toboo-lo arrived at the garden his communicator buzzed. It was Senoa-lo, the leader of the WMD committee. *Damn, not now.*

CHAPTER

4

ICE MOUNTAINS

A solemn air permeated the room. Jolocko-lo slouched in his chair and fingered the Earth map in front of him. Leela-lo was frowning and reading something on the screen of a small computer. Toobo-lo was smoothing out the papers in front of him. Inside he was as happy a kid with a new toy, but he was trying to remain quiet and subdued. It was obvious that no one else shared his joy. As Senoa-lo, the leader of the group entered the room, their furry ears stood up and they all looked up at her expectantly.

Senoa-lo sat down, looked around the table, and sighed. "They want us to do it. Our best option for learning about weapons is to go to Earth. It's the only way to do a thorough internet search for a weapon that we can use against the Palalans."

"When do we go?" Jolocko-lo asked.

"A Palalan ship is scheduled to leave on day 235. So we'll have to sneak aboard the ship the night before. We meet here in four days."

Jolocko-lo huffed, "I don't like it, but if it is to be done, I will go. It is an amusing twist of fate that we are going to be stowaways on a Palalan vessel in order to find a weapon to fight the Palalans."

Leela-lo turned toward him. "We'll understand if you don't want to go, Jolocko-lo. Your daughter is not quite an adult and you'll be leaving her alone. "

"It's not that. She is very pro-WMD. And she has all her aunts and uncles nearby to care for her. She'll be fine without me. I'm just not certain that acquiring weapons of mass destruction is the answer to our problem. I think we should explore the possibility of trying to communicate with the Palalans first."

Toboo-lo jumped up, fire coming from his eyes. "Let's get real here. We share this planet with beings nine times bigger than us. When they find out about us they are not going to like the fact that we have been stealing their technology for centuries. Nobody likes to look the fool. They're going to be very agitated when they find that all these years we've tricked them into thinking that we're just harmless cute little dumb critters. We've managed to hide our cities from them thus far. But, it can't last. Some day they're going to venture out of the tropics and discover us. And when they do,they could squash us like bugs. You want to call them up and invite them over for a little talk? No! Our whole Ume civilization is at risk. When we do finally meet them, I will put out my hand in peace, but I want to have a powerful weapon in the other hand."

"Please sit down Toboo-lo." Senoa-lo waved him toward a seat. "Basically, we all agree with you or we wouldn't be here."

"And, Toboo-lo." Jolocko-lo interjected, "we did not steal anything from the Palalans. We simply studied their technology and copied it or adapted it to our needs."

Senoa-lo held up her hands to get their attention. "Before we go any further, I want to thank you for volunteering to do this. I feel confident that if this can be done, you are the best qualified for the job. I need Leela-lo for her background in earth customs and languages. I need Jolocko-lo-lo for his computer skills, and Toboo-lo for his knowledge of plants and chemistry expert.

Senoa-lo's eyes scanned the group. "But, we will fault no one if any of you now change your mind about going. The odds are against any of us making it back alive. We will probably be either killed or stuck on Earth forever. So Leela-lo, Jolocko- lo, Toboo-lo, take a minute and think. We will be sneaking aboard a space ship that we can not operate and going to a planet full of violent beings. You could be saying good-bye to your life when we board that ship. Is this what you really want to do?"

"Yes," Toobo-lo said. "I will miss my garden, my children and my friends, but we need protection. It is unfortunate that, from what we know, the Palalans have no powerful weapons that we can copy. If going to Earth is the only way to acquire plans for a weapon, I'm going." His eyebrows went up and a little smile lit up his face. "And, I can't wait to see the Earth vegetation."

Beside him was Jolocko-lo. "Yeah, Toboo-lo's right, and I hate it when he's right. I also think we should have some type of weapon. So I'm going."

All eyes moved to slender little Leela-lo.

"I will miss my sisters and my parents, but I do want to go. What we are doing is very important. We, the Ume, must be able to defend ourselves. And you need me too. You guys aren't really that good at reading the Earth languages."

Senoa-lo nodded. "Then I suggest that you all go home and put your affairs in order. It's not going to be easy to say good-bye to everyone you know and love. I hope we will be able to find a way to come home. But if we don't come home, well… If we are successful and are able to send back plans for a WMD, then it will have been worth it." Her head went down and she wiped her hand across one cheek. "I'm afraid I'm letting it get to me." She straightened her back and raised her chin. "Can't do that now. We have things to do."

"I need one of you to make one more trip with me into the Palalan tropics. Not you Jolocko-lo. You go spend some time with that lovely daughter. So, who's volunteering?"

Toboo-lo nodded "I'll go."

There was silence.

Senoa-lo waited another minute, hoping Leela-lo or Jolocko-lo would insist on going, then said, "Thank you Toboo-lo." She looked them over again. "I will send you lists of what we need to take with us. Only bring one small personal item. We will be cramped in a small space as it is. Contact me with any questions." She paused as she studied the empty wall behind them for a second, then scanned the room as she said, "So, I will see you three back here in four suns, on day 233. Our transport leaves at three. Be here on time please."

Jolocko-lo spoke up. "Before we go, I have a question."

All heads turned toward him.

"Have we any new information about the size of the Earth beings?"

"Leela-lo, anything?" Senoa-lo asked Leela-lo paused, then said, "There have been four flights to earth. I haven't been able to access the reports from those visits. I think the reports are being kept secret because some Palalans don't like earthwatching. There are factions who want to stop all Palalans from watching the humans. They want to block access to the Earth television screens, computer monitors... everything. I doubt it will happen because so many of the Palalans watch humans for amusement."

"I agree," Toboo-lo said. "The Palalans have been watching Earth TV since the humans first invented it. Now they also observe the humans through earth computer screens and phone screens. I admit that we Ume spend much time observing the antics of the earth creatures, but earthwatching is a very popular entertainment with the Palalans."

"Back to the topic at hand," Leela-lo interjected. "I have not seen the reports, and I do not know how big humans are. But, as far as we know, all the other aliens that the Palalans have had contact with have been about the same size as the Palalans. So I guess we have no reason to think that the Earth beings are anything but near Palalan size." She grinned. "But, wouldn't it be wonderful if they are our size?"

Toboo-lo nodded enthusiastically. "Yeah, it would have been something if the Palalans had landed their ship on Earth and found it to be a world where the people are the size of their hands. Maybe that is why their reports are secret?"

"We don't know." Senoa-lo stood up and gathered her papers. "We have someone working on accessing those records. But more importantly, because there are two factions are at odds concerning their future relationship with Earth, this might be their last flight to the planet. And that's why we must, and I emphasize, *must* get on that ship."

"But about the size thing," Toboo-lo interjected. "If the Earth beings are our size, I think that will put us at a disadvantage, because we'll find it difficult to hide and spy on them."

"Or, it could be a good thing if they're our size," Leela-lo offered. "They would be more likely to understand our situation and maybe willing to share weapon plans."

Jolocko-lo stood up and put his hands on his hips. "Leela-lo, get real. If they are big or small, that doesn't mean they'll be friendly. They might shoot us on sight. You've studied the Earth beings. They are violent and easily frightened by the unfamiliar. I, for one, hope they are as big as the Palalans, so we have a better chance of hiding from them. And, from watching their movies and TV, it is a fact that they have an innate affection for small furry creatures. They keep many different furry small animals as pets in their homes and express great affection for them. So, if we are discovered, being small in relation to them, would be advantageous."

"You know," Toboo-lo added, "one of their main food sources are furry creatures called cows. These creatures are more than twice as big as a human. So size seems to matter if you are a furry animal on Earth."

Jolocko-lo huffed. "So we're not sure if the Earth beings are big or small. Wonderful."

Toboo-lo spoke up. "The fact is we don't know what we're getting ourselves into, but it's worth it if we can get plans for a weapon that can make us safe. So, we'll just see how big they are when we get there."

Senoa-lo picked up her papers. "I think we're done here."

Jolocko-lo stood up and headed toward the door. "Uh… yeah. I've got places to go. Lots to do."

The rest of the group shuffled out of the room leaving Toboo-lo and Senoa-lo alone.

5

ICE MOUNTAINS

Leela-lo could not remember being more uncomfortable. The room was full of people. Two tables were pushed up against the wall and stacked high with fruits, vegetables, breads, and sweets. Her mother had gathered cousins, and great aunts, and every sort of relative to be here to see her off. *I don't know most of these people. I hate this.*

She saw her mother winding her way through the crowd dragging a tall reddish man in her wake. *Now, who is that?* Her mother introduced the man as a third cousin on her father's side of the family. As she smiled and nodded, she spied her father standing by the side door. He motioned toward the door.

"I see someone I must talk to." she lied. When she joined her father at the door, he turned and went out. She followed.

She took his arm and they hopped off into the pipa grove. When they were far enough from the house that the pipa trees hid them, they slowed to a walk. "Thanks, Dad. I was going crazy in there."

"I thought you might want to spend some time with your housemates before you go." Her Dad hugged her, then stepped back to look at her. "I will miss you."

"Hey, we'll be able to send messages. We've set up a system just like the Palalans use. So even if we can't get back, we'll always be able to talk."

"I think you will come home someday."

"How?" She drew back.

He stepped closer to her. "I have studied the Palalans and I think they will continue to watch the Earthers and send more ships to the planet. The Earth watching is very popular among the Palalans. And, you're a very smart girl. I'm betting that you'll find a way to get home."

She hugged him. "I hope you're right."

"Of course I am. I'm your dad. But, I still worry. This is a dangerous thing you're trying to do. Once you get to Earth, no one knows what might happen to you."

"I wish you wouldn't worry. But I know I can't stop you from worrying." She glared at him. "It's your option to dismiss the worry or let it dominate your thoughts, but I'm not going to let it affect what I choose to do." She touched his hand. "But

I do appreciate that you are concerned. Thank you for getting me out of there. I'm going to see my friends now. Mom's not going to like it"

"I'll handle your mom. Go."

"I'm going. But I need you to stop worrying. Right now."

He nodded. "I'll try."

She gave him a parting hug and turned to go out the garden gate. Leela-lo took a few steps, then paused and turned to watch her father go back through the grove toward the house. As he disappeared behind a tree, she whispered, "Bye Dad." Then she touched the tree beside her and said, "Bye trees." A tear made its way down her cheek. "Bye planet."

CHAPTER

6

DESERT BETWEEN PALALA AND UME

The grey flying machine taxied up to a small domed building that was painted to blend in with the surrounding gray rocks and soil. The door of the plane opened and a short stairway dropped to the ground. Toboo-lo and Senoa-lo stepped off.

"No matter how many times I fly, I will never feel comfortable about it. It's so unnatural," Toboo-lo complained.

"You should be grateful that we have airplanes. It would've taken us days to have gotten here by land. And, it gives us one advantage over the Palalans."

"Yeah, no planes. I don't get that. They're usually so logical about everything." Toboo-lo grumbled, "As a scientist, I will never understand why they voted to stop the development of air travel. Why didn't their scientist just tell them to get over their fear of heights and fly. We do it. I don't like it, but I fly when I need to."

Senoa-lo sighed. "You've got to understand where they're coming from. They have no mountains. We were raised running up and down those icy cliffs." She motioned toward the glaciers and mountains in the distance. "They live in a hot flat jungle. And they're a pure democracy. So if the people don't want to fly, then no flying."

"But they fly to other planets."

"That's different. That's scientists doing exploration and research. They're all for that. But the general public refuses to even consider getting on anything that flies. They don't even like tall buildings. Have you noticed that they rarely build anything over two stories."

Senoa-lo picked up her bag. "Hey, can we drop this and move on? Our ground transportation is waiting for us."

Beside the mottled gray building sat a square, drab, six-wheeled, compressed air vehicle with a slender fellow standing next to it. As they approached, they recognized Huto-lo, the one-man staff of the little airport.

His fur was dusty and he wore a slate colored vest that matched the desert dirt. Huto-lo looked down at his vest. It was a maze of pockets holding an array of tools. "Been working outside all day. Guess I'm a mess. I'm alone so much, I forget to clean up sometimes." He shrugged and put the tool in his hand in a vest pocket. A cloud of dust came off the side of the vest. "Anyway, I hear you're going on a Palalan ship to Earth. What's up with that?"

"You got a better idea about how we can get plans for a WMD?" Senoa-lo replied.

"Yeah, I've been following all the discussions on my computer. We need a weapon. And you brave people are going to Earth to find plans for one. Thanks and I'm glad they didn't ask me to do it."

Senoa-lo handed him her bag. "Somebody's got to do it."

"Well, get in." He put the bag in the vehicle. "Let's go. I've been watching the radar and there's no Palalans on the desert right now. So I should be able get you pretty close to the green zone."

They rode in silence, with Senoa-lo watching the radar screen and Huto-lo trying to miss the bigger holes and rocks as they bounced across the rough terrain. Toboo-lo was curled up in back asleep. His head lolled back and forth as they careened over the rocks. The ground levelled out as they approached the distant wall of vegetation that marked the edge of the Palalans' world.

Suddenly, Huto-lo stopped. "I'm not supposed to get any closer. They figure that from here any Palalan who sees this buggy from the bush won't be able to see it clearly enough to be sure whether it's an animal or whatever. So you've got about a two hour walk or an hour hop ahead of you."

He turned to face Senoa-lo. "Why am I telling you this? You've gone in this way a few times."

As Huto-lo roused Toboo-lo, Senoa-lo got her bag out and removed two silver metal poles and two fake fur vests.

Toboo-lo tumbled out of the vehicle and wrestled his coat off; he then tossed it back into the buggy. Senoa-lo handed him one of the vests and a pole. Huto-lo helped Senoa-lo out of her coat, folded it, and laid it on the seat. They then put on the vests, tied them tight around their bodies, and slid the poles into inside pockets in the vests. The vest blended so well with their fur that they looked just like they were wearing nothing, just a bit fatter.

"You got everything?" Huto-lo asked.

Both Toboo-lo and Senoa-lo felt around inside their vest for the communicators and food packets that were supposed to be in the vests' inside pockets.

"I'm good." Senoa-lo nodded.

Toboo-lo yawned. "Me too."

"Then I'll see you in a couple of days." Huto-lo stepped into the vehicle and gunned it back toward the airport.

CHAPTER

7

UME

Crawling green and brown vines stretched out from the lush jungle onto the dry gray earth. They escaped the shaded bush to seek light on the bare soil. The vines were an introduction to a wall of green trees and ferns and vines. As Senoa-lo and Toboo- lo stepped into the bush, Senoa-lo's hand went inside her vest and grasped the handle of her silver charger. The weapon worked by emitting an electric charge; it had two settings: stun and kill.

Toboo-lo stopped and looked over at her, "Do you see something?"

"No. Let's keep moving please. I've found that it pays to be cautious in the less populated areas. No Palalans live in this area near the desert, so there are more wild animals here. Don't want to be some dumb animal's lunch, do we?"

Toboo-lo's hand flew inside his vest. "I hope you realize that this is only the second time I've gone into Palalan territory." His voice was high and strained. "So I'm depending on your experience to keep us alive." He stumbled over a stick, but caught himself by grabbing a limb.

"Just watch where you're going. We'll be fine. Keep your hand on your weapon anytime we're in areas not populated by the Palalans. And don't ever let a Palalan see you reach under your vest or see your charger. If you are threatened by an animal, pull it out, and shock him quickly. Then immediately put it backunder the vest.""Can't I just keep my weapon out in my hand? This walking or even worse hopping, with my hand in my vest is awkward and uncomfortable," he grumped.

"No, you can't be seen with it. We could easily come across some Palalans in this bush. And stay close to me, so I can see you."

"What if we are being watched by a Palalan and an animal tries to eat me?"

"Then you're somebody's lunch."

He stopped, turned, and stared at her.

"I'm joking. Probably never happen because the carnivorous animals stay away from places occupied by the Palalans."

They moved in silence for a while. Toboo-lo's neck swivelled back and forth as he scanned every bush and tree for any sign of life.

"Just put your ears up. You'll hear something before you see it," Senoa-lo advised. "We should come to a road soon."

The words were hardly out of her mouth when she heard a "Eeeh!" from Toboo-lo. She looked down. He looked up at her from where he lay on the cement road.

"I stumbled on the curb."

"You all right?"

He rubbed his hands over his legs. "I seem to be in one piece."

"Good, now that we're on a road, we can hop and make better time. I want to make it to the launch site before dark."

"Yeah, sure, no problem." He slowly struggled up and hopped after her. "Hey, slow down. I'm still recovering from that fall. You know I'm old, right?."

The average life expectancy for the Ume people is 300 years. The Ume year is slightly longer than an Earth year. It's about five days longer. When a child is born, he is said to be 300 years. They count age by how many years you are expected to live, not by how many years you have lived. The ancients said this method of defining age makes people more aware of the shortness of life and encourages people to use their time more wisely. After one reaches zero, age is irrelevant. They are just said to be old and every day is treated as a gift.

"How old are you?" Senoa-lo asked?

"I'm one hundred and twenty."

"That's not old. I'm eighty."

"Oh." He looked her over and racked his head for the appropriate reply. *Do not ask if she has planned her funeral ceremony yet.* "You look good. Do we just keep on this road now?"

"Yes, just follow me."

Toboo-lo was just getting into his hopping rhythm when a big six-legged reddish brown animal with no hair and a small head crawled on to the road in front of him.

Toboo-lo stopped and pulled out his charger as Senoa-lo yelled back, "Harmless. Only eats plants."

The animal was more than twice his size. It turned itshead, wiggled some whisker-like things beside its mouth and stared at him. Toboo-lo slowly edged around it and backed down the road, with his charger drawn, not taking his eyes off the monster. It lost interest in him and ambled into the bush.

Senoa-lo was sitting on a rock beside the road when he caught up with her. She looked up at him with a half-smile. "You're more the sit behind a desk type, aren't you?"

"Wow! how'd you figure that one out. If I'm not at my desk, I'm in the garden. And my garden does not have any carnivorous animals."

She stood up, put her hands on her hips and moved a step closer to him. "So… what motivated you to leave your desk and garden? Why did you volunteer for the trip to Earth?"

"I know it sounds like an ego trip, but except for my friend, Talado Sume, I am the country's leading chemist. Talado is too old and fragile for a trip like this. So here I am. You may not like me, but you need me. Didn't you read my file?"

She backed off. "Sure, I read it, but I didn't understand all of it. Lots of technical stuff. It's not that I dislike you. You're a pleasant fellow. I just wish that you were more, let's say… comfortable and capable outdoors."

"I'm trying. And I'm a quick learner. And I'm physically fit." He stretched up tall. "At least an hour in the gym, every day."

Senoa-lo sighed. "You'll do." She looked down the road. "We've got a ways to go yet. Stick close to me."

8

PALALA

Meanwhile, in another part of the lush green jungle, under an ivory sky in a round cement house on the planet, Eela lay on her sleep platform. Two of her arms were behind her head, her third hand was touching the computer keyboard and her fourth hand held a yellow fruit. A ray of sunshine came through the door and reflected off her light grey scales. As she listened to the sounds coming out of her computer, a puzzled look came over her face. She sat up. She pushed a button to hear it again. The sounds were like nothing she had ever heard, and the patterns of the sounds were like people speaking. Then she played it again. Eela smiled. She pushed three other buttons and waited impatiently to hear the tone that signified that her call was accepted.

Solang's green scaley figure appeared on the computer screen. She was knitting with two hands, holding a ball of yarn in a third hand and scratching her nose with her fourth hand.

"Solang, I have got something you have got to hear!"

Solang looked up from her knitting, "What have I got to hear?"

"I heard some jungle animals talk… " Eela took a closer look at the screen. "What are you doing?"

Solang held up the knitting so Eela could see it on her screen, "You mean this?"

"Yes, that."

"It is called knitting. It is a method of making fabric out of strings. I learned it by watching Earth beings doing it."

"Why are you making fabric? You never wear clothes. Not even shoes when you walk through the rough bush. Why do you need fabric?"

Solang replied, "I do not need fabric, I… "

"Oh, forget I asked," Eela interrupted. "I contacted you to tell you that I have recorded some animals talking, really communicating. So, of course, I thought of you. Maybe you can tell what they are saying."

"Talking animals? Interesting. What do these animals look like?"

"I have no idea. I just have sound recordings, not photos. As part of my research into oral communication among animas, I placed sound recorders in twenty-five locations and I am analyzing the sounds for patterns. I have identified some basic communications in three locations. Usually what I hear is just grunts and barks. This is different; it sounds like a language with a diversity of sounds, and the emphasis varies as it would when we talk. I am very excited to see who these animals are! Does that not excite you?"

Solang slowly put the knitting down on her desk and propped her chin on her upper two hands. She stared into the camera on the computer. "I am interested." She leaned back on her slantboard. (A slantboard is a large rectangular piece of wood, angled at 45 degrees, supported by braces, with a small perpendicular wood piece at the bottom. Palalans lie back on the board with their heels against the small bottom piece.) "I want to hear it. Can you send it to me now?"

"Of course. I am sending it as we speak. Then, I am going out to the locale where I recorded it to put some motion cameras around the area."

Solang looked thoughtful. "I suggest that you take great care in hiding the cameras. If these animals are talking, and I doubt that, but if they are, then they are definitely smart enough to avoid your cameras."

"They can not know what a camera is."

"Eela, even a dumb animal will avoid a mechanical devise that smells of Palalan. I suggest that you wipe the cameras with alcohol, then water, then rub them with leaves. Put them high in trees with leaves attached for camouflage and aim them down. Do not expect to see any animals on your computer for at least two days."

"I have to wait two days?" Eela tilted her head to one side. "How do you know so much about filming wild animals?"

"My first husband shot nature films. Remember Lalem? I selected him to father my first child."

"Yes, of course I remember him. He was… "

"I think the word you're looking for is difficult."

"Yes, but he must have been a good father. Your son seems very nice. So, according to Lalem, the animals will avoid them for two days?"

"At least two days. Even with the precautions, your smell can linger."

Eela sighed. "If you say so. Meanwhile, I will still access the sound recorders several times each day and send you any further talking sounds that I detect."

"Good. Now go set up the cameras, while I listen to what you just sent."

"You will let me know if you think it could be a language."

"Yes Eela. Go! Cameras… now!"

Eela nodded a farewell as her image disappeared from Solang's computer screen.

Solang stowed her knitting needles on a shelf and settled herself on her slant board to listen to the recording that Eela had sent. Solang had first met Eela when she took a university language course that Solang taught. Solang only taught advanced courses and was considered to be a leading language expert. The teacher-student relationship had grown into a friendship and they regularly chatted or played sports together. Solang took a patta fruit out of a bowl on the shelf beside her and nibbled on it as the recording played. She prepared herself to hear the usual grunts and barks of the jungle animals. The Palalans had lived in the jungles of Palala for many centuries and in all that time no one had ever heard any of animals uttering anything except simple sounds that warn of a predator or communicating that they had found food.

Solang stopped in mid bite as she listened. *It is language.* There was a pattern of one animal saying something, then another animal replying. She put the patta fruit down and played it again. *How could this be? Had some aliens landed and were hiding in the bush?* She played it again. *It is definitely a sophisticated communication in some unknown idiom.*

She stood up and paced the room, lost in thought. *Could Eela be playing a trick on me? Eela is not the type to play gags; she is much too serious. Should I share this with a colleague now or wait to see if we can get a photo of the animals?* Solang grabbed the patta fruit and finished it. *I had better protect my reputation by waiting until I see a video of these beings.*

CHAPTER

9

UME IN PALALA

"This is so weird," Toboo-lo remarked. "We're spies, but we walk around out in the open and when the Palalans see us they stop and watch us,then smile and point us out to their young. That's certainly not how spies in Earth movies operate"

"Hush, we're cute little fuzzy animals who hop around and eat grass." Senoa-lo growled at him. "Only talk when absolutely necessary."

Senoa-lo hopped out of the bushes and right up to the space ship. She hopped all the way around it, stopping occasionally to sniff the air. Two slick green Palalans were working on some equipment near the ship. One looked up and saw her. He smiled. The Palalan had tools in all four hands, so he nudged the other Palalan with an elbow and pointed toward her with one of the tools. The other fellow looked up, tilted his head and grinned. The sun reflected off his scales, making his green skin look silver in places. Senoa-lo turned toward him and sniffed the air. He said something to his partner and went back to his work. She hopped back into the bushes beside Toboo-lo, motioned for him to follow her and they hopped a bit further into the dense green jungle.

"We can talk here. Was there something you wanted to say back there?" Senoa-lo asked.

"Nothing important. So is everything all right with the ship?"

"Yeah, we knew that they were going to make some adjustments to the ship hull, and we were concerned that they might make some changes that would prevent us from being able to get in and out easily. I see what they've done. We'll be fine." Senoa-lo hopped off toward the road.

Toboo-lo looked puzzled. "Wait! That's it?"

She hopped back to him. "I said we were coming here for a final inspection of the ship. Done. We'll sleep in the bush tonight. Tomorrow, we go home and tell everybody good-bye and… "

Toboo-lo interrupted. "So why did you bring me? You didn't need a chemist for this!"

"Please don't raise your voice. We need to keep the illusion of being dumb, as in that we can't talk." She moved closer to him. "We needed two people. We always send two on missions, in case one has an accident. You volunteered, so you're my back-up."

"I know nothing about the building mechanics of the exterior of an interstellar vessel. What good could I have been if something had happened to you?"

"Well… You would have called the bureau and said you had a problem. Right?"

He nodded.

"My assistant would probably have told you to use your communicator to photograph the ship. Anybody could have done that, even you. Then the engineers would have looked over the photos. I volunteered because I wanted to see for myself that we'll have no problem boarding for the trip. Our engineers looked over the schematics for the changes weeks ago. We accessed the plans from the Palalan engineers' computers. It all looked good, but I needed to see for myself. Many of us are thinking that this is going be their last trip to Earth. We have to get on that ship."

"All right, I understand now. So where do we go from here?"

"There's a camp nearby where we can spend the night. Follow me." Senoa-lo led Toboo-lo to a spot in the jungle where some bushes grew next to an outcrop of big stones. She moved the bushes aside to reveal the narrow entrance to a cave. Inside the cave there was a huge Palalan lantern and a Palalan towel.

Senoa-lo went over to the lantern and kicked a button on the side of it. A glaring bright light lit up the cave.

Toboo-lo picked up the edge of the big towel. "This is it? This is a camp?"

"What did you expect?

"A bed, a table, some chairs would be nice."

"We can't take the chance that a Palalan might find it. If they find one of their towels and a lantern, no problem. But, if they found a very small chair, that could be a problem. So your bed for tonight is a towel. You should appreciate having that. I had to steal it from a nearby house and it wasn't easy dragging that thing through the jungle." Senoa-lo flopped down on the end of the towel closer to the entrance. "And it took four of us to carry the lantern. Hope you can sleep with the light on. I can turn it off, but we keep it on to discourage jungle animals from coming in here."

Toboo-lo glanced at the entrance to the cave. "No problem. The light definitely stays on." Senoa-lo lay down on one end of the towel and Toboo-lo lay on the other end. He tugged and fluffed until he had it just right. He laid still for a few ticks, then turned toward Senoa-lo. "Are you asleep?"

"Almost." Senoa-lo sat up.

"Oh, sorry. I was just thinking… "

"I don't sleep well here either. What were you thinking?"

"Being here is so unreal. I always thought it was amazing that we share this planet with such a different race. They're so big and scaly. It's weird that we evolved from warm blooded animals in the northern geothermal springs at the same time that the Palalans were evolving from cold blooded sea things in the tropics. But, seeing them, it makes more sense. They are fish- like, aren't they. I mean they've really come a long way from evolving from some water animal to having their four arms and big feet. And they're really smart. Look at all the technological stuff they've invented. Four arms must make working with tools a lot easier. Wish I had four arms." He paused. "You know, if they weren't cold blooded and incapable of travelling into cold places, their ancestors would have probably killed and eaten our ancestors."

"Probably. It's a good thing that genetics and chance prevented that from happening. I like being alive." Senoa-lo pulled her legs up and hugged them to her body.

"What puzzles me is how we developed such different lifestyles. Like, we have couches and chairs and other furniture in our houses, and they have only have slantboards and sleeping platforms. Their technology is sophisticated like ours, but they keep their lives really simple. They swim and walk almost everywhere. I'd hate that. Their houses are spaced far apart and are almost hidden in the jungle. They don't build tall buildings, even in their cities. They're so… odd."

"Different is only odd if you aren't open to a variety of ways of doing things. They have a simple, nature oriented lifestyle. I could live like that.

Toboo-lo scratched his head. "Really?"

"Yeah, really. I'd love to live in a simple hut in the bush, away from people. But with our population problem, it's not going to happen. Our lack of really strict birth control and limited inhabitable space makes that impossible."

"You could live like a Palalan?"

"Sure. Well, except for the walking and swimming. I like my little car."

Toboo-lo tilted his head, deep in thought. "So you don't find the Palalans to be so… different from us?"

"Both we and the Palalans revere water as the source of all life. We share that," Senoa-lo reminded him.

"Yeah, and they seem to be even tempered like us. So I can understand why some people believe that they would do us no harm." He hesitated." Have you ever seen any of them be violent or mean?"

"Sort of. I saw a Palalan squash an insect once. It was trying to get into the Palalan's food. I understand killing an insect that's in your food. We do it all the time." Senoa-lo made a sour face. "But the scary thing is that the insect was almost as big as me."

"You mean scary in that they could squash us just as easily as that insect, or scary in that big bugs live here?

"Both."

"Oh."

"Toboo-lo, we should get some sleep now."

Toboo-lo put his head down, but he had difficulty with the concept of closing his eyes. Just as he finally closed them, he heard a sound. The bushes at the mouth of the cave were rustling. He popped up into a sitting position. He heard it again. He rolled over on his stomach and crawled over to Senoa-lo. She was making little popping sounds as air escaped her sleeping mouth. He nudged her. She grunted and rolled over on her side. He pinched her arm. She rolled back over to face him. "That hurt. What?"

"I heard… "

"Hey guys, you got room for two more?" A deep voice called from out of the dark corner by the entrance.

"Is that you, Viro-lo?" Senoa-lo asked.

Toboo-lo sighed and fell back on the towel.

Two bedraggled looking fellows stepped out of the shadows. "Yep, it's me. Do you know Zenbaco-lo?" He motioned toward the fellow beside him.

Zenbaco-lo greeted her with a nod. His reddish-brown fur was matted and dirty. Then Viro-lo came over, flopped down on the towel beside Senoa-lo and stretched out. Zenbaco-lo shuffled over toward them and carefully sat down on the far edge of the towel.

"I am so tired," Viro-lo sighed. "We went to Calora and looked at a new cement-mixing machine and a few other machines. I didn't realize that it was so far into the interior. We have been walking and hopping and riding buses for days. I just want to go home."

Senoa-lo look over at Zenbaco-lo. "Hi, I'm Senoa-lo and this is Toboo-lo. As you probably know by now, your friend Viro-lo has no manners. Please make yourself comfortable. We have food. Would you like something to eat?"

"Thank you, but, no. We've eaten."

Toboo-lo held out a canteen. "Water?"

Zenbaco-lo lifted his eyes to look at Toboo-lo, then looked back down at his feet. "No thank you, I'm good."

"Where are you from Zenbaco-lo?" Senoa-lo inquired.

"I lived in a little village outside Risus until I went away to engineering school."

"Is this your first trip into the Palalan jungle?"

"It is. I guess I seem like a real rube. I'm not good with people, but I love machines. We saw a cement-mixer, an electric generator, a fabric manufacturing machine and a new type of bus engine." His face lit up. "We can learn a lot from their computer diagrams, but actually seeing the real things is so much better. I've drawn up a design for a... "

A loud snore interrupted Zenbaco-lo. All three turned to look at Viro-lo. He was sound asleep.

"Now, I remember hearing your name." Senoa-lo nodded and smiled. "You're the young, award-winning genius who is going to build our weapon when we get the plans."

Zenbaco-lo looked back down at his feet. "I... I'm uncomfortable being called that. I know a lot and I'm good at building things, but there are lots of people way smarter than me."

Toboo-lo jumped in. "So, Zenbaco-lo. It's good to meet the man we will be working with when we get to Earth. I understand that we're going to have a direct communication link between us and your lab."

Zenbaco-lo blinked. "You're one of the people going to Earth?"

"Sure am. And Senoa-lo is the leader of the team."

"Wow! I'm really glad to meet you two. If you're not too tired, can we talk for a bit?"

CHAPTER

10

UME AT HOME

Mera stood looking out the window at the white mountains in the distance. She was angry and proud. And she was confused about her feelings. She knew that they needed a WMD, but she was distressed that her father had chosen to leave her and go on this trip. She had listened without responding when he told her that he was going to fly to Earth, hidden on a Palalan interstellar ship. He was open with her about the fact that he would probably never return. After he left the room, she just sat down on the floor and cried. Everyone knew her father as a gruff realistic patriot. So she knew she shouldn't be surprised that he would be one of the people asked to go to Earth. Of course they needed him. He's an expert on Earth geography and brilliant with computers. She had just washed her face to clear away the tears, when she heard him come through the front door.

She ran into the front room and threw her arms around him. After a big hug, she released him but held on to one hand. "So, what are we doing?"

"Whatever you want. I'm free for the next two days."

"You said you wanted to visit the memorial before you go. Do you want to go there now? I'd like to get the sad stuff over with."

Jolocko-lo's shoulders slumped. "Let's do that. Let's go visit your Mom. I'll get our warm suits."

Mera chatted about school and her friends as they rode up to the edge of the glaciers. Jolocko-lo had let her drive. When they got to where the road turned to ice, they parked their vehicle beside a big storage building. Jolocko-lo helped Mera open a heavy door to the building, revealing a room full of ice buggies. He then handed her the key to their square, four-seated ice buggy. It was old, not streamlined like the new ones, but it was dependable. She took the key and tried to not look surprised, but smiled weakly. She had driven it a few times, but usually he drove. They put on their warm suits and climbed into it. They were quiet for most of the trip. So quiet that she could hear the crunch as the eight studded tires gripped the ice. She parked the vehicle beside the tall brown pole that marked the edge of the ice field where the dead lay frozen. They silently ambled toward the sign that marked the area where the bodies of their family and ancestors were interred under the ice. Mera felt the weight of the world come down on her shoulders. She would probably never see her father again. She could come here anytime, wipe the snow off the ice and at least see the face of her mother frozen in time. Her father was going to another planet and she would miss him in life and in death. They walked across the ice together, occasionally clearing the snow, looking down at the bodies of her grandmother, a cousin who fell mountain climbing, many of her ancestors from past centuries, and finally her mother.

"You know, if you really don't want me to go, I can easily get out of it," Jolocko-lo offered.

Her eyes reluctantly left her mother's face. "No, we both believe that our people need a weapon. I seem to be more convinced of that than you. And Mom, if she were here, she would tell you to go." Mera smiled. "Or she'd insist on going instead of you."

"She probably would. And then we'd be arguing about who should go and who should stay."

Mera took his big hand in hers. "You have to go."

"I really think the Palalans mean us no harm. But, just because I believe something doesn't mean it's true. It's just the way I feel about it. I wish I had some viable evidence to show." He ran his fingers through the fur on the sides of his head, then continued, "I understand that I could be wrong. But, we can't take that chance. Our scientists have found thirty- one planets with intelligent life thus far. On twenty-two of the planets there was more than one sapient species. And on all twenty-two, there was either fighting between the groups at the time of the study or a history of war. I can't envision the Palalans wanting to hurt us, but I can't ignore the evidence of what has happened on other planets. Anyone can see that we must have a weapon before they become aware of us."

Mera stepped closer and pulled him into a hug. "So my dad will fly off to save the world, like in the cartoons I watched when I was a child." She moved back, their hands met and they stared into each others' eyes. "I'll be alright. You've been a great dad. You've taught me everything and now you're needed by our people. Go without worries about me." She straightened her back and held her head high. "Go. I envy you. What an adventure."

Ume in the Palalan Jungle

A big green leaf slapped Toboo-lo in the face as he trailed along behind Senoa-lo. *I hate the jungle.* "So, where do we go from here?"

Senoa-lo reached inside her vest. "Let me check my communicator for the local bus schedule."

Toboo-lo sighed and plopped down on the ground. He had watched many of the James Bond movies, and this was not what he thought spying should be like.

Senoa-lo put the communicator away inside her vest. "Good. If we hurry out to the road, a bus will be by directly.

Toboo-lo had seen photos of the big vehicles the Palalans refer to as buses, but he had never been on one. The vehicles were just huge platforms with Palalan-sized seats and a roof. There was a computerized control box on the front. He followed Senoa-lo out to the road and they stood beside a tall orange post.

"Now get ready to hop quickly. It will not stop because the computer doesn't detect any Palalans at his stop. But it will slow down a bit at this corner. So just hop on as it goes by."

Toboo-lo hadn't hopped on a moving vehicle since he was a kid and he would never forget the trouble he got into for doing it. Just as he turned to Senoa-lo intending to object, a bus came into sight. *Can't talk now. Guess I'll hop on or die trying.*

They hopped on. *I made it.* Toobo-lo's heart was racing from the excitement. High above them, sitting on the seats were five Palalans. Two of them looked up from their communicators, and smiled. Toboo-lo tried to look cute and dumb. *I think this is what cute looks like. Maybe I should have practised in a mirror.* The Palalans went back to their work and ignored them.

Fortunately, Senoa-lo didn't make him jump off the vehicle while it was still moving. She nudged him when it stopped to let off one of the Palalans, and they quickly leapt off before it started moving again. The Palalan disappeared down a path, while the two Ume stood still working at looking cute.

After they had watched the bus go out of sight, Toboo-lo whispered to Senoa-lo, "Is it safe to talk now?"

"Sure, better here than in the woods."

"Why is that?"

Senoa-lo motioned for him to start moving. "I read in the research files that a Palalan scientist is doing a study on animal sounds and has planted microphones in several areas."

"Not good. That sort of relates to what I want to ask." They hopped down the road. "The Palalans see that we are smart enough to hop a ride on their buses. And they seem to study and analyze everything. Why haven't they captured some of us to study?"

Senoa-lo stopped, took his arm to turn him to face her and explained, "Fortunately, when Palalans went from being hunter-gathers to farming they started to respect other animals. They came to view us and other animals as unique beings that they share the planet with. So they quit killing and eating animals. Killing any animal is only allowed if the animal tries to take your food or threatens your life."

"Like bugs? They try to eat my fruit." Toboo-lo interjected.

"Yes. Also, the more intelligent the animal seems, the more they respect them. It would be unthinkable to touch or put us in a cage. In the past, some scientists have tried to watch and study us. But, we've always made it difficult. Sometimes, we would just disappear for a while. There was lots of speculation about where we went. It never occurred to them that we might live in the ice mountains. They decided that we could burrow in the ground and hibernate at will."

Senoa-lo turned away from him. "We should go. Less talking and more walking. We need to get off the road and into the bush now."

Toboo-lo and Senoa-lo were silent as they trekked through the jungle. Toboo-lo kept his ears up listening for creatures that might eat them. When they reached the edge of the desert, Toboo-lo whispered, "Can we talk now?"

"Yeah."

"You know, being frightened like that makes a fellow think. Are you spiritual?"

She turned, looked at him and paused. "Somewhat."

They continued walking. "What does that mean? Somewhat?"

"It means that I go to temple and float in the warm water and meditate, just like most people." She smirked, "I'm not devout, I don't spend hours sitting by a hot spring staring into the water in appreciation."

"And what do you think happens to us when we die?"

"Well, of course our bodies decompose eventually and our minds go into a state of perfect contemplation." Senoa-lo glared at him. "Did you sleep through your grade two mind& body classes? Why would I think anything else?"

"I just wondered if studying Earth had any effect on your spiritual beliefs." She huffed. "Of course not. I'm a scientist. Are you?"

"No, those Earth religions are silly. It just makes me think about our assumption that when we die we will go into a meditative state forever. That's not based on science. It's just what we've been taught.

"Yeah, and like anything else we've been taught, we can choose to believe it or not believe it. I know it's not science, but I choose to believe it."

"Why?" he asked. "Why believe something that can't be proven?"

"I... " her voice wavered. "I guess it's easier." She stopped and looked into the distance. "I think I see Huto-lo's vehicle."

Chapter

12

EARTH

In a park in a field on planet Earth sat a relatively small spaceship. It was shaped like a bullet and almost as tall as the trees that surrounded it. The ship was silver in color, but if any human looked at it with human eyes they would only see a group of trees and bushes. The ship was supposedly vacant. The two Palalans who had come to Earth in the ship were off exploring the area.

Inside the ship two screws on a wall panel started to unscrew. They slowly turned until they were all the way out, then they dropped to the floor. Then the other two screws that held the flat metal panel in place did the same. The panel fell to the floor with a loud clang. Two fuzzy brown Ume faces popped out.

Toboo-lo huffed and hopped down to the floor of the cabin. "I thought they were going to take forever getting their clothing on and getting out of here."

Senoa-lo hopped down. "All is going according to plan. Now let's get this ship unloaded and be on our way. Jolocko-lo, please start handing the cases down to Toboo-lo."

Jolocko-lo looked down at Toboo-lo. "Be very careful with this first one. The computers are in it."

"Just move."

Jolocko-lo's words were interrupted as Toboo-lo jumped down and ran over to a window. It was starting to get dark, but there was enough light to see the colors. "It's green and brown and yellow and red." Toboo-lo beamed with excitement. "Wow! I can't believe we're really here." He turned back toward Senoa-lo. "I know… you want me to help unload the cartons." He hopped over beside Toboo-lo and took a package from him and put it in front of the ship's entrance.

After all the cartons were assembled in front of the door and everyone was lined up behind the cartons, Senoa-lo climbed up on the control panel for the ship and pushed the button that opened the door to the outside. Then she reset the computer controlling the door so that it would close at a set time. They all peered out into the night; the trees were silhouetted against a fading pink sunset. Nobody moved until Senoa-lo hopped down beside them and yelled out. "Let's go. The door is set to close and lock in twenty Earth minutes." She took a little flashlight out of a vest pocket and pointed it into the grass below. She hopped down to the grassy field, careful to land between the clumps of grass. Senoa-lo reached out and ran a hand over a piece of tall grass. "Jump down one at a time. And pick your landing spot carefully. These plants are hard and sharp. I don't have the time or energy to be dragging an injured person through this stuff."

Senoa-lo continued, "Jolocko-lo, you will be the last one out. Make sure that panel is securely closed and that nothing is left behind." *I wouldn't want this ship to crash because of us.* "Leela-lo and Toboo-lo come on down. Then Jolocko-lo can hand the cartons down to us."

She heard two thumps. The last one was followed by a voice saying, "Ouch, that stuff is hard."

She shined her light in the direction of the voice and found Leela-lo's face. "Are you hurt? Do you need help?"

"No, I'm fine," Leela-lo replied as she limped toward Senoa- lo.

They unloaded the cartons.

"Right. Well, before we go any further, I'll remind you of a few things. First, keep your weapons handy at all times. They should be set at stun. We don't need to make unnecessary enemies. Second, as you walk, remember to look up. If anything threatens us, I think it will probably be bigger than us. Also, watch out for holes. Some animal could reach up out of a burrow and grab you."

As Jolocko-lo poked his head around a blade behind Senoa-lo, he grumped, "so we're supposed to look up, down and all around all at the same time. Yeah, no problem. You know... I've only got two eyes."

Senoa-lo had turned around to face him. She smiled, "But they're sharp eyes and fortunately they are connected to a very good brain. So quit fussing and use it."

Toboo-lo's light was focused on a leaf of grass. "Can't wait to examine these plants. They're somewhat similar to ours at home, but… "

Senoa-lo interrupted, "Toboo-lo, It'll have to wait. Your job right now is to grab a carton and follow me."

Senoa-lo had been scanning the area while she talked. She wanted to get into the treed area before sunrise. Her night vision was good enough to make out a stand of trees to their right. Since those were the closest, they would have to do. It was going to be slow travelling because they couldn't chance hopping in this hard grass in the dark. They would have to walk.

"No hopping."

"What?" Toboo-lo protested. "We have to walk?"

"As I said earlier, we don't want to have to drag your bloody torn body along behind us. So, as long as we are in this grass, we walk."

Each grabbed a crate by the handle and carried or towed it along toward the trees. As they moved away from the ship, they heard the door on the ship slide shut.

I'm scared, but I'm not going to let the others know. "Well, there's no going back now;" Leela-lo whispered to no one.

After weaving their way through the grass for a long while, they stumbled on a hard surfaced road. Toboo-lo sniffed the air. "This road smells bad, sort of like tree sap, but stronger."

"It's called tar. It comes from oil," Jolocko-lo informed them. "They take it out of the ground and use it for roads and burn it to run vehicles."

"They burn it? That must smell awful."

They were hopping down the road, with crates on their shoulders, when Senoa-lo yelled, "stop!"

Jolocko-lo bumped into her. "What?"

Senoa-lo held up her hand, "Quiet, there's something coming down the road."

Everybody's ears shot up.

Toboo-lo motioned right. "The bushes are taller over on this side. I strongly suggest that we hide quickly and see what... Ooh, they're big, really big."

They all followed Toboo-lo as he dashed into the bushes.

By moonlight, they were able to see three tall teen-aged Earth boys loping down the road. One had on a hockey jersey and a goalie mask. One had on a tee-shirt with a Superman insignia and a black red cape. The third one had a little pink tutu around his waist, a plastic tiara on his head and a pink plastic wand in his hand. All three carried heavy plastic bags. The six Ume peeked around the bushes and watched them pass by. They remained silent until the boys were out of sight.

Toboo-lo stepped out on the road and peered after them. "They're huge. They're bigger than the Palalans."

"Oh, yeah, I forgot to tell you. Just before we left, I was digging around in some Palalan documents and found that the Earthers are about one fifth taller than Palalans," Leela-lo winced. "Sorry."

Senoa-lo jerked around to face her. "Anything else you forgot to tell us?"

"Uh... no. It seemed that we were assuming that they were big so... It didn't seem to be that important."

Senoa-lo was steaming. "Leela-lo, everything is important. Don't you get it? We are risking our lives to try to ensure the future of our people. I... I... "

Jolocko-lo interrupted, "No harm done. We all knew they were big when we saw the size of this road. So let's get going." He nodded toward the trees. "We need to be well-hidden before first light."

After stumbling around in the woods for a while, they found a hollow under a big root. There, they set up a temporary camp.

C H A P T E R

13

EARTH

Jane closed the door and glanced at the bowl on candy on the table by the door. There were only about twenty pieces left in the bowl. She turned and looked at the clock in the hallway. *It's almost nine o'clock. Time for the trick-or-treaters to go home and stuff their little faces with sugar.* Jane reached out to hit the light switch for the front porch when she heard a loud knock on the big oak door. She looked through the glass panel beside the door. On the porch, stood three boys from her class. She agreed with her parents that fourteen was too old to be out collecting candy on Halloween, but obviously these guys hadn't got the message. She knew them well because they had gone through school together since kindergarten. Everybody had known everybody in that little school. Jane had been happy to move up the high school this September and be in a bigger school where everybody didn't know her. Jane quietly backed away from the door. *Maybe they'll just go away if I ignore them.*

The door vibrated as all three pounded on the door. "Trick or treat," they yelled. "Hey, Plain Jane, we want candy! We know you're in there. We saw you giving candy to some kids."

Jane sighed and looked down at the Oriental rug at her feet. She clasped her hands at her waist. She let her eyes follow the twist and turns of the intricate design of the rug. She stood rigid and motionless, letting time stand still. They banged on the door again. She peeped out. Of course, the boys hadn't put much effort into their costumes. George had on a hockey jersey.

Anthony wore a tutu and was holding a pink wand. She didn't know what Bart was supposed to be. Again she stood like a statue and traced the rug design with her eyes. "Whack!" More banging on the door brought her back to reality. She reached for the bowl of candy and slowly opened the door. She shoved the bowl out in front of her, staring into the bowl, not looking at the boys' faces, not hearing what they were saying, but watching their hands grab all the candy. Then she pulled the bowl back and quickly closed the door. She reached up and flipped off the light for the porch.

Jane stood perfectly still until their footsteps and voices faded away. Then she walked across the hardwood floor into the living room and curled up in a big overstuffed chair and stared off into space. *Will they ever quit calling me that? Probably not. I will always be "Plain Jane" to them. But I look okay. In the magazines, some of the models look a lot like me. I'm not ugly.* Jane twisted around and threw one leg over the arm of the chair. *When I go to University I'll use my middle name. I'll be Amelia Thomas. Even better, I could go by Amy.* For the second time this Halloween night, she smiled. Her first smile, earlier in the night, had been inspired by a little girl in a fish costume. You just don't expect to see a green fish at your front door.

Halloween had never been a good holiday for Jane. When she was little, her shyness had made the night into a thing of horror. Her mother had insisted that she put on a costume and go out. She was dragged from house to house. Her mother would shove her up to the door and glare at her until she mumbled the expected three words: "Trick or treat."

Jane thought that she'd be able to stay in her room and avoid the whole Halloween thing this year. But, today, when she came home from school, exactly at three-fifty, as she always did, her mother had said, "Your supper is in the fridge; there's candy on the counter. Stay downstairs and give out the stuff. I'll be in my room on my computer all evening. And don't you dare eat even one piece of that candy." Then her mother had stomped off up the stairs. At least she didn't yell. Her mother yelled at her a lot. She yelled about anything and sometimes about nothing.

Jane understood. She didn't like the yelling and the hostility and the strict rules, but she understood. Life had not been easy for her mom, and it had worn her down. Her mother's life dream was to be a great musician. She had played the violin since she was four and at twenty-two, just weeks after being accepted in the London Philharmonic Orchestra, her arm was smashed in an auto accident. It was a serious break that left her with limited use of her fingers. She was pregnant with Jane at the time. Her mom blamed the driver of the other car for Jane's

Asperger's and the abrupt end of her musical career. Her mom had sued the other driver, but he had no money and it brought her no satisfaction. As far back as Jane could remember, her mother had always been an angry woman working in a job she hated. Dad's moving out had been the last straw. After he left, her mother lived in a state of permanent tension, strung as tight as her old violin. And she just could not accept the fact that her child, her *only* child, had Asperger's.

Jane had read and researched her disorder. Fortunately, her Asperger's symptoms were relatively mild. Most people wouldn't know she was different. She didn't flap her hands or repeat words over and over. She worked hard at looking interested when people spoke to her. She knew she tended to say certain favourite phrases often, but she tried not to. Looking people in the eye was still difficult for her, but she worked at it. Sometimes she would just look at their noses and hope they didn't notice. Now that she was older, she didn't blame her mother for trying to make her normal. Jane wanted so badly to be normal.

A loud ring made her jerk around in the chair and lunge for the phone. She knew that if her mother answered the phone, she'd have no chance of getting the call. Her mother usually told people who phoned in the evening that, "Unless it was an emergency, one is not to call this house after supper." It was one of her mother's rules. Jane's mom had decided that a person with Aspergers needed a lot of rules.

"Hello?"

"Wow! You're quick. You got it on the first ring."

"Luckily, the first ring doesn't usually penetrate the haze of cognition that surrounds my procreator when she's on her computer.

"Luckily, you have a friend that's smart enough to understand you without consulting a dictionary."

"And I do appreciate you, Ava. I just wanted you to know that. I've read that Asperger's people often lack facial expressions and body language to show our feelings. Consequently, I thought it appropriate to tell you that I appreciate you." Jane glanced at the stairs to see if her mother was coming down. Her shoulders relaxed when she saw the empty staircase. "So… what did you find to occupy your evening?"

"Well, I'm sure you'll disapprove, but I put on my old witch costume and hit up a few houses for candy."

"You could still get in that dress? You wore that in the… was it the third or fourth grade? Do you really think it appropriate to… "

Ava interrupted, "I got taller, not fatter, but it was tight. See, I knew you'd fuss at me for going out. Don't care. We have different opinions about a lot of things. Still, I'm sure you'll not refuse a bit of my candy tomorrow. Will you?"

"I relish the thought of candy, and I will delight in breaking one of Mom's rules. I hate rule number three: no sweets. Since it will be the day after Halloween she'll probably sniff for the smell of chocolate on my breath."

"Are you serious?" Ava gasped.

"No. I jest. She doesn't go that far. But I dare not show up for my well-balanced supper tomorrow with no appetite."

"Wow! I *so* wouldn't want to be you. How do you stand living with her?"

Jane sighed. "I have analyzed my other options and find this abode preferable to a foster home or group home. And she is my mother. I do feel affection for her."

"Yeah, she's your mom."

"And the future looks quite favourable. I achieve very good grades and my university education will be paid for by the bursary left to me in my grandmother's will."

"You never told me about that. That's great. My parents are sweating bullets over how they're going to put me and my stupid brother through college."

"I hope we can attend the same university. The University of Idaho has the preeminent forestry program in North America. From my research, there are several that I could attend. There are good syllabuses at Laval in Quebec, the University of Toronto and UBC in Vancouver."

"So you're still intending to specialize in trees?" Ava exclaimed. "I was hoping, really hoping, that some day you'd get over your obsession with trees. There are so many other interesting things in the world. I mean, I haven't heard any tree facts out of you for weeks so I thought… "

"Obviously, you don't remember our conversation on October fourth. After I told you that the Ava Tree in Australia has a root system that takes up more than an acre, you became quite exasperated and indicated that you never wanted to hear anything about trees out of me ever again. Wanting to retain our friendship, I have refrained from talking about trees for the last twenty-seven days. But, I still find them the most fascinating thing on earth and I intend to make them the basis of my life's work. They are the oldest living things on earth. There is a bristlecone pine in California that is 4,841 years old. How can you not find them interesting?"

There was silence on Ava's end of the line. "All right. Trees are neat. How's this for a compromise. If you can just keep it down to one tree fact per day, I can live with that."

"Thank you. I read so many amazing things about trees and I want to share them with someone. I don't dare mention the T-word to my mother. She quit listening years ago. The very word starts her yelling."

"All right, I've heard my tree fact for the day. Back to university. So you've got to go to a school with a good forestry program, right? Some day, give me a list of acceptable schools and we'll go from there."

"I just realized that we've never seriously discussed your proposed future. What do you want to major in?" Jane asked.

"That is a momentous factor in choosing a school. You can't get a degree in reading sci-fi books. But, you could major in literature. You could teach literature. Or do you want to write? You might write sci-fi?"

"That would be wonderful. But I don't know if I can write. It's a talent thing. How do I know if I can do it?"

"You just do it," Jane replied forcefully. "Just write.

Write descriptions of your surroundings. Write up a dialogue between me and you. Write about a world you picture in your mind. Imagine a perfect society on a perfect planet and then write a plot in which things go wrong."

"Wow! You've put a lot of thought into this."

"No. Not really," Jane retorted. "I read a book about writing yesterday. All those methods were in the book. I'll lend it to you."

"But, what if my writing style is... um, not good? Who can I get to read my stuff and evaluate it? Not our English teacher. She's not really a brain. You're way smarter than her"

"So therefore, I will read your prose and indicate my opinion."

"Jane, you know a lot. But what makes you an expert on writing?"

"Last year, I read 253 books and this year, since January one, I have read 189. I would think that this consumption of literature has made me aware of the quality of things I read."

"That does make some sense. You'll tell me if it's bad?"

"If you want, I will write out an analysis of the positive and negative aspects of the writings. From that, you can attempt to improve the text. If this still results in prose that is unacceptable, then you will know that it would be prudent to consider another career."

"All right, I'd like that. Can you bring the writing book to school tomorrow? I think I should read it before I start anything."

"Definitely. I'll bring the book with me tomorrow. Right now, I should end this conversation. I have homework to attend to and don't want to hear the bellowing that would ensue if my mother were to find me on the phone."

"Right. So I'll see you tomorrow. It's really nice of you to help me with this writing thing. I'm sort of scared cause I could be lousy. I usually get mostly Bs on school papers and… "

"Bye Ava. I hear Mom on the stairs."

CHAPTER

14

UME ON EARTH

The sun rose casting a red glow over the fall leaves on the forest floor. After digging out the back of the hollow to make it a bit bigger, the Ume had covered the opening to their little cave with green and brown camouflage fabric. Toboo-lo and Jolocko-lo scattered red and gold leaves over the fresh dirt. Senoa-lo stepped out and looked back at the camp. *Well done.* They gathered inside, all wondering what the day would bring.

Senoa-lo sat them down and reminded them of the plan for their first day on Earth. "If we go out, we go in twos. If we see human or animal activity, we stay inside. At all times, someone must be on lookout at the door. We'll take turns. Our goal today is to examine this area to determine what could be a threat to us or an asset, and to scout around for a more permanent camp. Always have your weapon ready. Any animal might just see us as a possible meal. Humans could think we are small Earth rodents and possibly try to kill us. Hopefully, we will be able to escape their notice most of the time. And remember, if you are captured by an Earth person, never speak or show any intelligence. And, try to hide your hands. Here on Earth only apes have fingers and apes are not native to North America. I almost forgot, if you are in an area where there might be humans, make sure to hop. Do not walk. None of the native animals walk upright. We want them to think that we are just cute fuzzy harmless creatures. Now, let's unpack and get to work."

"Why?" Leela-lo asked. "Why not speak to the humans if we are captured? They might help us."

They all turned and stared at her.

Senoa-lo shook her head in disbelief. "If they think we are just some forest animal, some weird rabbit or rat that they are unfamiliar with, they might just release us. But, if we show them that we can talk, we'll spend the rest of our lives in a lab being prodded and experimented on."

"You're right. What I was thinking? Bad idea." Leela-lo stared into to space with a wistful look on her face. "I wish we could just communicate with them. I have so many questions." She picked up one of the crates. "So… let's unpack these things."

As they pulled equipment out of the crates, Toboo-lo nudged Senoa-lo. "I have watched much Earth TV, but it seems that the attire worn by those young male adults we saw yesterday was rather unusual for this part of Earth."

Senoa-lo stopped what she was doing and turned to him. "Yesterday was Hallowe'en; it is a holiday when children and some adults roam the streets in abnormal clothing and ask for sweet foods. We discussed this in one of our meetings. The Palalan only visit here on this holiday."

"Oh."

"You weren't listening, were you? That's right, I remember, you had your computer in front of you all the time."

He turned his back to her, pulled a carton of tools out of his crate and put it on the ground. "Well, I got the gist."

Senoa-lo took his arm and tugged on it until he turned to face her. "Toboo-lo, you're smart and you get things done. That's true. But, you're one of those easy going people who float along in his own world, not strictly following the rules, and doing things your own way. Maybe it's because you're only interested in things that concern plants." She moved closer to him and grabbed his other arm. "That might work for you at home. But here, we're on a mission to save our people. We need you to listen carefully and be one of the team." She stood glaring at him.

"All right, I wasn't listening." He hung his head. "I'll do better. So are you going to tell me why this Hallowe'en day is so important to the Palalans?"

"It's simple and sort of ingenious." Senoa-lo smiled and let go of his arms. "They came to Earth on this holiday so that they could go out among the Earth people disguised in Earth-type Hallowe'en clothing."

Toboo-lo tilted his head and asked, "You're saying they came all this distance to just stay one day?"

"Yes, and you'd know that if you had been listening at the meetings. Of course, they take air samples, soil samples and plant samples. We and the Palalans already know lots about Earth from watching their TV and computer screens. I guess the Palalans just wanted to really be here, even briefly just to see what it's really like. They can't stay longer because the Earth people would discover them, and Palalan law forbids communicating with the Earth people."

Just as she got the last word out, Leela-lo, who was near the door hushed them. "Quiet, there's an animal out there. A dog."

Toboo-lo whispered, "What kind of dog?"

"I don't know. Not my specialty."

Toboo-lo moved over to the doorway. "I think it's a golden lab. They're supposed to be very nice. I've seen them on computers and in films. But, it's wonderful to see one live. I'm so excited!"

"If he sticks his big nose in here, he won't be live much longer," Jolocko-lo growled and waved his weapon.

"Really, we must stop talking; dogs have very sensitive hearing. Just be still 'til he goes away." Senoa-lo motioned for everyone to move away from the doorway. "I'll watch and tell you when he goes away," Toboo-lo whispered. The others quietly moved to the back of the cave and sat in silence. Long minutes passed until Toboo-lo announced that the dog was gone.

Senoa-lo took charge. "Jolocko-lo, unpack your computer please. We need to know exactly where we are in relation to houses, towns and military bases. I hope we can use Google from here."

Jolocko-lo actually smiled for once. "I've been looking forward to this. It's been so difficult to gather information when I could only see sites that the Earth people pulled up. Now, I can hopefully access the entire web."

Jolocko-lo put his computer on his lap and typed and paused, then typed and paused some more. He twisted his mouth to on side and went at it again. Everyone else continued to unpack, but they all kept an eye on Jolocko-lo. He put his head down and moaned. Suddenly he perked up and quickly typed in a series of numbers. "Yes, finally!" He threw his arms up in the air, and grinned. "We have Google!"

A sigh of relief passed through the room. Senoa-lo smiled, then peeked out the door. "I need someone to go out scouting with me."

Toboo-lo jumped up. "I'd really like to go."

"Fine. But remember, this isn't a botanical survey. No plants. We're going to see what's here and look for a better camping spot. Pack some food bars, a weapon and some water in your vest and let's go."

CHAPTER

15

UME ON EARTH

Toboo-lo was sitting on the ground rubbing his leg when Senoa-lo got to him. "Toboo-lo, if you're going to hop, then you have to pick a level landing spot before you leap. Have you always been accident prone?"

"Not really. I know. How many times did I hear my mother say, ' Look before you leap'? This is so different from the Palalan jungle and not at all like the vegetation at home. These huge trees have big surface roots all over the place." He continued to rub his leg. "The Palalan jungle has huge trees but the roots are all underground, so the jungle floor is pretty level. And at home, we don't have this problem because we don't have trees this big. Did you know that the height of our trees is limited by the cold air that blows off the ice."

Senoa-lo rolled her eyes, "So if you're thorough with the science lesson… are you good to go?"

Toboo-lo pushed himself off the ground and stood up. "Give me a minute." He took a few steps, stopped, stretched his left leg, then said, "I'm fine."

Senoa-lo took the lead. "The bush is a bit denser over that way. Let's see what's over there." Toboo-lo followed.

They had only gone ten steps when Senoa-lo's ears went up. "Stop. Listen."

Something was rattling the bushes in front of them. They both stayed perfectly still. Then slowly Senoa-lo took her charger out of her vest. A huge red furry head poked out of the bushes. It had a long pointed snout that ended in a wet black nose. The nose seemed to be almost as big as Senoa-lo's head, and it was moving as it sniffed at them. Senoa-lo whispered to Toboo-lo, "Back up. I don't want to have to hurt it."

Toboo-lo whispered as he backed up, "Hurt it? I don't want to be eaten." In a flash, his charger was in his hand. As they backed up, the animal continued to advance.

Senoa-lo whispered, "What is your charger setting?"

"Low. You said to keep it at the stun setting. Maybe I should I turn it up?"

"No. That should be enough to make it go away. What kind of animal is it? Is it another dog?" They backed up as it slowly moved toward them.

"I think it's a fox. It's like a dog, but wild," Toboo-lo replied.

"Then it eats creatures like us every day." She reached down and set her charger to max.

As they continued backing up, Toboo-lo glanced back to see what was behind them. "Uh, Senoa-lo, there's a tree, with huge roots spreading out on each side just behind us. We can't go much farther. We're going to have to, uh, deal with it. What do we do?"

"Stay beside me. It's really interested in us. Soon, it's probably going to lower its head to sniff us or eat us. When it does, we both go for it."

"Alright, if that's the plan, then let's back up a bit more so we'll have our backs up against the tree when he attacks. I don't want him to be able to get behind us. From what I've seen on nature shows, these types of creatures can move very fast."

Just then, the animal lowered his head and rushed toward them. Both stabbed at it, but only Toboo-lo's charger made contact. The animal winced and jerked its head back. It took a step back and stood with its head twisted to one side studying them.

"Toboo-lo, put your charger on max. He's not going away." Toboo-lo quickly turned the knob, making his charger into a lethal weapon. They stood with their chargers aimed at the huge animal, waiting for its next attack.

The animal stepped toward them, bared his teeth and growled. They stood their ground. They had no choice. With the tree and roots behind them and the creature in front of them, there was no place to run. Toboo-lo's hand started to shake, so he reinforced it with his other hand. As the monster opened its mouth, its lower jaw came down a bit. Senoa-lo ran forward, leapt up and touched the jaw with her charger. The animal's body twitched. It staggered. Then it slowly tilted to one side and fell over. The ground shook. Toboo-lo eased his weapon down to his side, and looked over at Senoa-lo. "You killed it."

"Yeah. And would you rather I hadn't killed it?"

"No, you were great. I've just never seen anything killed. It was him or us and I'm glad that it was him. Wow! That was intense. I mean, I had been told that these chargers could kill anything, but… Wow! One touch and he was done for."

"It was amazing." Senoa-lo flopped down on a rock. "I guess we had better get out of here. I understand that the smell of a dead animal attracts other animals."

Toboo-lo noticed that Senoa-lo looked a bit dazed. "We can sit for a few minutes. I think it'll be a while before the flesh deteriorates enough to allow the carrion-eating animals to detect it. Let's just sit on these rocks and get our heads together." They sat still, glancing up at the dead animal occasionally. After a few minutes, Toboo-lo got up. "I want to see it up close. I have to touch it." Senoa-lo nodded approval and watched as he approached the dead animal.

Toboo-lo moved cautiously over to it. He touched the fur on one leg, then quickly drew his hand back. He walked over to the end of the leg and touched the rough skin on the bottom of one paw. He held his charger out in front of him as he approached the head.

He jumped when Senoa-lo called out, "It's dead. Really. No animal, not even a Palalan or an Earth person can live through a maximum charge. So get on with your examination so we can go. Now we'll have to find another section of the woods for our permanent camp. We certainly can't put it anywhere near this thing."

"Right, we're going to have to really distance ourselves from this. Not only because of the smell and animals, but because if a human finds it there might be a police investigation."

Senoa-lo jumped up. "A what?"

Toboo-lo came over and faced her. "If this is a red fox, and I think it is, from what I remember of the animal charts. It's a protected species."

"So?"

"So if an Earth person sees that it is dead with no obvious injuries, then they might take it to a lab and do an autopsy. And if they find that it was killed by an electrical charge, then… They, the police, or some authority, could come looking to see who who killed it."

"You've watched too much CSI." Senoa-lo wandered over toward the carcass.

"No, really. We don't want policemen or park rangers stomping around in these woods right now."

Senoa-lo turned back toward him. "And what do you suggest we do to prevent that?"

Toboo-lo studied the situation for a moment, then walked over to the creature's head. "I think we should cut holes in it so that it will look like it was attacked by some other forest animal."

She stepped back. "Are you serious?"

"Think about it. We can't take that chance. They could send sniffing dogs in here. We'd be found in no time. And the thing is dead. It's not going to be any deader if we poke some holes in it."

Senoa-lo hesitated. "Where should the cuts be?"

Toboo-lo took a knife out of his vest. "In the Earth nature shows, when wolf-, dog-, or fox-type animals attack each other, they kill by biting the neck. I can try to stab holes that will look like teeth marks."

Senoa-lo shook her head and turned away from the dead creature. "Just do it and let's go."

CHAPTER

16

EARTH

As she did many nights, Jane lay in her single bed thinking over everything she had said that day. She analyzed what had been said to her and what she had replied. It was like watching a movie. As she reviewed the day, she speculated on different ways she could have handled things. She had decided to approach the girl with the new hair style like she would a scared rabbit. *I will always stay five or more feet away from her and try to do a slight but not full smile when she looks my way. If there is no negative reaction from her, I will come a foot closer in a few days. She seems to be someone who trusts no one, so I will refrain from any actions that could look like I am trying to be her friend. I doubt she will ever be my friend, but maybe in a few weeks I can get her to go from hostile to neutral. It feels bad to have antagonistic people around.*

Jane was so glad to have Ava for a friend. *I can talk to Ava about anything. She tells me if something doesn't interest her. But she says it in a nice way. Why can't more people be like her? Truthful, but considerate. She's the only person in the world that I can relax with.*

Jane went back to reviewing the day. At lunch, two new girls had plopped down at her table without asking. Ava hadn't arrived yet so she had had to handle it alone. *I looked up, smiled and said."Hello." They just glared at me and continued their conversation. I just looked at my food and continued eating. What should I have done? I could have asked their names and told them mine. I could have told them one of the jokes I've memorized. I could have complimented one of them on something. That's what Ava did. Ava came over and told the blonde that she liked how her blue bracelet matched her skirt. Then she introduced both of us and started asking what classes they were taking. In two minutes, she had them laughing.*

As she drifted off to sleep, Jane was thinking… *I guess my mantra should be, "What would Ava do?"*

CHAPTER

17

EARTH: THE UME CAMP

It had been two Earth hours since Jolocko-lo had first accessed the internet. Leela-lo glanced over at him and saw that he was still smiling. *The old grump is actually happy. I can't remember ever seeing him smile like that. Not once, ever.* Leela-lo looked out the door scanning the area in front of the camp. "Hey, here they come." As Senoa-lo and Toboo-lo brushed past her, she exclaimed, "Toboo-lo, what is that on your fur?" That got Jolocko-lo's attention. He turned to look at Senoa-lo and Toboo-lo.

Senoa-lo raised her arms to halt the flurry of questions she knew would follow. "It's blood, but not his blood. We're fine. Let me sit down and we'll tell you what happened." Jolocko-lo rose and motioned her toward his seat on a crate. They were all ears as Senoa-lo told them about their encounter with the animal.

Leela-lo pointed to her computer screen. "Is this what it looked like?" She had pulled up a photo of the North American red fox.

Toboo-lo looked it over. "That was it, but it was big, really big."

Leela-lo threw her arms around Toboo-lo. "I'm so glad that you're alright."

Senoa-lo rose from her seat and sighed. "I am wiped. I am feeling old and I need to rest."

Toboo-lo smiled at her. "Maybe a nap will help."

Senoa-lo sighed. "Yeah. If you need me, I'll be laying down in the back for a few blips, I mean, minutes."

Toboo-lo's ears perked up. "So we are using Earth time delineations?"

"Yes," Senoa-lo replied. "That was indicated in your information material. Didn't you read it? We would find it difficult to divide time on this planet into twelve parts day and twelve parts night since the length of their light and dark times vary. I think using Earth time delineations will make it easier to understand the internet and coordinate our bodies to their sun rotation. Your computers should already be set to Earth time."

Senoa-lo moved to the back of the shelter. "So Jolocko-lo, please wake me in twenty Earth minutes." She spread a cloth on the ground between two crates and lay down.

CHAPTER

18

UME ON EARTH

Senoa-lo closed her eyes, but sleep was impossible. Her body was tired but her mind was spinning. *I wish Mom were here and could be part of this.* Her mother had died six years ago at the age of two hundred. Ume scientists had been able to devise medicines for many maladies and many medicines had been borrowed from the Palalans, but the muscle-destroying disease that killed her mother had no cure and quickly made her mother's life unbearable. Her mother had chosen to have a traditional living funeral. Friends and family gathered in a ceremony to say goodbye and stand by as chemicals sent her mother drifting off to sleep and a painless death. It had been a beautiful ceremony. The music and poems were exactly what her mother had wanted. But Senoa-lo was bothered by something her mother had said during the ceremony. Just as the chemicals were injected, she said, "I never did anything of significance."

Those words hurt. Years ago, before her mother's illness struck, Senoa-lo had noticed that her mother smiled less and seemed troubled at times. One day, Senoa-lo and her mother were in their petra orchard sitting on the ground, resting after picking a basket of fruit when her mother said to her, suddenly, out of nowhere, "I'm nobody. I've done nothing of significance in my whole life."

Senoa-lo had been shocked to hear her mother say this. Her mother had always worked in the government's administration of food distribution. She was respected and seemed to be appreciated at work. Her mom had been a caring and encouraging mother to her and her older brother, Heno-lo. And, from Senoa- lo's viewpoint, her mom had had a very good relationship with Senoa-lo's father. Senoa-lo was puzzled by what she was hearing.

Tears had flowed down her mother's face as she spoke. "When I die of course you and those who know me well will mourn. But there will have been nothing that I have done that is of any significance to our people or our planet. I have never cured a disease or invented anything. I have not written books or created a building. This saddens me. I wish I had lived differently."

At first, Senoa-lo was stunned and sat in silence. *What do I say?* She watched a tear drop off her mother's chin. "But Mom, your genes created me and Heno-lo. Your care and teaching skills helped us develop into… " She paused. "We're good people because of you. And about your work. Everyone admires how efficiently you kept the department running."

"I'm a bureaucrat." Her voice became harsh. "I shuffle papers and type on my computer. I can and will be easily replaced."

Senoa-lo was grasping at straws. "You are loved by many people because of your generosity and kindness."

"A few people will miss me when I am gone. And I will be sorry to leave them. I appreciate that you laud my parenting skills, but your father was also a big influence on your development." She paused. "But I will die, as we all do and I have done nothing."

Senoa-lo hadn't known what to say. Fortunately Heno-lo appeared on the scene with drinks and food. Her mother had quickly wiped her tears and nothing more was said about it. Several times Senoa-lo thought about discussing it with her mother. But, to say what? So she let it lie.

Senoa-lo thought to herself, *I am here on a foreign planet trying to do something of importance for our people. I am who I am in part because of her.* I would like to think that what I do here lends significance to my mother's life. *I wish she were here so that I could tell her that.* Senoa-lo then drifted off to sleep.

CHAPTER

19

UME ON EARTH

Senoa-lo woke to to the sounds of loud voices arguing over something about a guide to Earth. As she pushed herself up off the hard ground, she could feel her body protesting her choice of a bed. She turned to see who was making the racket and her neck reminded her that next time she should find something softer to sleep on.

Jolocko-lo was waving a fist in the air and saying, "We don't have time to waste with this nonsense. Delete that from your computer and get to work!"

"I am working," Toboo-lo replied. "I just took a ten minute break to write a few lines. I get breaks, don't I? When did I become your slave?"

"This is not something worthy of your time or brainpower. Science fiction is just… "

"Have you ever read any science fiction?" Toboo-lo shouted as he planted his hands on his hips and tilted his head.

"Of course I have. I wanted to see what thoughts Earthers might have written about people from other planets. And it's all silly stuff. They seem to think that either we want to suck out their brains or that we are going to come to Earth and teach them about technology that will solve all their problems."

"But doesn't sci-fi make you think about things?"

"I've been thinking about things since I was born. It's just ludicrous speculation based on nothing. They've got some crazy ideas about other species. It never occurred to them that we're just neighbours with our own problems. But from what I've seen of their news broadcasts, there's a lot of '*it's all about me*' thinking on this planet." Jolocko-lo paused, then he got loud again. "Anyway, I don't care what kind of book you're writing. We don't have time for this foolishness. We are trying to save our people and you… "

"Stop!" Senoa-lo yelled as she approached the two of them. Holding her hand up, she lowered her voice to almost a whisper. "First, there should be no shouting in this camp, ever! The animals and people here might hear us. Remember, this is a covert operation. We should always be speaking in hushed tones. And second, Toboo-lo, what are you doing that has Jolocko-lo so upset?"

Jolocko-lo stepped up to her with both hands in the air. "He is wasting... "

Senoa-lo raised a hand to interrupt him. "I was speaking to Toboo-lo." Jolocko-lo turned his back on her and stomped over to his computer with his shoulders hunched. Senoa-lo paused, then turned back to Toboo-lo. "Well?"

Toboo-lo looked a bit sheepish as he replied. "I'm writing a book."

Senoa-lo peered at him. "Here? Now?"

Toboo-lo shuffled his feet. "It's like this. I really like Earth science fiction books and movies. My favorite is 'A Hitchhiker's Guide to the Universe.' It's really funny. So when we started talking about this trip I started writing a novel sort of based on what we're doing. I call it 'A Hitchhiker's Guide to Earth.'"

"Jolocko-lo's right. We don't have time... "

"Wait," Toboo-lo cut in. "I'm not letting it interfere with my work. Really. I'll just write down a couple of lines once or twice a day. I'm just making some notes so that I can work on it when this is all over. Jolocko-lo saw the title and my notes and went wild. Maybe he doesn't like Douglas Adams. Probably doesn't even know who he is. It seems that he hates sci-fi in general. But what it comes down to is that I should be allowed to write a couple of lines once or twice a day."

Senoa-lo glanced over at Jolocko-lo. Then, turned back to Toboo-lo. "All right. We're all free to take occasional breaks. It keeps us fresh. I'll talk to Jolocko-lo. Just promise me that you won't let it interfere with your work."

"Of course. I take this mission very seriously. Speaking of which... "

"Yeah, tell her about the message, already," Leela-lo piped up.

Senoa-lo's head bounced back and forth from Leela-lo to Toboo-lo. "We got a message?"

Jolocko-lo looked back over his shoulder. "Yep, six minutes ago we received our first communication from home."

Senoa-lo sighed and sank down on the nearest carton. "I am so relieved. Why didn't you wake me? What did they say? Did you send a reply?"

"Reply sent six minutes and twenty seconds ago," Jolocko-lo stood up and delivered a mock salute. "They just wanted to know if we received the message and if we were all right."

Senoa-lo smiled. "I was beginning to worry. It would all be for nothing if the communication system hadn't worked."

Toboo-lo jerked around in his seat and glared at Senoa-lo. "You mean there was a possibility that we could have been stranded here with no way of ever getting in touch with our people?"

"Uh, even though we duplicated the Palalan equipment very carefully, there was always a small chance that something could go wrong. It's never been done before."

"Is there any other experimental part of this mission we should be worrying about?"

Senoa-lo threw up her hands. "This whole thing's an experiment. You knew that. But we're here and the next part is relatively simple. We find a weapon that fits our needs, and then we contact our people with specifications on how to build it."

"And then we work on finding a way home." Leela-lo added.

Senoa-lo wandered over to stand beside Jolocko-lo. "Jolocko-lo, what did you say in your reply to our people back home?'

"I said, 'We received your message and all is well.'"

"In English?"

"No, in Ume. They sent their message in Ume."

Senoa-lo reared up and snarled at him. "In Ume! What are the Palalans going to think if they hear a message coming from Earth in a non-Earth language? Do you have ice for brains? I want you to stop what you're doing and pull up the mission manual and carefully read every word of it. All correspondence with our planet is to be in English and in code. It's a simple code that substitutes specific words. It's programmed into the computers under the heading code conversion. Weapon is ice cream. Steel is putty. Hair is spaghetti. This way whether Palalans or Earthers intercept a message coming from Earth, it's just jumbled meaningless English words coming from Earth."

"Let me get this straight." Jolocko-lo cocked his head to one side. "Messages from our planet are sent out in Ume and we only communicate back in coded English? What are the Earth beings going to think if they intercept Ume messages coming to Earth?"

Senoa-lo hesitated. "Well… "

Leela-lo jumped in. "Some of them will think their dream has finally come true. They'll think aliens are trying to contact earth. We are going to make them so happy. They'll be dancing in the streets."

Jolocko-lo huffed. "Some might be dancing, but there will be others who will be scared, really scared."

Senoa-lo raised her eyebrows at Jolocko-lo. "Better that, than if they hear an Earth language being broadcast from space. If they intercept an Ume message they are going to be thrilled to hear an alien voice from outer space. But they'll have no idea what it says because they have nothing they can relate it to. And because their astrophysics studies are way behind ours, they will have only a vague idea about where the message comes from.

Jolocko-lo nodded. "So… no problem. There will just be some very excited, confused Earth scientists. I've always felt sorry for those humans who have devoted their lives to looking and listening for us. This is like the Earth saying about 'throwing them a bone', which means we give them something, but not anything of any worth."

Leela-lo tilted her head to one side. "I wonder what the Earth religious groups will say about it?"

"Not our problem, but it should be interesting. So… " Senoa-lo concluded, "From now on, Leela-lo will handle all Earth to Ume communications and all of you are to review the mission manual. That includes you Jolocko-lo, especially you.

CHAPTER

20

PALALA

In a house in the Palalan tropics, Kebeck flipped over on his padded sleep platform and smiled to himself. He lay on his back and stretched his four arms and both legs up toward the ceiling, then flopped them down on the platform. *Finally, I can relax and get back to a normal life.* After he had returned from his brief visit to Earth, his life had been chaotic and tense. Accusations and bad feelings had dominated the Earth study committee meetings. He was so glad to have everything settled. He was sad that as a consequence of breaking the Earth non-communication rule, he was banned from any further trips to Earth or any other planet. But he could live with that because his forbidden communication had saved the life of someone he cared for. He realized that most Palalans would not understand why he was so attached to Adeline, the Earth female that he watched. He had observed Adeline from birth. She was like a daughter to him. He was pleased that she would soon enter into a lifelong contract with an Earth male that he thought to be considerate and dependable. He hoped he would be able to watch the wedding. Surely, someone at the wedding would record it on their cellphone and then he would be able to view it on his home computer.

Earth watching had been the most popular amusement for Palalans for a number of years. The Plalans could watch anything that happened in front of TV or cell phone or computer screens on Earth and they could watch all the Earth TV shows. At first, language was a problem, but soon most Palalans had learned at least one human language.

Some people worry that the Earth violence and their disregard for nature is having a bad influence on the Palalans. And now there is a faction trying to pass a law banning Earth watching. Kebeck was happy to learn that the group did not have the required number of members needed to force a vote. For now, he would be able continue to watch Adeline whenever he wanted. As he stretched his neck to one side, he noticed his travel bag sitting on the floor by the door. He had been so busy and so tense that he had forgotten to unpack it. *Today, I am going to straighten up the house, get my papers in order, and go back to living a life free of strife. No problems.*

As Kebeck stretched his limbs one more time, he noticed the smell of a female. The aroma grew stronger. He sat up as he recognized the scent and Sheme walked in the door.

"Greetings, my friend," he said as he jumped up and faced her. He extended his arms with his palms facing up, in the traditional greeting. She then placed a map in his upper right hand and smiled. He unfolded the map and studied it. It was the map he had given her when they changed the landing location for his last trip to Earth. It was evidence that he had done more than just lie to the committee. If this had been shown to the Justice Council when he came before them a few days ago, he would probably be locked in a psychiatric medical facility by now. He had lied. That had been proven by the recorded voice communications he had sent to the committee. But if they had known that in addition he had changed the landing location and given a note to a human, it would have led to more questions and a lot more trouble.

"Sheme, thank you for your discretion." *I am so relieved.* "I appreciate that you did not tell on me or show this map to anyone. I think it best that I destroy this now and we just forget everything that happened on that trip."

"I took it as evidence of your trust in me. You knew that you could rely on me to keep this from the Justice Council. We Palalans may not lie, at least not when we are visible, but some times we do avoid the truth."

"True. Fortunately they had no reason to inquire about where our ship landed and you have done me a great favor by not bringing it to their attention. No one would care that I landed in Canada, instead of Florida."

Sheme hopped up on the edge of the sleeping platform. "I respect that you took such a chance to save the life of a human.

I will never forget that. It is confirmation that you are the good person I thought you to be."

Trying to relax, Kebeck sat down beside her on the platform. But a tension started in his shoulders and crept into his neck. *Now she is going to ask about contracting with me to have a child. What do I say? Do I want to live with her for the next twenty years? Do I want to be a father again?* He looked over at her and forced a smile.

She stood up and faced him.

Here it comes. What do I say?

"Kebeck, we have been friends for many years. Now I am at a stage in my life when I am ready to have my second child, the last child that I shall produce. We speak of avoiding the truth. I must speak a truth to you now. I do not know if you are ready at this time to be a father again but I think you to be… "

Sheme stopped speaking and they both turned toward the door. A pungent male scent wafted in. Then, Prigo, Kebeck's son walked through the doorway. For a moment, they silently stared at him. Then Kebeck said, "Well… nice to see you. I… "

"Hi Dad. Hi Sheme. I know I am covered with mud; I've been on my bicycle for three hours. I am so glad that we duplicated that Earth invention. It is a wonderful machine." He looked down at the floor. "Sorry to track mud into the house. I will just step out back and rinse off." Prigo strolled past them, grabbed a towel off the shelf by the rear door, and disappeared through the back.

When he was out of sight, Kebeck quickly moved away from Sheme and grabbed his travel bag off the floor. He held it up in front of Sheme. "My son came for this. I brought some foliage back from Earth for him. He mentioned that he planned to come over and stay with me a few days." Kebeck lowered the bag. Their eyes met. He shrugged his shoulders. "Maybe we should continue this conversation later… some time soon?"

Sheme's body sagged as she nodded in agreement. "You are right. This is not a good time for this conversation. I wish you clear water." She turned and went out the front door.

Kebeck collapsed on the sleeping platform and released a sigh of relief. *I have some big decisions to consider.*

Prigo ambled in the back door drying his grey scales with a towel. He looked around. "Where is Sheme?"

Kebeck picked himself up off the platform. "She had to go."

"Oh." He put the towel back on the rack by the door then turned to face his father. "Is Sheme moving in with you?"

"No. I mean, I do not know." Kebeck held up the bag, then put it on the platform, and started pulling stuff out scattering it over the platform. "I have your leaves here somewhere."

Prigo shuffled through the collection of empty food wrappers, clothing and other odds and ends. He opened a notebook and a pile of dried red and yellow leaves fell out.

Prigo smiled. "Ah ha, my leaves. Very nice."

Kebeck started sorting the stuff into piles of trash and possessions to put be put away. A small piece of paper caught his eye. It seemed to have writing on it. He held it close to his face to examine it. The tiny paper had tiny marks on it that looked like foreign writing. He handed it to his son. "Look at this."

Prigo examined it. "It looks like someone wrote something in a language I don't recognize, then shrank it. This is curious. Do you have a magnifying instrument?"

Kebeck went over to a shelf and rummaged through a jumble of bits and pieces until he came across a piece of round glass. "This will do."

They took turns looking at the tiny paper through the glass.

"Dad, this is writing. Where did you get this?"

Kebeck thought for a blip. "I think I picked it up off the floor of the vessel we took to earth. I remember collecting all my stuff off the floor of the ship just before we landed back here. I certainly did not want to leave the vessel untidy, so I just tossed everything in my bag."

"Dad, could this have been left behind from another expedition to some other planet?"

"Maybe. But I doubt it. The vessel is cleaned and sanitized after every trip. The people at the intergalactic station are very fussy about germs. They sterilize the whole thing after every flight."

"So this paper somehow got on the ship on Earth."

"I guess it could have been in with the candy we collected from the Earth beings. But I do not see how? We stood outside the ship and sealed the Earth candy in a sterile container before we brought it in the vessel. When we landed here on Palala, we gave the sealed container to the scientist who debriefed us and sterilized us. He then took it to his lab to examine it. We did not open the container in the ship. We had been told not to open to it and we did not. I have no idea how this paper got here. This is a mystery."

Prigo examined the paper with the magnifying glass again. "It is writing. We should take this to a language expert to see if the language can be determined."

"Yes. That is what I will do. Tomorrow I will consult the directory and find the top language person in this region and contact them for a consultation." Kebeck took the paper from his son. He crossed the room and laid it on the shelf beside his computer. "Now, you probably want food and we finally have the time for a leisurely chat about my trip to Earth."

"I have been looking forward to this." Prigo grabbed a tongoo fruit and jumped up on the sleeping platform. "Tell me everything… "

21

PALALA

The next morning, streaks of pink peaked through the white clouds as the sun was rising in the grey sky over the Palalan jungle. Kebeck quietly rolled off the sleeping platform, moving slowly to keep the wooden boards from creaking. He watched his son's breast rise and fall as he continued to sleep. The boy, now a man, was never an early riser. Kebeck eased over to the shelf where the tiny piece of paper lay beside his computer. He examined the paper. *Still, no idea about what it is.* He flopped down on his slantboard and started a search on his computer. *Peelam is the nearest big university, I will check their directory.* It listed Solang Folint Creda as the senior language professor at Peelam University. A picture of Solang appeared beside her contact information. Her green scales had a bit of a red tint and her facial features were pleasing. *She looks nice and friendly. I will send her a message to inquire if she is interested in looking at this odd little paper.* Two blips after Kebeck finished typing his message, his computer bleeped indicating that he was receiving a request for live communication from Solang Folint Creda. Kebeck had just taken a bite out of a kebaa fruit, but he put it down and moved back over to the computer.

A voice behind him called out, "Dad, I am trying to sleep here."

"Sorry. I was trying to be quiet. I have a language expert wanting to discuss the little paper we found."

Prigo popped up and jumped off the platform. "That is different. Be right there. I am anxious to see what a language specialist thinks of the note."

Prigo was standing behind Kebeck's slantboard when Solang's face appeared on the screen. "Greetings. Being contacted by the famous space explorer, Kebeck, caught my attention, but my curiosity was really piqued at your mention of this mysterious language. May I see the paper?"

"I will send it now," Kebeck replied. He waved a hand at Prigo and Prigo took the tiny paper and put it in the scanner at the back of the computer.

Solang's lips puckered as she studied her screen. "I do not recognize this language at first glance. I will have to study it further. Why is it so small? Where did you find it? Is it from Earth?"

Prigo twisted his head around to look at his father.

"Uh… I think I picked it up off the floor in the ship as we were heading back from Earth," Kebeck replied.

"Did you let Earth beings come aboard the ship?"

"No!" Kebeck exclaimed. "I would never do that. The Earth beings did not even know we were there."

"I asked because I remember there was some kind of irregularity on your voyage."

"The incident you refer to consisted of me sending a message to an Earth being in order to prevent the death of another human. I must explain. For amusement, the last twenty-five rotations I have watched a human female as she matured. Here name is Adeline. At the time of my flight to Earth, I found out that a mentally sick human planned to kill her. It was necessary for me to send a message to one of Adeline's friends to prevent the murder. The message that I sent was transmitted without anyone being aware of where it came from. As I said, the humans were never aware of our presence on the planet and no one entered the ship."

"Then, how did th note get on the vessel?"

Kebeck made a face. "I do not know," Kebeck said curtly. There was silence on both ends.

"I am sorry," Kebeck apologized. "I should not display my frustration about this mysterious paper in my conversation with you. It is no excuse, but my life has been in turmoil since I came back from Earth. I thought everything was back to normal and then yesterday, we found this note among the items I took off the ship."

Solang smiled. "Apology accepted."

Kebeck continued. "I appreciate that you are willing to examine this paper for me, and I will not treat you with discourtesy again. I… "

Solang broke in on what was beginning to sounding like a lengthy repeat of his apology. "Really, I appreciate that you have given me the opportunity to examine this strange writing. I can see that this is of some importance to you, so I will work on it today and talk with you again tomorrow." She smiled again to reassure him that she had no animosity toward him.

Kebeck sighed. "Thank you. I look forward to talking with you again tomorrow." He turned off the communicator on his computer and shifted on his seat to face Prigo.

"Why is it that there is always something? I just want life to go back to normal."

Prigo smiled at him. "Normal is overrated. Interesting is better and more fun."

CHAPTER

22

PALALA

When Solang studied language in university many years ago, her studies consisted of regional variations of the Palalan language. Then about ninety years ago, scientists developed methods of receiving oral and visual information from other planets. That changed everything. Suddenly Solang was called on to examine and translate many different languages. With the help of her colleagues, Solang became proficient in two Poret languages, four Kiurt languages and six Earth languages. To Solang, a new language is just a fun new puzzle for her to play with and unravel.

Solang studied the note Kebeck had sent her. A feeling in the back of her head said something felt familiar about it. Then she realized what it was some of the characters were similar to the Palalan alphabet. Most of the graphic symbols were totally new to her, but a few were almost Palalan. She had seen something sort of like this somewhere. Then it hit her. Many years ago, one of her colleagues had shown her a tiny piece of paper with writing resembling this note. The paper had been found ten or fifteen years ago in a computer factory. Somewhere in her files she had a copy of that paper. She looked over at the shelves of files that lined the walls of her office. To anyone else, it might look like a disorganized mess. Her mate accused her of being a 'gather-hunter.' She did tend to gather lots of papers and then have to hunt through them to find anything. She started to dig.

CHAPTER

23

EARTH

After school, Jane finished her homework and was out the door in record time. Wandering through the woods, she wore heavy hiking boots, a checked flannel shirt and finished off her fashion statement with a pair of brown cargo pants. Her pockets were weighed down with notebooks, pens, a magnifying glass, a compass, and plastic bags for samples, everything and anything she might need to examine trees. She considered herself really fortunate to have a semi-wild park just behind her house. These woods were the only place where she could really relax and let her guard down. She knew the trees, bushes and mosses by their common and scientific names. A sound caught her attention. She looked up and there was the red-bellied woodpecker pecking on an oak tree. She smiled. His rapping was like an old friend saying hello. Jane checked her watch. She had to be home in fifty- seven minutes. She set her watch alarm to go off in fifty minutes, giving herself seven minutes to run home. Then she took out a notebook, checked her compass, pressed her shoulders back and headed north, examining trees and taking notes.

As usual, the time passed quickly. When the alarm rang, she stuffed her notebook in a pocket and galloped off for home. Jane ran in the front door and found her mother standing in the foyer. Jane scanned her watch. "I'm not late."

"No, you're on time. Come into the parlour. We need to talk."

Jane's heart skipped a beat. *Something's up. Something big.* She chucked off her muddy boots and followed her mother down the hall to their pristine parlour. The fact that her mom wanted her to come sit in the room usually reserved for important guests, surprised and scared her. Jane's mind was spinning with possibilities. *Grandma? Cancer? Moving?*

Her mother sat down in the imitation Tudor chair that they had inherited from Aunt Sadie. She motioned for Jane to sit on the couch. Then she put her hands in her lap and interlaced her fingers, looking quite prim and proper. Jane cautiously crossed the room and perched on the edge of the white whale of a couch that had usually been forbidden territory. "Jane, I have invited a guest to dinner tomorrow night. He is a very nice gentleman and I want you to meet him."

"So… this is someone I've never met? Where did you meet him? At work?"

"No." She looked down at her hands, then back up at Jane. "I feel awkward telling you this, but I met him on the internet." Her mother squirmed in her seat. "We've been chatting back and forth for months now. We've met for coffee several times. Yesterday he took me to lunch. He's very nice."

Jane worked at not showing surprise or disgust. *The internet? Her mom got picked up by some weirdo on the internet.* She looked down at the floor, taking a moment to let the news sink in before she spoke. "What does he do for a living? Where does he work?"

"He doesn't work anywhere. He's sort of self-employed. From what I understand, he was left a lot of money and he spends his time managing his investments." She paused. "So he does work, because managing money is a difficult job." She took a deep breath. "He's very nice."

"Right… At this dinner tomorrow, should I wear anything special or is it just a regular dinner?"

"I think, uh…, maybe your pink dress. Something casual but nice."

Jane could not wait for this conversation to be over. She didn't dare say any of the lines running through her head. And, no way was she going to wear that silly frilly pink dress. Jane kept her eyes on her lap, not daring to let her mother see the panic in her eyes. "I look forward to meeting him. Maybe I should wash up for supper now?" Before her mother could get another word out, Jane was off the couch and flying up the stairs.

CHAPTER

24

EARTH

Jane got up earlier than usual the next morning. She rushed
through her breakfast so that she could avoid her mother and
get to school a bit early. She was pacing up and down on the
side walk in front of the school when Ava saw her.

"Hey. What's up? You're strung tight as a piano wire."

Jane stopped, faced her and took a big breath. "I have a major, colossal, mind-blowing problem. I am reticent to broach it now because we don't have time to deal with it before class."

"So, how about a one sentence summary for now and we can tackle it in-depth at lunch?"

Jane looked down at the sidewalk for a second, then grumbled, "My mother seems to have acquired an internet boyfriend and has invited him to dinner tonight."

Ava stepped back. "Oh! Yeah, that's heavy. Definitely. We'll talk at lunch."

Jane glided through the morning, not listening to her teachers or paying any attention to the students around her. She hadn't slept well and her mind buzzed with the possibilities of how her mother's 'nice man' might affect her life.

At noon she rushed through the line and was halfway through her lunch when Ava joined her. "So, who is this guy your mom is having over for dinner?"

Jane sighed. "I don't know. She said she's been conversing on the internet with this man for months. You know there are all sorts of unsavoury types on the internet. I was too stunned to even ask his name. If I had his name, I could check him out on the internet. Or maybe not. He could have given my mother a fake name. Who knows who he really is?"

Ava put her hand on Jane's arm. "Slow down. Could be that he's not a bad fellow. Your mother's not stupid. She wouldn't fall for some Romeo who's just after her money. I'm sure that working at that divorces-are-us law office has had to make her a bit cautious about men. Sure she's rigid and tightly strung, but you have to admit that she is a smart woman. This could be a good thing. You know, if your mother had someone in her life besides you, she'd probably ease up on the rules."

"Right, as usual you bring up some sterling points." Jane stared at the surface of the table.

"Jane, look at me."

Jane lifted her head.

"At dinner tonight, you are going to meet someone your mother likes. And she doesn't seem to like many people. So, be friendly and courteous. Maybe treat him like... like you would want your mom to treat me. Give the guy a chance. Don't condemn him before you've met him. He must like your mother. How rare is that? And, of course, as soon as you can get away from them and to a phone, I want a full report on this dinner."

25

UME ON EARTH

Leela-lo sat working away on her computer while Toboo-lo stood looking out into the dark woods, guarding the doorway.

"There's nothing happening out there. This guard duty thing is a waste of my time," Toboo-lo complained. "They're taking forever. How long does it take to carry a few boxes over to the new camp?"

Leela-lo looked over at him. "Please be quiet, Toboo-lo. I'm trying to read."

"So tell me what you're reading. My mind's turning to mush from just staring into the dark."

"Sure, if it'll keep you quiet. Saying it aloud will help me remember more."

"Please. I'm going crazy here."

"Well… the only use of a WMD on Earth was the bombing of Japan at the end of their second World War. The destruction was amazingly awful. Oh! These pictures… they are disgusting and painful to look at." Leela-lo turned away from the screen, closed her eyes and made a sour face. "It scares me that we're looking for a weapon that could do something like this."

Toboo-lo moved toward her. "Let me see."

"No. I'm dumping this site." She deleted the image. "I can't stand to see any more. Fortunately, as far as we know, there is no uranium on our planet. So we can't make an atomic bomb."

"You're right about us not having uranium, but surely there are other lethal substances that can be put in a bomb."

"You know, now that we're here and I look on the internet and see the devastation caused by their wars, I… I… well, it scares me. I want to have a weapon to prevent the Palalans from hurting us, but I wouldn't want to use it and kill thousands of Palalans."

Toboo-lo glared at her. "I don't want to kill anyone either. But think of it like this. The Palalans are logical, intelligent beings. They probably want peace as much as we do. All this WMD stuff is probably for nothing. However, we can't stake our lives on 'probably'. This is just insurance. We need a big stick to wave at them, just in case they're not as logical as we think they are."

Jolocko-lo stumbled in the door and brushed past Toboo-lo. "I gotta sit. I'm exhausted. This lugging boxes thing is too much. I'm not a muscle bound grunt; I'm a scientist." He nudged Leela-lo over and squeezed in beside her. Senoa-lo trudged in behind him and threw herself on the floor.

Senoa-lo put out her hand to Leela-lo. "Could you hand me one of those water bottles beside you?

Leela-lo got up and distributed water to everyone.

"Thanks." Senoa-lo took a sip from her bottle. "We can pack up this stuff and if we all carry something, this will be our last trip. By tomorrow morning we should be all sorted out at our permanent camp and we can start devoting all our time to searching for a weapon. But for the moment, let's just rest a bit." Senoa-lo flopped back down and sighed.

CHAPTER

26

EARTH

Jane went straight to her room after school and succeeded in avoiding her mother until dinnertime. She tried on four different outfits before settling on a white long sleeve blouse and green A-line skirt. She topped it off with her grandmother's gold watch necklace. She found it comforting to fiddle with it when she was nervous. At ten to six, she descended the stairs to find her mother wearing a beautiful red dress with a draped neckline.

Inside, she was flabbergasted to see her mother wearing red. Her mother never wore red. Her whole closet was brown and tan. And she had never seen her mother in anything this flattering and fashionable. But Jane controlled herself and with a slight smile just said, "Nice ensemble."

The doorbell rang and, for a second, they just looked at each other. As her mother moved to open the door, Jane wanted to yell, 'Don't open it.' But she didn't. She just looked down at the floor and tried to disappear into her mind. When she heard her mother call her name, she smiled politely as her mother introduced her to Walter Fitzgerald. He was tall, pale and slender, except for a little pot belly. He had an English accent that reminded her of the Harry Potter movies. At first glance, he seemed to have a full head of light brown hair. But as he turned his head, chatting with her mother, she saw that it was a toupee blended into his real hair. Jane made a mental note to avoid looking at his hair. *If he sees me looking at it, he will know that I know and we'll both be embarrassed.*

The dinner wasn't as bad as she had thought it would be. He asked her a few questions about school, but otherwise he spent the whole evening talking to her mother. It was as if he didn't see her as a real person. When she tried to enter the conversation, he would reply with short answers and turn back to charming her mother. She felt like a third wheel or a fly on the wall, listening to a private conversation. When her mother mentioned after-dinner coffee in the parlour, she asked to be excused, saying that she should go to her room and study.

She closed her bedroom door and stood thinking for a minute. *Her mother was quite different tonight. Was this beginning of a divergent aspect of her life? Was life with her mother going to be different from now on? Enough speculating.* She reached for her phone and dialed Ava. "I survived the dinner."

Ava was all ears. "What does he look like?

Jane thought for a second. "If you took a Ken doll and stretched it, aged it 30 years, then with some clay gave it a little pouch stomach and a big nose, then bleached the whole thing and stuck an old fur hat on its head, then you would have Walter Fitzgerald."

"So he's not going to be modelling for Esquire magazine. Tell me more."

"He's quite tall. When he first came in the door and stepped toward me to shake my hand, I looked up at him and there was a clump of hair sprouting out his big nose. I stepped back a bit and tried to ignore the nasal bird's nest. Then there is the brown wig perched on his head. So the whole dinner I tried to look at him without looking at his nose or the fake hair. That was a challenge. Do I dislike him? I don't know because I don't know him. Except for a few courteous inquiries, he hardly acknowledged I was there. I was an accessory, like the salt shaker. Oh, and you'll love this… he sounds like one of the villains from the Harry Potter films. Remember the teacher with long black hair? Sounds like him, with maybe a bit of Monty Python thrown in."

"So he has a British accent. Did he say what part of England he was from?

"London, of course. He practically struts when he mentions London. Like a turkey with a beaver hat on his head. He lives in Toronto now for business reasons. He said it as if we were supposed to feel pity for the unfortunate fact that he's not living in London. Poor man stuck here in the colonies."

"So he's not terrible?"

"No," Jane paused. "He seems like a decent person. He appears to enjoy talking to my mother. He was charming her socks off, as the saying goes. And she's looking happier than I've ever seen her. It's just that it's so blatantly evident that he has absolutely no use for me.

"So maybe that's a good thing. If he makes your mom happy and keeps his big hairy nose out of your life, wouldn't that be nice?"

"That would be phenomenal. Alas, I must hang up now. I hear a car starting. Walter has left the building. I plan to Google him the minute I get off this phone. Please do the same. His full name is Walter Duncan Fitzgerald. Bye for now."

CHAPTER

27

UME ON EARTH

As the first pink light of dawn crept into the new Ume shelter, Jolocko-lo rolled over and bumped into Toboo-lo. "Hey! I'm trying to sleep here."

Jolocko-lo moved a bit and mumbled, "Sorry, didn't mean to hit you. I'm not used to sleeping in such close quarters. I need more room."

"Yeah, we know." Toboo-lo piped up. "Your elbow was in my stomach half the night."

Senoa-lo sat up. "Since we're all awake now, we might as well get up."

As they crawled out of their sleeping bags, a red light flashed on one of the computers.

Leela-lo rushed over to her computer. "They sent a message."

Everyone crowded around Leela-lo as she read the message aloud.

"Sayba says that our security team has reason to believe that the Palalans have discovered evidence that we exist. A note in Ume writing was found and is being studied by their experts. We know this because we intercepted a Palalan message about it. Also, one of their scientists has acquired a tape of two Ume speaking. They have not linked these two communications to our existence in the frozen region, but it means that they could be getting closer to discovering us. We are removing all non-essential Ume from the jungle and stepping up our audio and video surveillance of the Palalans. And she says that this development makes our job even more important and more urgent."

Jolocko-lo flopped back down on the ground. "Like we weren't under enough pressure. What idiot lost a note in Palalan territory?"

Toboo-lo piped up. "Some years ago, the Palalans found a paper with Ume writing in a factory. Some dim-wit had dropped it. They had their language experts study it, but they got nowhere with it. Why would another paper cause such a fuss?"

"Because" Leela-lo explained, "if they have multiple examples of a language, they have a better chance of deciphering it. So this oral sample just helps a bit more."

Senoa-lo moved to face the group. "Nothing we can do about that. Leela-lo, please reply that we received the message. And, remember to reply in English. After a morning bite, we need to get on our computers and continue our research. Now that atomic weapons have been eliminated as a possibility, we need to see what chemical bombs might work for us. Jolocko-lo is checking out napalm. He will assign each of you some other chemical compound to research. Toboo-lo and I will go out and hunt up some more edible plants. Leela-lo, please keep a watch on the doorway."

"Hey, I never get to go anywhere," Jolocko-lo complaimed. "What if I go with you instead of Toboo-lo? Why not?"

Toboo-lo just looked at him, then said, "Because we'll starve or be poisoned if we eat anything you bring in."

"Oh, right," Jolocko-lo confessed. "It is more logical to have our chemistry and plant expert find our food. But if you need me for anything else, I'd love to get out of this tent."

"Maybe next time." Senoa-lo gathered a water bottle, a weapon and a fake fur vest, then turned to Toboo-lo. "Do you want to eat now or shall we nibble as we gather greens?"

"Let's nibble." Toboo-lo picked up his vest, put it on and pushed instruments and mesh bags into the inside pockets. He twirled around to show off his round figure. The stuffed vest made him look like a big ball of fur. "Good thing we go out in pairs. If I were to fall over in this, I might need someone to roll me back to the camp."

As they went out the door, Leela-lo set up her computer so half her screen showed the area just outside the door and half her screen was available for work. Rigging a camera that focused on the area near the door had made life a bit easier for the door guard. After a few minutes Leela-lo looked over at Jolocko-lo's screen and saw a photo of an unclothed Earth being running down a road. The young female looked to be in pain.

"Jolocko-lo, what is that photo about?"

"It is of a young human female who has been sprayed with the chemical I am researching, napalm. It was used in a war some years ago. It burns the clothing and skin. I'm looking to see if I can find its chemical composition. Here is a photo of where it was used on a small town." He put another photo up.

Leela-lo looked at it and flinched. "It's not right that any one would do such horrible things to another being."

Jojocko-lo shrugged his shoulders. "That's war."

"I know from my history studies that we Ume warred during brief periods of our primitive development. Those battles were fought with stones and clubs. I understand those battles. We were unsophisticated. But I have difficulty understanding how an advanced society can kill their own kind in this way."

"And they don't just kill each other in wars, they kill by withholding food. That amazes me. When humans lack credits they don't get to eat. I don't understand their rules of morality. Even the ones who profess to be good because they follow a religion, allow starvation. Their religions have rules about killing and stealing property, but none of their belief systems say, 'Thou shall not allow other people to starve.' There is more than enough substance on this planet to feed them all."

"Jolocko-lo, I have accepted that this planet is not a pleasant place. If it were a compassionate world, we wouldn't be here looking for a WMD. We've come to an evil world in order to find an evil weapon." Leela-lo ran her hands through her head fur in frustration. "I wish I had never volunteered for this mission. The implications of what we are doing here make me feel dirty."

"Leela-lo, did you think we're working to find a nice weapon? We have to have a weapon so awful that the giants we live beside won't dare to harm us. I don't like it either. But that's the reality. Strong will kill weak. In many cultures, they kill beings just because they look slightly different from them."

"I see that's happened on earth, but our planet is not like Earth. We and the Palalans are not like Earth societies."

Jolocko-lo sighed. "We may be peaceful, but we can't be sure about what the Palalans will do. They also had wars during their primitive development. For many centuries, all the Palalans have been one homogeneous group. They have had no one different to fight against. And we are weak. We are the perfect victims: we are small and different." Jolocko-lo shrugged his shoulders again. "Anyway… that's our mission and I've got to get back to work." Jolocko-lo turned away from her, stared at the floor for a moment, then went back to his computer.

Chapter

28

PALALA

Kebeck stood in his doorway and watched as his son disappeared around the curve. As the lush tropical greenery enveloped Prigo, Kebeck let his mind wander. It had been a nice visit, but Kebeck was glad to have his house to himself again. Before he could turn around, his computer buzzed. It was the leader of his Earth study panel, Samot, asking to talk with him.

Kebeck tapped a key and faced the computer and extended all four hands, palms up. "Greetings, my friend. How can I help you? You look disturbed."

"Just when I thought all is back to normal, I was contacted by a member of our Earth panel, Jarrell. He is coming to my home today to discuss an aspect of your journey to Earth. He claims to have proof that you broke our laws when you were on Earth. He was ranting about a note. What do you know of this?"

Kebeck's mind was racing. *How could Jarrell know about the note that I sent to Adeline's friend? That note had saved her life. I do not regret sending it. I accept the fact that I broke Palalan law by sending it, and I was ready to pay the penalty if necessary. But I seemed to have gotten away with it. And now this? How did Jarrell know?*

"Kebeck? I asked a question? Is there a problem with your computer?"

"I am trying to think." *Which note is he referring to? Computer problem. Sure. That'll work.* Kebeck hit the key that disconnected the visual portion of the communication. "Oh, my screen has kicked out again. Sorry." Kebeck knew that if Samot could see him, he would not know by the redness of Kebeck's neck that he was lying. *I had hoped to never lie again.*

Samot sighed. "Jarrell has a copy of a tiny note in an unknown language that he claims is proof of your wrong-doing."

Kebeck fell back against his slant board. Waves of relief washed over him. *Oh, that note... the one I found in my bag.* He took a deep breath, stiffened his shoulders and punched a key to turn the video back on. "That's better. I need to get this computer fixed. Sorry about the interruption. Samot, the paper Jarrell refers to has nothing to do with humans. When he comes over, look at it. It is not an Earth language. It is an unknown language that has the experts puzzled. We are trying to find the origin of the thing. It is quite a mystery."

"I will look at it. I am familiar with the major Earth languages, but I do not know them all."

"I have asked one of our leading language experts to look at it. She agreed that it is not a human language."

"Good. Then it is not a problem appropriate for our Earth panel. We will talk later. Meanwhile, please get your computer fixed. I find it disconcerting to talk to a blank screen."

Samot signed off and Kebeck leaned back and exhaled.

CHAPTER

29

EARTH

A dull sun made its way through the grimy window of the school lunchroom. Ava was seated at a standard tan cafeteria table, all alone, reading a faded blue library book entitled, "Writing For Fun and Profit." Jane plopped her lunch down on the table beside Ava. The loud sound made Ava looked up. Jane resembled a dark cloud, full of thunder and lightning.

"What's wrong?"

"Everything and nothing."

"Spill it."

Jane flopped into a chair. "Mom is spending so much time with Walter Fitzgerald. It's like I don't exist any more."

"You wanted her off your case."

"Yeah, that part I like. But they're together all the time, I mean all the time. Either she's home and he's there or they're out together. I'm glad that she's happier than ever, but… "

"What's the worst that can happen?" Ava elbowed her. "Would it be so bad if they got married?"

"Isn't that moving a little fast?"

Ava grinned. "They're old. They haven't got time for a long romance."

Jane stared at the floor.

"I'm sorry. You're really troubled and I'm making jokes. My bad."

Jane looked up at her. "My mom and I have never had a commendable relationship, but it was a relationship. Now, I get nothing from her. I am just an object, like a chess piece to be moved around at will. I now understand why some teenagers exhibit disruptive behaviour in order to get their parent's attention. I will not resort to that. I can deal with this. It doesn't feel good, but I will endeavour to view it as an opportunity to become more independent."

Ava wanted to put her arm around Jane and hug her, but doing that in the cafeteria would just stir up silly rumours. She moved a bit closer to Jane.

"I understand… well, I shouldn't say that. I don't *really* understand. My mom is almost the opposite of yours. I thought you'd be glad to not have your mother yelling at you and telling you what to do all the time. But, I see that you're hurt by your mother's behaviour. How can I help?"

"Come over after school today. Now that mom's so busy with Walter, she's loosened up some of her rules. Suddenly, I'm allowed to have a friend over. I almost keeled over when she dropped that one on me. All these years of no… no… and no."

"She feels guilty for ignoring you. Hey. That's a good thing. Let's see what else her guilt might get you. See if she'll buy you a cellphone."

Jane let a hint of a smile cross her face. "Yes, that would be nice, but I'm dubious that her guilt could be stretched that far. Asking for a phone might be a bit ambitious."

Ava glanced at her watch, grabbed her book off the table and got up. "I'm supposed to be at a school council meeting. Sorry. Gotta go. I'll be by after school."

CHAPTER

30

PALALA

Solang stood in the doorway of her house, with a cup of tenga juice in her hand, and surveyed the lush Palalan jungle that surrounded her house. Some people liked to tame their yards, but she preferred the intertwining vines and untamed growth of nature. She had found the fifteen year old mystery note that had been buried in her papers and compared it to the new note that Kebeck has sent her. She found it odd that, except for a few characters, it was written with the Palalan alphabet. Both notes were definitely the same language. And five of the words seemed to be Palalan, but with odd spelling. Solang's eyes glazed over as she thought it through. *The first note was found years ago in a computer factory and it contained words close to the Palalan words for 'computer' and 'screen'. This new note was found on the floor of a space vessel that had been to Earth. It contained Palalan words very similar to 'bottle' and 'notebook'. And some of the other words are similar to certain Palalan nouns. The second note looked like a list. I am sure that they were written by two different people.* Solang took a sip of her juice. *Could the two notes be the same language that was spoken in the recording Eela had sent her? Maybe? It seems like just too much of a coincidence that we found this second note just as we hear a new language being spoken on our planet. This needs more research. This could be happenstance but maybe not. If the oral and written are the same language, who are these very intelligent creatures who have been in our jungle, inside a factory and inside one of our spaceships?*

Solang had talked to several people about this mystery. She had discussed it with some of the members of the Earth research panel, trying to determine how the recent note got in the vessel. And she had talked to the manager of the computer factory. Solang decided that now it was time to tell a higher authority in the government about her findings. After a bit of research, Solang decided that the appropriate person to contact was the head of the Foreign Planets Department. The department had an office in the Science Research Center. She put in the call and got a recording. "The entire department, all three of us, will be away on day 286 and day 287 at our annual waterball tournament. Please leave a message and we will return your call on day 288. We wish you pure water." Solang left a short message and mused, *I guess nothing urgent ever happens in the Foreign Planets Department.*

CHAPTER

31

EARTH

After Ava rushed out of the cafeteria to her meeting, Jane pulled a book out of her backpack. *Maybe reading will get my mind off the British invader in our house.* She had heard it said that everyone should read "Catcher in the Rye" in order to understand the male mind. Thus far she was halfway through the book and as she read, her opinion of the male mind was deteriorating. She looked around the room at the boys in the cafeteria. *Do they really think like that?* She shook her head and went back to reading.

"Hi, may I sit here?"

Jane looked up to see Peter Hooper Dickson, the tall, handsome prince of the school looking down at her. She looked back down at her book. *This isn't happening.*

He spoke again. "If I'm disturbing you, I can sit somewhere else."

Jane slowly raised her head, reminded herself to smile, and nodded, then ducked back down.

"Does that mean yes, I'm welcome to sit here or does that mean yes, I should go away because I'm interfering with your reading? Words would be helpful."

Not taking her eyes off her book Jane replied, "Have a seat, please."

Jane continued to look at the words on the page, but of course, they now had no meaning. She just saw an incoherent series of letters. *What does he want? Why is he sitting here?* She could hear him crunching potato chips. Then she heard the sound of him drinking something. All around them, the normal cafeteria chatter continued. Some guy at a nearby table called to him, "Hey, Hoop, come join us."

"Later, I'm good here for now." His fork clattered against the plate.

"Jane, I just wanted to see if you were all right. Remember us bumping into each other in the hall a few days ago? I got the feeling that those guys were picking on you. So, I talked to them."

Jane's head jerked up. Her anger overcame her shyness, "You what?"

"I asked them to leave you alone."

"Why?" she sputtered. "Who do you think you are? What do you care about me? Now they'll be even worse." Her nostrils flared. "Maybe you should have talked to me first."

"I'm sorry." He blurted out. "I was trying to help. I understand… "

"You understand? You can't understand my world. We live on different planets. You live in the world of hanging out with the guys, and standing on the stage receiving sports awards. A world where girls who look like they belong in a fashion magazine flirt with you. How can you?"

"My brother has… "

Jane stopped her rant and sucked in her breath, "Has what?"

"He's autistic. I mean, I know you're not anything like him. He barely talks and has to have round the clock care. But, I guess what I'm trying to say is taking care of Josh has given me a little understanding of the Autism-Asperger's thing."

Jane stared at him. The thought hit her that this might be the first time that she had sat beside a boy her age and looked him straight in the face. He had a kind face. He looked sincere. She wasn't sure what to say next.

"I just thought we could be friends. I thought you probably needed a friend. Well, you can't have too many friends." He looked down. "Now I sound like an idiot."

"No Peter, you sound like a nice person. How old is your brother?"

"He's seven. You know everybody calls me Hoop. Well, that's what my friends call me. Just the teachers call me Peter."

"Hoop, I appreciate… "

The end of period buzzer interrupted and drowned out Jane's words and made them both spring into action. They gathered up their books and stood up.

Jane mumbled, "Gotta go"

And Hoop called out, "Later" as he headed toward the door.

CHAPTER

32

EARTH

Jane went straight home after school. She unlocked the door, thankful that her mother would not be home til five thirty, and flopped down on the living room couch. She had bumped into Ava in the hall after lunch. She was buzzing with excitement and her big smile had told Ava that something was up. Ava had followed Jane down the hall, trying to get her to talk. She had just grinned and said, "See you at my house after school."

Jane was just snuggling into the cushions, so happy that she had actually talked to a boy without doing something stupid, when there was a knock on the door. She jumped up and peeked out. *Should I tell her everything?* Ava came through the door, grabbed Jane's hand and dragged her over to the couch.

"So… What's the big secret?"

Jane bounced on the seat as she told Ava, "Hoop sat down and talked to me. He wants to be friends."

"Who?"

She stretched out every word as she whispered, "Peter Hooper Dickson."

"Oh, Hoop. The Zeus of South High. The god of sports and academics, worshipped by all who gaze upon him. Wow!"

Jane could no longer restrain herself. She told Ava all about it, every detail and every word.

Ava was stunned. "You go from 'can't even look at people' to 'lunch with the school hunk' in one day. I'll say it again… wow!"

"Well, it not like he's trying to court me. He just wants to be my friend. You know, he just sees me as an acquaintance with whom he can share thoughts."

Ava sighed. "You're doing it again. Nobody says 'court' or 'acquaintance.' If you want to be thought of as normal, watch the vocabulary. I'm only mentioning it because you asked me to tell you when you're doing it. But, back to Hoop. I never knew about his brother. I guess that does give you two something in common."

Ava paused and scrunched up her face, obviously in deep thought. "How to handle this? Well, first, be very cautious around the other girls at school. There's going to be some jealousy. And if some of them are suddenly friendly, be nice, but cautious and don't tell them anything about him. When they ask about him, and they will, just say you're friends. If they ask about what you and he talk about, be vague or suddenly say you have to go to the bathroom."

"I hadn't thought about the implications of having a popular male friend. Ava, I'm so lucky to have you as my pal. I… " They both turned at the sound of the front door opening.

Jane's mother's sturdy thick one inch heels clicked on the floor as she strode into the living room. She looked surprised to see the two of them sitting there. "Oh hello, Ava." A tight smile appeared on her face, then faded. Ava had noticed that Jane's mother's smile often turned off and on like a light switch. "Very nice to see you, my dear. Jane, I have to go change now. Walter and I are going to Toronto for dinner and a show. Please see to your own supper. The fridge is quite full. We will be back very late, but I expect you to be in your bed by 10:00." With that, she switched her smile on for a second, then turned and click-clacked her way up the stairs.

Ava and Jane looked at each other, puzzled and surprised by what had just transpired. Their minds were abuzz with ideas about what they might do with an evening free of Jane's overbearing, strict mother.

Jane whispered, "Music that's not classical, like loud, really loud hard rock."

Ava smiled and whispered, "Candy and chips."

Jane looked toward the staircase. "Beer?"

"No. I tried it. You wouldn't like it." She studied Jane for a second. "But if you really want some, I can sneak a bottle out of the house."

"Well… maybe next time. I am quite inebriated by the prospect of an evening with my best friend and the possibility of having a male friend."

"But I'll get some pop. I know she doesn't allow it. Remind me to take the pop cans home with me. We must leave no evidence behind."

Jane's eyes lit up. "We can order out for a pizza. I've never done that. And get a horror movie!"

"I'll bring a garbage bag and take all the evidence home with me."

"She's not that bad. She doesn't check the trash."

"I'm not taking any chances. One pizza box found in the trash could make her sprout horns again."

Jane sighed. "You go home: I'll call when she leaves."

Jane spent the next fifteen minutes smiling and humming as she zipped through her homework. A tapping sound caught her attention. She looked up to see her mother come down the stairs wearing a silky light blue dress, with a triple set of pearls at her neck. And she had on tall spiked heels. "Jane, you are not to leave the house while I'm gone and you're not to have anyone in either. Is that clear?" She stared at Jane for a second, then turned to get a coat out of the closet as Jane answered, "Perfectly. What are you going to see?"

Her mother turned back to face her, glaring intensely. "I'll have my cell phone with me. Of course it will be off during the performance. Otherwise, it'll be on. So call me if you need to." She switched on her smile. "We're going to see 'Phantom of the Opera.' Walter's seen it but he wants to take me. He's a very considerate man."

33

UME ON EARTH

A chilly fall wind blew in through the doorway as Toboo-lo and Senoa-lo entered. The others peered up from their computers. Both Senoa-lo and Toboo-lo were looking grim. The atmosphere in the room suddenly changed from convivial to dour.

Jolocko-lo broke the ice, "What's up?"

Senoa-lo took off her vest and threw it on a crate. "We have a problem. It's like this. When we planned this trip, we had no options about where the vessel would take us, but we needed to get to earth to research how to make a WMD. Originally, they were supposed to land in the southern warmer part of this land mass, but for some reason they changed the plan and here we are in Ontario, Canada. Our problem is food. We are in an area where the seasonal change is going to make it very cold here. And it will soon be impossible to find green edible plants."

Senoa-lo took a tired breath and continued, "If we had landed in the original place, we wouldn't have this problem. The last couple of days, Toboo-lo has been analyzing the plants here to see if we can eat roots when the last of the green plants die off from the cold. Most of the roots are not edible. A very few are. They taste terrible and there's not enough to last until spring. When we first landed, I thought this change in landing location would be a minor inconvenience. But, no, this is a whopping big problem. Leela-lo and I have discussed the possibility of finding a way to travel south to avoid this cold period. Now that we've looked around and researched the area, I think it would be very difficult to travel without being discovered. The population is dense in this locale. I fear that if we were to leave these woods, we would be noticed."

The silence was deafening.

Leela-lo tentatively spoke up. "I researched the possibility of going south by train. The problem with that mode of transportation is the fact that we would have to change trains in a major city. We might sneak on a local train, but that wouldn't get us far enough south without changing trains in a big city."

Jolocko-lo interjected, "Well, that kills that option. Flying is out. Too many people in an airport and it would be impossible to sneak on a plane. So, what do we do? Call a cab?"

Senoa-lo glared at him. "Unless someone comes up with a better option, we're stuck here. We can probably get the job done from here. We just have to figure out a food source."

Jolocko-lo looked at the dried gaba fruit in his hand, then asked, "If we conserve, how long can we last on the food we brought with us?"

Senoa-lo looked at Toboo-lo. They all stared at Toboo-lo.

Toboo-lo looked down at his feet, then raised his head to meet their eyes. "Three or four weeks. But we can still gather some greens, before the frost comes. The problem is preserving them. If this area were consistently cold, we could gather greens and freeze them. But here the temperatures will fluctuate through the winter."

Senoa-lo's voice took on a tone of authority. "You all were selected for this assignment because you are smart. We can solve this problem. Jolocko-lo, I want you to research methods of preserving foods. Leela-lo, I want you to go out and gather greens. Toboo-lo will go with you and show you which ones are edible. We will live on the local greens as long as possible and keep our dried food in reserve until we need it."

Toboo-lo stuffed the remainder of the dried gaba fruit in his mouth and looked around to see if anyone had noticed.

After Toboo-lo and Leela-lo left, Senoa-lo sat down beside Jolocko-lo. "So from your research, what are the options with poison?"

Jolocko-lo sighed and stared at her.

"I'm sure you're upset by what I've just told you about our food situation. But we must continue with our mission. We've got to work even harder and faster now."

Jolocko-lo sighed again. "As you know, there are three main rivers in Palala. If we were to put a poison in those rivers a lot of Palalans would die."

"And other animals?" Senoa-lo asked.

"Of course. Anything strong enough to kill a Palalan will kill any animal on the planet."

Toboo-lo stood up and walked to the tent entrance, then turned to face the others. "I don't want to poison the water. Really, I don't think that our people would allow us to poison water. It's sacred to our people, especially the traditionalists."

Senoa-lo asked, "Could we spray a poison in the air from an airplane? That would only cover a small area.

"Yeah, but because they all live near the water, some of it would get in the water. Poison in the water or in the air would wipe out whomever happened to be in the area. You can't aim it at specific people unless you hand it to them in a drink."

Senoa-lo heaved a sigh. "I guess what we're talking about here is really terrorism. Killing some random innocent Palalans in order to show that we have a weapon would be terrorism." As soon as the words were out of her mouth, Senoa-lo wanted to take them back. "We shook our heads in disgust when we saw the effects of terrorism here on Earth." The word 'terrorism' echoed in her head. She had avoided thinking about the real significance of their assignment. Now, she was repulsed by the whole thing. "We just want something to threaten them with."

Jolocko-lo scratched the back of his neck. "Will it work to just threaten the Palalans with a poison or bomb? Don't we have to show the Palalans that we have something, some WMD, that could kill a big proportion of the Palalans. And we would have to demonstrate our weapon by killing some of them. Right?"

Senoa-lo slowly rose from her chair and moved over to the doorway. As she stood looking out at the fall leaves she said, "Everyone just talked about having a WMD as a deterrent. But you're right. Why should they believe that we're strong enough to defend ourselves if we don't demonstrate our power?"

Jolocko-lo's shoulders slumped forward. He ran a hand through the fur on his head. "Maybe we're getting ahead of ourselves. Our job is to find a WMD that could be used on Palalans. How it's used or whether it's used isn't our decision to make. That determination has to be made by the general council."

"Right." Senoa-lo turned back toward Toboo-lo. Her head was spinning with thoughts of duty and guilt, with images of dead Palalans laid out like the bodies at the train station in 'Gone With The Wind.' *Can I live with myself if I give our people a weapon that they will use to kill with? But I would feel so awful and guilty if the Palalans were to attack us because I failed to deliver a weapon.* "You're right. It's not our decision. Our job is to find a usable WMD. Let's just do our job."

34

EARTH

As Jane rushed through the dull taupe halls, zig-zagging past herds of teenagers, she heard a familiar voice behind her say, "See you at lunch?"

She dodged a gaggle of girls and turned to see Hoop walking behind her. "Sure." She glided into her second period class with a smile on her face. Jane floated through her next two classes, with the teacher's words going in one ear and out the other. She was a bit tired from last night's pizza, pop and movies with Ava. But it was a good tired. *Last night I was just a normal teen doing what normal teens do.*

As she entered the lunch room, she saw Hoop seated at her usual table in the corner. She sped through the lunch line, impatient with the people who were in front of her. They seemed to be chatting and meandering along in slow motion. When she finally got to the table, three of Hoop's friends had joined him. *Oh no. His pals are with him.*

"Guys, meet my friend Jane. Jane, this is Roger, Ivan the terrible, and Aaron. I've known these fellows since kindergarten. They're nice guys, most of the time."

Aaron examined her. "Uh, yeah. I know you. You're in my chemistry class. Hoop, she should be called 'Jane, the Brain.' This girl knows the answers before Mr. Stevens can ask the questions."

Jane suddenly found the food on her tray very interesting. "Uh… " she mumbled, "thanks."

Hoop quickly changed the topic to football and Jane ate her lunch as the guys bantered on about who should win what. When Hoop asked her opinion about a team, she had to admit that she knew nothing about football.

Hoop let her off easy, "Hey, you can't know everything."

She made a mental note do a little research on the topic. As their voices buzzed around her, she realized that she enjoyed being part of the group and she was grateful to Hoop for including her. *So, this is what it feels like to be part of a group of friends. It feels comfortable, like I feel when I'm sitting out under the trees listening to the wind blow through the leaves.*

Hoop's voice brought her out of her reverie. "Hey, earth to Jane, the bell just rang. We've got to get to class."

She jumped to her feet and gathered her things. "Sorry, I was thinking and… "

Hoop was almost out the door as he called, "No problem, later."

Jane drifted out the door, wearing a shy smile.

Chapter

35

EARTH

The sky was blue, the birds were singing and Jane was still smiling as she unlocked the front door to her house. She paused and looked around before she entered the house. Their house and neighborhood looked like the set for the old TV show, "Leave It to Beaver." It was one of the shows on her mother's list of appropriate TV. She was only allowed to watch shows on the list. The list was short, very short. So over the years, she had probably seen every episode. Between the house and her mother's archaic rules, Jane had often felt like she was living in the 1950s. So every morning, there was the culture shock of leaving her time-warp house and jumping into modern reality. Now with the easing of the rules, the distance between her two lives was getting smaller.

Every school day, her first action when she got home was to go directly to the kitchen cork board and see what chores her mom had assigned her for the day. She looked at the board. *No notes from mom.* Jane plunged her fist into the air and danced around. *Yes! No chores.* She yelled out,"Free at last." As she heard her voice echo through the house she thought, *Well, maybe 'free at last' was overdoing it.* Since she was caught up on her schoolwork, she had two hours of glorious freedom before her mother came home. Usually, Jane came home to a schedule of tasks that her mother had written out the night before. But lately, there was just an occasional note directing her to do a few tasks. She didn't care much for her mom's new beau, but she loved the way her mother had changed since he had appeared on the scene.

What to do? I saw a fashion magazine around here somewhere. My mother, my practical mother actually bought a glossy magazine. Never thought that would happen. I'll make a snack, something chocolate, put my feet up and decadently thumb through a silly fashion magazine. As Jane searched through the house for the magazine, a thought hit her. *I saw it in mom's hand when she went into her office last night.* Jane proceeded into her mother's office and immediately spotted it on her mother's desk. As she lifted up the magazine, she noticed a brochure for a private school in Calgary and another brochure for a private school in Montreal. She scanned the pamphlets. Both schools were for students with Asperger's Syndrome. Jane was flabbergasted.

She wants to send me away. Or maybe, he wants to send me away. She had realized from the start that Mr. Fitzgerald had no desire to be her friend, and she suspected that he had little use for kids or teens. But she couldn't believe her mother would even consider doing this to her. *Maybe he brought the brochures over in an attempt to get rid of me. Maybe this is his idea. Her mother wouldn't… would she? She does spend more time with him than she does with me. She seems to be in love with him. She talks about him all the time.* Jane wandered over to the window and looked out at the neighborhood. *If she had wanted to send me away to school last year, I probably would have considered it. I would have missed Ava, but just having one friend in the whole world is difficult. A school with others like me might have been a chance to make more friends. But now I have more than one friend at school, and a relationship with a fantastic boy. I'm sure he just sees me as a friend, but I feel a little rush of joy when he looks at me. I don't want to go. I want to stay here in a normal school with normal people.*

Jane backed up against the wall and slid down into a crossed leg sitting position. She looked down at her hands. She was still holding the pamphlets. She wanted to yell as loudly as possible "No! It's not fair!" But Jane was not the type to yell much; instead, she slumped her shoulders forward and shrank into herself. She didn't know how long she had sat there when she was brought out of her stupor by the sound of a phone ringing. Like a robot, she stood up and lurched toward the phone.

"Jane, what is up with you? This is the third time I've rung your house in the last half an hour and the other two times it just rang and rang. You had said you were going to go home and stay there, so I knew you had to be home. Were you home? Are you sick?"

"I, uh, I'm here… for now. I guess, uh, I'm upset, actually really, quite distraught."

"Is your mother yelling at you again?"

"I wish. At least that would show that she cared about me. I'm feeling quite unloved right now."

"Please, just tell me what happened."

"I found brochures for private schools for students with Asperger's on my mother's desk. Schools in Alberta and Quebec. One could get the impression that they plan to send me away, far away."

"Oh," Ava paused, "she wouldn't do that. You're the center of her life."

"Not any more. Walter is the sun she orbits around now. I have become Pluto."

"Just because the publications are on her desk doesn't mean she's considering sending you away. My mom has books about Australia, but that doesn't mean… Forget I said that. That analogy doesn't fit at all. Anyway, let's not jump the gun."

"You're right. Maybe some well-meaning friend gave them to her. It could mean nothing… or everything." Jane paused. "What were you saying about a gun? What does 'jump the gun,' mean; it makes no sense."

"Yes it does. It started out as a racing term. A gun is shot to start a foot race. Anyone who starts running before the gun is shot is said to have 'jumped the gun.'"

"Oh. Now that you have distracted me with an interesting bit of idiom etymology, I'm settling down. But finding those brochures was very disquieting. What should I do about this? Confront her? Ignore it? They were laying under a magazine on her desk. So I don't think she wanted me to see them. Ava, what do you suggest?"

"Maybe give it a day or two and see if she mentions it. And if she doesn't say anything, then that gives you some time to decide how to bring it up."

"That's probably what I should do. But it's going to be extremely difficult to act as if I'm not aware of these pamphlets. There's a part of me that wants to yell at her the minute she walks through the door." Jane paused. "But that would be rash and unwise. The prudent thing to do is to say nothing and wait and think. This situation calls for an Oscar- winning performance. I hope I'm up to it."

"You can do it. You've had years of not saying what's on your mind."

Jane's voice softened, almost to a whisper, "I can't believe how much she's changed since Mr. Wonderful came into her life. Most of the changes are great. But this… this is so unfair."

"I know. It hurts. Unfortunately, I have to tell you some more bad news. But, if I don't tell you, someone else will or you'll see them."

"See who?"

"Hoop and Sophie. They're dating. They're a couple now. I know you like Hoop and I don't want you hurt. So I thought you should know."

"Is Sophie the Asian girl with the beautiful long black hair?"

"Yeah, she was in math class with us last year."

"She seems nice. She never picked on me or stared at me like some of the others." Jane leaned against the wall and hung her head. "Oh well. Really, Hoop and I are just friends, so I shouldn't feel bad."

"Get real. You like him."

"As a friend, but… I was hoping that eventually we might be more."

"Sandra Thomas, I'm sure you know Sandra; she says men are like purses. You should think of them as just nice things to hang on your arm and use for a while."

"I could never adopt that type of casual attitude toward boys. And I think she only said that because of an unrequited love situation. I admit to being a bit of a romantic. I hold on to the expectation that some day I will stumble upon someone who understands me and cares about what I think and how I feel, someone I can share my life with."

"And you probably will, just not today. So moving on. Is your school work caught up?"

Jane was puzzled at the question. "Yes."

"So you can probably get your mother to release you from prison and come over to my house tonight to watch a movie. Say that you're coming over to help me with math. Practice your acting skills. I'm sure you want to examine every possible aspect of this brochure situation. And, I have a tearjerker movie that might take your mind off your semi-dire situation."

"This is way beyond semi-dire. This is one of those critical decisions that could totally change my future life. I'll talk to the warden and call you back. But since you mentioned it, I saw your grade on that last math test. We could spend a few minutes… "

"Just come over. We need some serious girl time together."

36

PALALA

Solang was sitting at her computer writing a Spanish lesson plan with her lower hands and stretching her upper hands up over her head. Sitting at the computer too long had given her a kink in her neck. A name flashed in the upper corner of her screen, notifying her that someone named Kebeck wanted to talk to her. She took a second to let her mind change gears. *Oh, yeah, the space traveller who found the note in the transport.* She opened a portal to him. "Greetings." She pulled her upper hands down into the traditional greeting, with her hands in front of her, palms up.

Kebeck replied with the customary hand gesture. "I thank you for taking my call. I am curious to know if you have any further information about the note I sent you."

"I am still working on it, but the writing is somewhat similar to a piece of paper found years ago in a factory. Some of the words are similar to archaic Palalan words. I think your paper could be a list of items. Do you have any idea why a list of objects might be on the interstellar vessel you took to Earth?"

"No. All I did was pick it up off the floor." He paused. "I do not mean to appear gruff. I have been called to appear at a meeting with my superior to discuss this tiny paper. And there is nothing to discuss. I picked it up while cleaning up the ship and I contacted you about it."

She could see that Kebeck was upset. *I will not bother to mention the language that was recorded in the bush. He has problems enough.* "Because the note was on a space vessel, I contacted the Foreign Planets Department. So, you will probably hear from them as well."

Kebeck grabbed his head and closed his eyes. *Now they are going to be asking questions too.* Kebeck forced a little smile to his face and thanked Solang for talking to him. As soon as he had said, "I wish you clear water," he jumped up and started pacing back and forth.

As Solang cut her link to Kebeck, she discovered another call notice and immediately accepted the connection. A beaming young female with dark green scales greeted her. "I am Nacoo Beram from the Foreign Planets Department. How can I be of assistance?"

Solang told her about the two notes and the strange language heard in the jungle. As Solang spoke, Nacoo's smile turned into a look of puzzlement. "You conclude from this that we may have unknown aliens on our planet. This is disturbing and needs to be investigated further. I think I should authorize an interstellar craft to fly over the planet to look for signs of these people."

"You can do that?"

"Certainly. I am the chief of the Foreign Planets Department. It is our job to manage all relationships with foreign beings. We need to know if we have aliens here. We have visited other planets and communicated with aliens, but we have never allowed them to come to Palala. I will schedule a flight for tomorrow. We have to pursue this. They may be here for nefarious purposes. I find this quite disturbing. Meanwhile, please contact me if you have any new information. This is very important. I will talk further with you after tomorrow's flight. May you swim in clear water."

Solang was delighted. *Should I call Kebeck and tell him about the fly over?* She stretched her arms again. *Better to wait and see if they find anything.* With that, she turned off her computer and went to see what she might find to eat.

PALALA

As Kebeck meandered down the hall toward the meeting room, his stomach was dancing a jig and his head was buzzing with 'what ifs.' He was not looking forward to meeting with his colleagues of the Earth Committee to explain the odd note found on the space ship. The note baffled him, but that wasn't the problem that made him worry. He had gone to Earth and had broken the law by communicating by way of a different note, with an Earth being. He thought he had gotten away with it. He had harmed no one and the Earth being who received the note would never know that it was from an alien. He had sent the note to save the life of a human. He had prevented her murder and he would never regret that. *Had his flight partner, Agra, divulged his secret?* As he approached the meeting room, he felt his neck muscles tighten. Kebeck stopped in front of the door and took a big breath. He opened the door and stepped into the meeting room. This was the first time he had seen his colleagues in person since his appearance in front of the law committee.

The law committee had heard his explanation about why he had lied to his colleagues before his last trip to Earth and had released him without a trial. There is no Palalan law against lying. Falsehoods are rare and awkward, but not illegal. The Palalan legal system is unique, but fair. In the Palalan justice system anyone accused of a crime goes in front of sixteen law specialists who question him in casual conversation in order to decide if a law has been broken. They vote and if twelve or more of the specialist vote that a law was broken, there is a trial. The trial is viewed by 64 randomly selected jurors who listen as a law specialist explains the law broken, and the accused explains his actions. Jurors get to ask the accused questions. Then they vote on whether his actions harmed an individual or the society. If judged guilty by 51% or more, then sixteen of the 51% are randomly chosen to meet and determine the punishment. Punishment is usually shunning permanently or for a designated period of time. When shunned, red paint is applied to the face and everyone avoids the person. If the crime is determined to be caused by a mental health problem, the person is placed in a mental health facility. The jurors also have the option of designing a punishment to fit the crime. If the accused wants to appeal the decisions of the court, he can meet with a different group of sixteen law specialist. They determine if justice is being served or not.

Crime is rare because Palalans necks turn red when they lie or get nervous or get angry. From the time they are young, Palalans are accustomed to avoiding lying because they will be found out. In school, they are taught that anger is a waste of energy and they learn methods for negotiating through problems and coping with difficult people. When a citizen notices a law being broken and reports it, a law researcher, armed with a stunner, investigates and determines if the person breaking the law might harm people. Rarely are people arrested, usually they are given a ticket that indicates that they must contact the law office to arrange a meeting with the law specialists.

As Kebeck stepped into the room, five of his six colleagues stood up and came over to greet him. Jarrell was the only member of the Earth Committee who remained on his slantboard. After catching up with talk of families and events, Samot, the leader of the committee, asked that they all be seated for the formal meeting.

"We are here because I was notified by the Foreign Planets Department that Kebeck found a small note on the ship after his last flight to Earth. A language specialist has determined that the note is in an unknown language. Because the note was found on the vessel, a team of scientist carefully examined the ship and discovered bits of brown fur in the engine section." With that, Samot sat back on his slantboard and waited to hear reactions.

Kebeck was taken aback. "How can that be? We locked the ship when we left it and unlocked it when we went to get back aboard. We did not see any furry animals."

Agara, Kebeck's companion on the trip was equally astonished. "We did not bring any Earth animals on the ship. We saw some feline and canine pets as we walked through the residential section, but we dared not go near them." He jumped up off his slantboard. "I concur with Kebeck. The vessel was securely locked before we walked away from it and it was still secure when we returned to it."

"Then how did the fur get on the ship?" Jarrell asked of Kebeck. "You lied to us before your flight, saying the camera on your computer was malfunctioning, thus not allowing us to see the redness of your neck. Thus you deceived us and avoided a meeting that could have cancelled the trip to Earth. Standing here in front of us now, I see that your neck is starting to glow."

"My color stems from anger, not falsehood," Kebeck promptly replied.

Samot moved to stand between Jarrell and Kebeck. "We are not here to accuse Kebeck and Agra of anything. We meet to discuss possibilities. How might an animal have entered the vessel? Did the fur belong to the creature who left the note? Where could this literate being have come from? Was the life-form intelligent enough to have opened the locked ship and then lock it back? Why was it on the ship? Since we are the Earth experts, we have been asked by the Foreign Planets Department to think on these things and get back to them with possibilities and ideas. So… let us confer and examine possibilities."

38

PALALA

The next morning the leaves sparkled where the sun reflected off the drops from last night's rain. Kebeck glanced at the note in his hand and at the number on the door in front of him. Samot, the leader of his Earth Studies Committee, had sent him the address and instructed him to report to this location for a meeting at the Foreign Planets Office.

Yesterday's meeting with his Earth Studies group had achieved nothing. They had thrown around all sorts of ideas, but had nothing solid to hang any of them on. The only good thing that came of the meeting was the fact that it was made clear to Jarrell and everyone else that Kebeck and Agra had no idea how the little note got on the ship.

He shuffled into the meeting room thinking, *I wish I had just left that little note on the floor of the ship. No. The cleaners would have found it and I would be just where I am now. And destroying it would have been wrong.* As he came through the door a familiar voice greeted him. "Greetings Kebeck, I was glad to hear that you volunteered to work on this project with us."

He looked up to see Solang, the language expert he had been communicating with, holding her hands in the traditional greeting pose. *Maybe this will not be so bad; she seems like a nice person.*

Solang introduced him to the other person in the room, Nacoo Beram. "Nacoo is the head of the Foreign Planets department. We have been asked to work with you on this problem of the unknown aliens. So, shall we relax on the slantboards and get started. I am quite anxious to learn more about this. With that, Solang grabbed a piece of fruit out of a bowl on the table and hopped on a slantboard.

After Kebeck related all he knew about the note, Solang took the floor. "The note found in the factory and the note Kebeck found are definitely the same language. And the voices my colleague taped in the forest could be speaking that same language, but I cannot be certain about it. My friend set up cameras in the area where the voices were heard, but no one was sighted, just the usual forest animals. Nacoo, have you learned anything that might help us find out who these people are and where they come from?"

"Possibly. I ordered a flight over the planet. I thought an aerial view might be one way to see if an interstellar ship had landed somewhere. It will take a few days to cover the whole planet. But today something was spotted in the northern ice fields. You can see some irregular shapes beside a thermal spring. But because the pilot was so high and because of the steam, it was not possible get a clear picture. There seemed to be buildings around the spring, but those could be just odd ice formations caused by the heat. Tomorrow the pilot will go back and give it a closer look. I think it probably is just ice; no one could live up in those cold mountains."

CHAPTER

39

EARTH

A chilly fall wind was making the students scrunch down in their coats and rush across the sidewalk into waiting cars. Jane was sitting on the low wall that surrounded an ill-kept little garden bed beside the school entrance. She was ignoring the fleeing students and the cold wind. Her eyes were focused on the ground, as she moved her foot tracing figure eights in the dirt that was trying to reclaim the cracked sidewalk. She looked up when Ava's feet appeared inches in front of her toes. "Life is weird, Ava. Sometimes I can almost believe the old idea that fortune is always followed by a fall. The Greeks and the Chinese both believed that if the gods saw that you were prospering, they would send some disaster to knock you down. Why can't people be happy and nice?"

Ava pulled her coat up around her ears and sat down beside Jane. "What happened?"

"Laura and Melissa and Char have been trying to make my life miserable. I have been noticed now that Hoop talks to me, and they have selected me as their current victim. And, I saw Hoop's girlfriend. She's beautiful. I'm alright just being his friend, but it seems that the gang of three doesn't want me to even speak to him. The witches have been whispering little snide remarks as they pass me in the hall. In biology class, Melissa drew a picture of a broken heart and dropped it on the floor beside my desk as she went by. And when we were changing classes after third period, Char elbowed me and giggled as she walked by. I'm trying to ignore them, but they're everywhere. They enjoy torturing me. What kind of people like to hurt people. Oh yeah, they're called psychopaths. I'm being tortured by psychopaths." She paused, "I've read that some girls go through a sadist stage around this age and that they usually mature into normal nice people. I understand that this is normal in the development of some girls. But why do I have to be the victim?"

"Because... "

"Because I'm not normal," Jane interjected. "I'm an easy target because of my Asperger's. I hate that," Jane raged. "And sometimes I hate myself."

Ava touched her arm. "No. You can't do that. Hate them. Hate their parents because they didn't teach them better. Hate this stupid school for letting them get away with this crap. But, don't hate yourself. You're my friend and I would only choose the very best type of person to be my best friend. I was afraid this would happen. They, the 'in' students, don't want to see us lowly 'non-in' students associating with upper caste. We are untouchables because we aren't one of them. It's a control thing. They've established the castes and you're breaking their rules by being friends with Hoop. It seems that boys are hardly aware of the high school caste system and just float through in a cloud of sports and cars. The girls decide who can hang out with whom and function as the enforcers."

"Yeah, I see that now."

"Jane, the only way you can disarm them is by ignoring them or being super nice to them. When they figure out that their methods aren't working on you, they'll quit wasting their time and choose a new victim. It's only fun for them when they get a reaction or force you to do what they want."

Jane brought her head up and looked at Ava. "You think so?"

"Sure. If you don't believe me, go do some research on bullying." Ava stood up and grabbed her bag. "I've got to go to a Drama Club meeting. I'm already late. Hey, before I go, did you talk to your mom about the private school pamphlets?"

"No, she hasn't said anything and I haven't mentioned it. That's still hanging in the air like the Sword of Damocles."

"The what? Forget I asked. I'll call you later. Okay?"

Jane nodded and Ava rushed off into the school. Jane just sat and reflected on what Ava had said about the gang of three. *Tomorrow, I'm going to walk though the halls with my head up and a smile on my face. I'll think about pleasant things, like the sound of the wind blowing through pine trees. I will be invincible.* Suddenly, she had the feeling that someone was watching her.

She looked up. Standing in front of her was Hoop and a kid who looked to be about ten years old. He had rich brown hair like his brother and anyone could see the family resemblance.

"You looked like you were deep in thought and considering how smart you are, I didn't want to interrupt you. You could be inventing a cure for cancer or devising a way to end all wars and establish world peace."

Jane shook her head. "I'd be happy with just a little peace here at school."

Hoop turned his head to one side, like an inquisitive puppy. "What's wrong?"

"Laura, Melissa and Char are being a pain."

"That's normal. Ignore 'em. If you've got a minute… This is my brother, Ted." Hoop moved to one side so he could see Ted's face. "Ted, this is my friend, Jane. Please say hello."

Ted's right arm jerked back and he turned his head away from Hoop and Jane. His face showed no expression. Slowly and deliberately Hoop repeated, "Please say hello." Ted's arm jerked again. He turned his face, still with no expression, toward Jane but looked over her shoulder and said, "Hello."

Jane remembered reading that people with autism usually don't like eye contact, so she looked at Ted's left shoulder and replied, "It's nice to meet you Ted. Hoop told me about you. He said that you know a lot about the weather."

Ted looked up at the sky and declared, "Windy… twelve miles per hour, Altocumulus castellanus clouds."

"Will it rain today?" Jane asked.

"Fourteen percent chance of rain."

"Ted, I'm impressed that you know the name of the clouds."

"Yesterday, there were some cumulonimbus that went up 20,000 feet."

"Were those the tall ones that looked like they were stacked up?"

Ted face still remained frozen. but there seemed to be a bit of sparkle in his eyes. "Yes."

Hoop moved so that he was directly facing Ted. "Ted, we should start toward home now. Say goodbye."

Ted's right arm jerked again and he looked down at the ground. "Bye." Then he pivoted around and started slowly walking down the sidewalk.

Hoop took hold of Jane's arm and quickly whispered, "I wish we could talk longer, but I gotta go. It's rare to find someone who is smart enough to figure out how to talk to Ted. We have to be home by five for supper. Ted gets upset if he doesn't eat exactly at five." Then he rushed off after Ted.

Jane sat back down on the chilly hard stone wall. She no longer felt the cold. She was thankful that chance and genetics had not cursed her with Ted's type of autism. *Really, according to the doctors, I do have autism. Asperger's syndrome is technically no longer a diagnosis. Now it's part of a category they call autism spectrum disorder (ASD). So I have autism… what they call a "high-functioning" type of ASD. Whatever they want to call it, it's a nuisance. But I can handle it and I will become an independent adult and live on my own after university.* She felt like crying as she thought about Ted. He would probably always be dependent on others. Now, she understood why Hoop wanted her friendship. The other people he hung out with would probably feel awkward around Ted and not even try to talk to him. She was sure some of Hoop's friends would make fun of him. And the witches who had been torturing her could have a field day with Ted. She wished she knew a way of getting through to those self-centered vicious girls.

Is there anything I could say to them to get them to understand that Ted and I are human and sensitive and deserve a chance at happiness? Is there any way to get them to care about the feelings of others? Mom once told me that some girls go through a mean stage and usually outgrow it and become nice people. Meanwhile, we, who are in the lower castes, have to suffer the damage brought on by their cruelty. I think I can handle it and come out okay, but, from what I've read, some people leave school with permanent scars. And I don't know anything I can do to change that.

Jane suddenly realized that the chill from the cold stone wall was penetrating her body and turning her into an icicle. The thought of her warm house sent her to her feet and rushing home.

CHAPTER

40

UME ON EARTH

As the North American side of the Earth rotated away from the Earth's sun, the Ume gathered around Senoa-lo. Green grass and leaves filled one side of the shelter. "First, let's discuss the food problem. I see that we've gathered enough greens for a few days. Jolocko-lo, have you found a way to preserve this stuff?"

"Yes and no. I discovered several ways to preserve food. Here on Earth, in the past, the primitives used to use sugar, salt, vinegar, alcohol, and smoke to preserve food. Now, they use mostly complicated chemicals. The problem is… we don't have any of these ingredients."

Toboo-lo perked up. "We can make smoke."

"You have ice for brains," Jolocko-lo roared. "If anyone saw smoke coming out of these woods, the city fire department would be here in minutes."

Toboo-lo stood up to face Jolocko-lo. "We could do it at night and hide the flame so it's not seen."

Senoa-lo stepped between them. "That's a possibility."

Leela-lo spoke up. "From my Earth studies, I have only heard of meat being preserved by smoke. I'm not sure if it'll work on greens."

Toboo-lo shuffled his feet, looked down at the ground and softly said, "I have never eaten animal flesh, but I guess if we're desperate, we could kill some animals and eat them.

Leela-lo exclaimed, "I'd die first."

Jolocko-lo declared, "You have that option. I'll eat almost anything if it means survival."

Senoa-lo held up a hand. "This is not something that has to be decided this moment. We can do a little more research and thinking before we come to a decision. Now, let's talk about our mission. Now that the Palalans are aware of the fact that they are not alone on our planet, we need to speed up our search for a weapon. We cannot be unarmed when they discover us. We've ruled out atomic bombs and TNT. Jolocko-lo has been doing some research on poisons."

Simultaneously, both Leela-lo and Toboo-lo jump up and exclaimed, "Poison!"

While Leela-lo stood there looking stunned, Toboo-lo said, "Do you realize what will that do to the plants and the water system? We can't even consider using chemicals that could destroy the ecology of half our planet. Blowing up buildings I can understand. They can be rebuilt, but… "

Leela-lo interrupted. "Poison is just unacceptable. It's such an underhanded way to kill people. I remind you that even though the Palalans are different and they are big, they are sentient beings."

Jolocko-lo sighed. "Leela-lo, all killing is bad. But, our mission is to find a powerful weapon that can kill a lot of Palalans. What did you think a WMD was?"

"Something like an atomic bomb, that kills the beings in an area."

"We don't have any uranium. So we can't make an atomic bomb," Jolocko-lo replied. "Or any thing that would be powerful enough to hurt the Palalans."

Senoa-lo held up her hands to get their attention and waited for the chatter to end. "I also hate the idea of poison, but… "

Toboo-lo barged in, "Here comes the 'but', the part no one wants to hear."

Senoa-lo glared at him with threatening eyes. "But, it seems chemical poisons are our only option. Jolocko-lo has been digging around on the internet and has found a couple of chemical formulas that our scientists might be able to replicate. Leela- lo, I want you to send our scientists the details of these chemical compounds at the usual communication time this evening."

They sat in silence, most looking at the ground and lost in their own thoughts. It was so quiet that they could hear a light breeze rustling the dry fall leaves outside. Leela-lo's soft voice expressed what they all thought. "Maybe we'll never have to use the poison. Maybe just letting the Palalans know we have it will make them leave us alone."

41

UME ON EARTH

The little Ume group camping in the Earth woods had discovered that the humans who walked in the park had regular schedules. The dog walkers came in the early morning and in the late afternoon. Between three and four, school kids cut through the park. Late at night, sometimes cars parked in the edge of the woods. Noises came from the cars, but usually no one got out of the vehicles. Keeping those busy times in mind, the Ume tried to schedule their trips out of camp so that they avoided the humans.

Leela-lo rose from her computer and stretched. "Senoa-lo, I think this would be a good time to go gather greens. The young ones have probably left the woods and the ones with dogs aren't due for a while. I'd like to go with Toboo-lo and get some fresh greens."

Senoa-lo stood up and turned to face her."Yes, I was so involved in this Vietnam war site that I forgot the time. Good idea." Senoa-lo tapped Toboo-lo on the shoulder. "I want you to go with Leela-lo to gather some food."

Toboo-lo pushed himself up off his seat. "It will be a pleasure. I can't stand being penned up in here." He rubbed his behind. "My rear is numb. Give me a minute. Let me see if I remember how to walk."

"You think any of us want to be here?" Jolocko-lo barked. "Quit complaining and do your job. Life would be a lot better here if you, the plant expert, were to find us something to eat besides these tough grasses and hard leaves. We need some real food. And don't you dare drag in any of those bitter roots you brought us yesterday."

Senoa-lo could see that the food problem was getting to some people. "Toboo-lo is dealing with his task very well considering our situation. If we can find a method of preserving the grasses, we'll still be able to get through the winter. Toboo-lo is working day and night to solve the problem of preserving the greens. If it can be done, he'll find a way. Meanwhile we will eat fresh greens while they're still available and keep our food from home in reserve. And Jolocko-lo, if you do not have anything helpful to say, please just keep your unpleasant thoughts in your head where they will only bother you and not the rest of us."

Jolocko-lo grunted and went back to his computer. Leela-lo quietly rose from her seat and started toward the door.

"And Toboo-lo," Senoa-lo added. "While you're out I want you to practice your English with Leela-lo. Your pronunciation could be better."

"Why?" Toboo-lo asked. We're not supposed to talk to any earth people."

"That's true," she replied. "But if you are somehow overheard talking, it is important that you are speaking English. Speaking Ume would attract attention. And we all need to be capable of communicating with our colleagues at home in English."

Toboo-lo shrugged. "All right." And he followed Leela-lo out the door.

Toboo-lo and Leela-lo walked in silence for awhile, both thinking about what kind of future might lie in store for them. Finally, Leela-lo broke the silence and said in English, "Where are we going?"

Toboo-lo nodded toward the big trees in front of them. "On the other side of those trees is an area where seedlings have sprouted. We can find some small tender leaves there if we're lucky and if the rabbits haven't found them yet."

Leela-lo frowned because Toboo-lo had spoken Ume. "Please speak English while we're out here."

"Sorry, I forgot." Toboo-lo said in English. "But I might be a bit slow, because I think in Ume while I speak in English." They climbed over some rocks and wound their way around the bigger roots.

"Toboo-lo, I have thoughts that trouble me and I need to talk to someone. You have age and wisdom. Can we sit and chat for a bit?"

"Of course, but we can't stay long. We have to watch the time so that we aren't out when the dog walkers come out. We can sit on those roots."

They sat. Leela-lo wiggled around and looked down at her hands. "Toboo-lo, first you have to promise that you will not tell anyone about what I'm going to tell you."

Now Toboo-lo felt uncomfortable and shifted on his seat. "All right. I promise."

"Will you make a sacred promise on water?"

Toboo-lo took a water bottle out of his vest, unscrewed the top and poured a little on his right hand. "I swear on the water that flows through our bodies and gives us life that I will keep our conversation secret." He put the bottle back in his vest. "Satisfied?"

"Thank you. I have been thinking about the WMD. If we make a weapon and let the Palalans know we have it, doesn't that give the Palalans a good reason to destroy us? If we threaten them, or if we poison a bunch of their people, they're going to try to squash us. I don't see how having a WMD can result in anything but war. Our settlements are scattered around the frozen mountains and the Palalans are all located together in the tropic equator area. We are at a geological disadvantage. I don't see how we could win a war with them."

Toboo-lo looked both sad and confused. "Why did you volunteer for this mission?"

"Our leaders said that it would be suicide to not have a WMD. I thought they were wiser than me and I didn't understand all the implications. Now that I've been able to research wars and political theory here on Earth, I see things differently."

Toboo-lo looked off into the distance. "I've mixed feelings about it too. I always have. And like you, I let our leaders seduce me to their viewpoint. But I can't justify using poison on animals or plants or sentient beings." He turned to face her.

"I was always taught that one should not just hope that things went right, but that it is our duty to our planet and our people to work for the right things. What can we do?"

"With your help, we could send our scientists a poison formula that doesn't work. Toboo-lo has written out the formula I'm supposed to send this evening. Do you know enough chemistry to change one or two elements and make it harmless?

"I could probably do that. But the scientists will test the formula and see that it's flawed. That might delay things, but it wouldn't stop this. And, if they didn't discover that it was defective, and tried to use it to defend us... that would be awful."

They both just sat, their bodies slack and their minds picturing scenes of doom and gloom.

CHAPTER

42

EARTH

Jane scurried home from school as fast as her feet would carry her. When she had headed out this morning, she hadn't expected it to turn so cold. A welcome warm blast of air greeted her as she came through the door. She dumped her coat in the hall as she sped to the kitchen to make something warm to drink. She searched through the cabinet, but there was no hot chocolate mix, so she settled for a tea and put the kettle on.

Jane had said nothing to her mother about the school brochures, but she couldn't get them out of her mind. She had grabbed the mail out of the mailbox as she unlocked the door and she had dropped it on the kitchen table. She shuffled through the mail, while she waited for the kettle to boil. She recognized the return address on one of the letters. It was one of the schools in the pamphlets. Steam was starting to come out of the kettle. She took the letter from the Asperger's school over to the cabinet and held it over the steam. She grabbed a knife and carefully pried the letter open. The kettle whistled as she read. She had been accepted into the school. *I'm being sent away to…* Her eyes travelled up to the letterhead at the top. *Alberta.* Finally, she noticed the screaming kettle and turned off the burner. It continued to whistle. Shrieking "Your mother wants to get rid of you." She took it off the burner and wandered into the living room. The letter dropped out of her limp hand and landed on the floor. She looked down at it and let it lay there.

The ringing of a phone brought her out of her trance. She ran to answer it.

She heard Ava's voice. "Hello… hello. Jane… Jane, I can hear you breathing. Say something or I'll think something's wrong."

"Oh nothing's wrong. My mother, the woman who gave birth to me, is planning to send me away, far away, to a special school for defective teens."

After a moment of silence, Ava said, "Did she say… "

"She hasn't said a word about the schools. But she obviously sent in an application because she just got a letter accepting me into a school in Alberta."

"If she didn't tell you… How?"

"I saw the return address when I picked up the mail and the kettle just happened to be steaming, so I steamed it open."

Jane plopped down on the couch and laid her head back. "Why? My grades are great. I stay out of her way. I don't cause any problems."

"It's not you. It's her and him probably, the British Mr. Wonderful."

"Should I grill her when she walks in the door? Should I ignore this and wait for her to bring it up? Should I just go shoot myself? I don't know what to do."

"I'm going to ignore that last option. As you would say, 'It's inappropriate for this situation.' I'd come over if I could. Mom is mad about my math grade and I can't leave the house until I do the homework and show it to her."

Jane beat her fist on the couch. "Expletive! Expletive! Really big expletive!"

"All right, I get that you're upset" Ava blurted out.

"Weird way to express it, but whatever." The line was silent for a minute. "How's this for a plan? Seal up the letter and put it back with the mail. Then… go somewhere like… the woods.

You're comfortable there. Sit and think carefully about what you want to do and phone me later tonight. With this homework, I doubt I'll get out of the house tonight. But Jane, I'm sending you a mental hug right now. Whatever happens, we'll always be friends, really close good friends."

"Thanks."

"So hang up the phone and get out of there right now! Your mom might come home early and you really shouldn't talk to her right now."

CHAPTER

43

PALALA

Swimming always made Kebeck cheerful. He liked to stretch all four of his arms out to pull his body through the water and feel the caress of it flowing past his slick green body. It was exhilarating. Kebeck was just stepping into his house, grabbing a towel to dry off from his swim, when his computer buzzed. He swiped at his arms as he sped over to his desk. A series of puddles left a path in his wake.

As he tapped the keyboard, he blurted out, "Greetings." Nacoo's serious countenance stopped him from saying more.

"Kebeck, you are needed here at my office as soon as possible. We have a problem."

Kebeck rubbed the towel over his head and neck. "What kind of problem?"

Nacoo hesitated. "I feel it would be more appropriate to discuss it in person."

Kebeck dried his stomach. *What could be so important?* "Could we just meet later this afternoon? I told my son that… "

Nacoo interrupted, "This is urgent and it is crucial that we meet as soon as possible. Please just get over here."

"Alright. I am walking out the door right now." Kebeck clicked off the computer and headed out.

When he arrived at her office, a very grim security officer was standing in front of her door. The officer greeted him and asked his name. As soon as he said, "Kebeck," the officer opened the door and indicated that he should enter. *What is going on?* Once inside, Nacoo quickly introduced him to three other people who worked with her in the Foreign Planets Department. He heard the names, but they didn't sink in because he was so distracted by the sober atmosphere in the room. Nacoo thanked them for their help, and they disappeared into an adjoining office. The tension in the room was palpable. Then he noticed Solang standing by a shelf, looking at some photos. Before he could say a word, Nacoo led him over to the shelf and pointed at one of the photos.

"We have neighbors. There seems to be an intelligent, industrialized society of small beings living in the ice mountains."

He stepped back and stared at her. "What? How could anyone live there? Why have we not seen them before?"

Solang held up a photo. "They live around hot springs. Our interstellar ships have found five cities thus far."

Kebeck was stunned. He suddenly felt like he couldn't breathe. "What?"

Nacoo put a hand on his shoulder. "Do you want a seat or a drink? I was also shocked when my pilots came to me with this. I just sat and stared at the photos for quite a while. Getting your mind around this means changing your worldview. These are not foreign visitors who just recently dropped in. These buildings and the infrastructure look like they have been here a long time."

"I would sit." A slantboard appeared behind him and he fell on it and held out a hand. "May I see one of the photos?" He studied the photo. There were buildings and roads and vehicles on the roads. Steam rose from the center of the settlement and at regular points around the town. He saw bodies of water and fields growing something green. All this was in a deep valley surrounded by high icy mountains.

"Why?"

Nacoo handed him a cup of water. "I'm assuming that you are asking why we have never seen them before? I suppose that in our arrogance, we Palalans thought that because we could not live in the cold regions, no one could. These beings must have a warm circulatory system like some of our forest animals.

We should have examined our own world more closely before we ran off to other planets. But, we did not. Our scientists wanted to explore other worlds, so they developed ships to fly to other stars and planets. It is unfortunate that our people rejected flight as a normal mode of transportation. Our history cites several occasions when it was voted down. We live in a flat world and feel insecure in anything over two stories high. We had no interest in the frozen mountains. In my youth, I remember someone suggesting that we send people to survey and better map the frozen regions. It was voted down by a huge margin.”

Kebeck stood up and handed Nacoo’s empty cup back to her. “What do they look like? I just see little dots in the photo.”

“We have no photos with enough detail to show them as anything but vague figures. Because our ships were built for long range flights, they are not suitable for flying low. Just before you arrived, we were discussing whether to land one of our ships briefly beside one of these villages, take some pictures and fly away. Solang thinks it would not be the right way to introduce ourselves to the beings.”

“Solang, could they be the ones that were heard speaking in the woods? Could they have written the notes?” He looked at the photo again. “They would have to be able to talk and write in order to have built this city.”

“They would have to have a written language,” Solang replied. “I also doubt that they could have constructed those intricate buildings without sophisticated communication skills. I have no way of knowing if the notes are in their language, but I intend to find out if they are.”

“So, we know nothing about them. They could be isolated and know very little about us or they could be watching us like we watch the Earthers. They might even be sneaking around spying on us.” Kebeck concluded.

“And one could have been on your ship that went to Earth,” Nacoo added.

Kebeck looked stunned. “You think I could have had one of these beings hiding on my ship when I went to earth?”

“That would explain the note and the fur.”

Kebeck stared at Nacoo. "Sounds crazy, but not any crazier that there being whole towns of intelligent beings living in the ice mountains."

"If that's true... If they were on the ship... " Solang pondered, "Then... they know a lot about us, but prefer that we not know about them."

There was a moment of silence as everyone contemplated the possibilities.

"We are doing a lot of speculating on very little data," Solang noted.

Kebeck turned toward Nacoo. "How big are these ice mountain people?

Nacoo put one of the photos in front of his face. "We don't know their exact size yet." She bit her lip and paused. "We should be able to determine their approximate size by comparing their buildings to one of the tall ice mountains in the background of these photos. And... from what I have noted, beings on most planets in sophisticated societies usually build their abodes about to be one and a half to two times their height. We surveyed some of the ice mountains from space long ago. Let me pull that up on my computer." Nacoo rushed over to her computer and started typing.

Solang held a photo up in front of Kebeck. "Look. This could be a steel mill." She held up another photo. "This looks like rows of homes down a street, similar to how they set up residences in parts of Earth. And notice the tall buildings in the background. Looking at the rows of windows, some buildings seem to be more that fifteen stories high. And... "

Nacoo cut her short as she yelled out across the room. "They are little things! They are tiny."

Everybody stopped what they were doing and rushed over to Nacoo.

Kebeck blurted out, "How tiny?"

"About one hand tall," Nacoo replied. We are about eight times taller than these little guys."

"Really?" Kebeck held his two upper hands one hand's distance apart. "Only that tall?"

"Well, that could be one reason we did not notice them before," Nacoo declared.

"Yeah, that fifteen-story building in the photo is probably about the height of my house," Solang mused.

Nacoo flopped back onto a slantboard. "Good. I had been envisioning the possibility of conflict with these people. But if they are that small, then there is very little chance of them being a threat to us. I am so relieved."

"Do you think it wise to assume that their size makes them harmless?" Kebeck pondered. "We have small animals in the bush that can kill with one bite or sting."

"But these beings are not wild animals." Nacoo insisted. "Look at what they have built. They are sophisticated and creative."

Solang spoke up. "There is still the question of how to start communications with them."

Nacoo speculated, "You know, we do not have to contact them. Maybe they are not aware of our existence. Or it could be that they know about us, but do not want us to know that they are there."

Both Solang and Kebeck stared at her in disbelief.

"Are you not curious?" Kebeck bellowed.

"I am." Nacoo replied. "But note that they have not dropped by and introduced themselves. Why is that?"

"Good point." Kebeck said. "Small does not mean that they are harmless. We must consider the security of our people. We need to know who and what they are. I suppose that they are aliens, but… ”

“Whatever they are, we need to know more about them.” Kebeck added.

“And what do they know about us? Are they the animals that have been recorded talking in the woods and dropping notes?” Solang asked. “If some foreign creatures are sneaking around on our lands, we need to know about them.

“Yes!” Kebeck stepped up in Nacoo’s face. “We must find out why they are here and what their intentions are.”

“Right, you are both right,” Nacoo admitted. “We need to know more about these creatures and we probably should attempt to communicate with them.” She paused. “This is a lot to absorb. I have to contact the Senior Council about this. We only represent the Earth Studies Committee and the Foreign Planets Department. Technically, since they are here on our planet, neither of our groups have the power to take this further. I will consult with the Council and get back to you.”

CHAPTER

44

UME ON EARTH

The two little Ume, Toboo-lo and Leela-lo had their arms piled high with grass and leaves as they stumbled through the woods. "I think we overdid it. This is too heavy," Leela-lo complained. "I need to sit, just briefly, and catch my breath." She placed her bundle on a flat rock, sat down and leaned against a big root coming out of the tree behind them.

Toboo-lo stood and glared at her for a second, then dropped his grasses and sat beside her. "You're right. I'm just afraid that it might frost tonight and it'll kill the grass and we won't have any food and we'll starve."

"Oh, that's reassuring. You're the person who is supposed to find food for us for the winter so we don't starve. What about eating roots? You said some of them are edible. We can put up with the terrible taste, if we have to."

" About that… now that I've had time to do some tests on the roots, I see that they have very little nutritional value."

"Have you told anyone, besides me?"

"No, not yet. I just finished the tests this morning. But I was on the internet earlier and I found a list of trees that are supposed have edible nutritious bark. Now I have to figure out if any of these are pines, slippery elms, spruce, hickory or black birch. After we get back to camp, I'm going to study up on trees so that I can identify those specific ones.

Leela-lo yawned. "When I was little, I looked up at all the suns in the sky and tried to imagine what it would be like to travel to some other solar system. I dreamed about shiny steel cities with buildings that reached up through the clouds. I thought I might meet strange intelligent beings who swim through the air. I never imagined starving to death in a cold forest.

"Leela-lo, we will be all right. If the bark of certain trees is quite sufficient as nutrition for Earth beings, they should fit our needs too."

"What if those specific trees don't grow here?

"There's a pine right in front of you."

Leela-lo and Toboo-lo jumped up and turned around to find the top half of a human's face peeking over a big root. They froze. *What to do?*

"Please don't be afraid. I would never hurt you. As a matter of fact, I can help you." Jane had been lying in a pile of leaves, contemplating her future, when she had heard Leela-lo and Toboo-lo's conversation.

Leela-lo and Toboo-lo were too scared to move.

"I'm going to slowly sit up now, but I'm not going to move toward you or touch you. I just want to move to a more comfortable position and then maybe we can talk." Jane shifted her body so that she sat facing them. She crossed her legs like a yogi and smiled at them. *This is like a dream, but I'm awake. I'm sure I'm awake.*

While Jane moved, Toboo-lo put his hand under his vest and wrapped it round the handle of his weapon.

They stayed like that for a while, nobody moving a muscle.

Nobody said a word. She stared at them and they stared at her.

Finally Jane broke the silence. "I understand that you're frightened. I'm frightened." She paused. "From what I heard, you seem to be from another planet and need food to survive the winter. I can identify the trees you mentioned. I can probably supply the food you need. And if you want, I could keep your existence a secret. I can understand why you might not want our people to know you're visiting our planet. After watching 'E.T.' and some other alien movies, I'm dubious about how the government and the scientists might treat you. Are you just here visiting, like tourists, or is there a reason for this visit?"

Leela-lo and Toboo-lo looked at each other, then looked back at Jane.

"I think you two need a moment alone to discuss the situation. I'm going to get up and walk over to that stream, so that you can talk without me hearing. You could run away into the woods," Jane paused and tilted her head. "I don't suggest you do that. I know these woods really well and I can probably find you. I know there are more than just the two of you and that your camp is close enough to the houses to pirate an internet signal. Or, I could tell others about you and the woods would be full of people searching for you. But I don't want to do that. I hope you'll talk to me and let me help you. I'll go over there… " She nodded to her left. "And let you talk together. Wave at me, when you're ready to discuss your situation." Jane got to her feet and walked away.

"What should we do?" Leela-lo whispered.

"I don't know. I have my weapon in my hand. We could call her over and kill her, but a dead human in these woods would cause big problems. And I don't want to kill her. She's being nice."

Leela-lo glanced over at Jane. "And there's no way we could hide that enormous body."

"We need to talk this over with Senoa-lo and the others."

"Yeah. How do we do that? Leela-lo asked.

"I have an idea." Toboo-lo stood up and waved both hands at Jane.

Jane came back over and resumed her sitting position.

Toboo-lo moved a step closer to Jane. "I have a proposal.

We need to confer with our colleagues. If you will agree to keep our existence secret for one day, we will meet you here tomorrow and bring our leader to talk with you."

Jane nodded, then glanced at her watch. "Do you have a system for telling time, Earth time?"

Toboo-lo huffed, "Of course. We have studied your planet. We are aware of the rotation sequence of this planet and your system of time-keeping."

"How have you been able to study Earth? Do you have surveillance satellites watching us? Have your ships been here previously?"

Leela-lo elbowed Toboo-lo. He looked at her and she shook her head.

"I can not answer those question without consulting our leader. Tomorrow you may ask her. We need to get back to our camp now. Soon the humans who bring their dogs to this park will be arriving."

Jane thought for a second. "Tomorrow is Saturday. Can we meet at this spot at ten o'clock tomorrow?

"We'll be here."

Neither of them moved.

Jane spoke up. "I guess you want me to leave first so that I can't see which direction you go."

Toboo-lo replied, "Yes. That would be nice."

Jane turned and left.

CHAPTER

45

ICE MOUNTAINS

Mera made a face as she put her spoon down. *This just isn't as good as my father's spoku soup.* After her father Jolocko-lo had flown off on the mission to Earth, Mera had moved in with her aunt. She missed her father. Life was good and school was good, but her aunt was not a great cook and she couldn't really talk to her, unless it was about plants and sports. Her dad understood her. He didn't always agree with her, but he understood. Mera looked out the window and thought about how to handle this cooking situation. *Maybe I'll have to learn how to cook?* Something caught her eye that made her forget about the sour soup. She moved closer to the window. Something was flying past the ice mountains. It wasn't a plane. The shape was wrong: the wings were too small for it to be a Ume airship. And it was fast. She got up and went outside. Several other people were standing outside looking up. A neighbor came over to her. "That's the third time that thing has flown over. What is it? Where's it from? Is it a Palalan ship?" Mera was too stunned to answer. It was a Palalan ship just like the one that had taken her father to Earth. Jolocko-lo had shown her a photo of the vessel.

Finally she found her voice. "They've found us. The Palalans know we're here."

The woman grabbed her arm. "What should we do?"

"Nothing. There's nothing we can do. We're doomed. We don't have a WMD yet. The only weapons we have are electric shock sticks. All we can do now is hope… hope that they don't destroy us."

46

UME ON EARTH

A cold wind blew through the woods and made the canvas door of the Ume camp flutter and wave. Senoa-lo was sitting by the entrance and heard footsteps as Leela-lo and Toboo-lo neared the camp. The minute they got inside, Senoa-lo could tell by their faces that something was wrong. She stood and watched them as they put the grass in the back of the enclosure. Then she asked, "What happened?"

Leela-lo and Toboo-lo looked at each other, each wanting the other to drop the bomb. By this time, Jolocko-lo had stopped what he was doing and had turned to watch.

"Toboo-lo, sit down here." She motioned toward her empty seat. "Tell us what happened out there."

Toboo-lo sat. He slumped forward and studied the ground. Then he looked up at her. "Try not to get angry. We didn't mean for it to happen."

Speaking loudly, but trying not to yell, "What happened?"

Standing beside him, Leela-lo blurted out, "We met a young human female and talked to her."

Suddenly everybody was waving their arms and yelling. Jolocko-lo bellowed at Toboo-lo, "You've got ice for brains. He howled, "We said not to talk to them. Never. How could you not understand that? Do you know what you've done?"

Senoa-lo clapped her hands and shouted, "Quiet! Quiet, everyone! We need to hear more about this." She waited until they all stopped talking, then again asked Toboo-lo, "What happened? Tell us exactly what was said by you and every word uttered by this Earth person."

Slowly, Toboo-lo told them the whole story of their encounter with the Earth being. When he finished, no one spoke.

Senoa-lo stared off into space for a minute, then said," You say she is young. Is she a child?"

"No. Her body is adult size, but she looks to be what they call a teenager."

"Then the judgement part of her brain isn't fully developed yet. Too bad." Jolocko-lo shook his head.

"But she seems to be very smart." Leela-lo added.

"Smart could be good or bad for us " Senoa-lo said.

"Tomorrow Toboo-lo will take me to the location and I will see what she wants."

"No, let me go." Jolocko-lo insisted. "It could be a trap."

"I will go with Toboo-lo early tomorrow so that he can show me the place where they met her. He will return and I will stay there, hidden until the set time. Then I will show myself. If it is a trap, it's better that they get only one of us, and if she is sincere, I should be the one to negotiate with her."

Jolocko-lo grumbled, "I don't like it, but you're probably right."

Senoa-lo nodded, "Of course I'm right."

"What should I say about this in my communication with the home base this evening?" Leela-lo asked. "Should I tell them?"

"Not a word.. Say nothing about the Earth female. There's no way that they can be of any help. It'll only upset them. We will deal with it and then inform them of whatever results from this encounter."

"I agree," Jolocko-lo added.

Senoa-lo glanced at him and with a slight nod of her head continued. "Now, we need to sit down together and make some plans. As I see it, we need to plan for three possibilities and decide how to proceed in each case. If she wants to help us, how should we handle it? If she captures me and goes looking for the rest of you, what to do? And if she has already told a government authority about us and they come looking for us, how should we proceed? Lots to decide. And, I'm hungry. We should eat some of these fresh greens before they start to wilt. We can eat and talk."

CHAPTER

47

PALALA

The lush green grass beside the river was shaded by kaba trees. Three Palalans were in their shadow engaged in a lively discussion, with all arms flying as they gestured to make their points. They stopped talking and one nudged another as Kebeck came out of the river. Kebeck's meeting with Nacoo and Solang had left his muscles in knots. The swim had helped loosen them. One of the fellows under the shade trees stood and nodded as he performed the traditional greeting toward Kebeck. Kebeck returned the greeting. *I do not know who he is, but he knows me. I suppose my photo was made public when I flew to Earth. I do not think I like being known by so many people that I do not know.* He shrugged his shoulders and wiped water off of his scales as he strolled down the path toward the meeting room. Nacoo had contacted Kebeck after her meeting with the Senior Council. The Council had decided that more information was needed, and assigned the job to Nacoo, with the suggestion that Kebeck and Solang assist her.

Nacoo and Solang were studying some new photos so intensely that they failed to notice Kebeck's entrance. "Anything new?"

They both looked up and Nacoo handed Kebeck a photo. "They stand vertical and are covered with red, brown or grey fur. Kebeck studied the photo. "I have seen this animal in the bush, or an animal that looks very similar. We called them hop-hops. I have no idea what their scientific name is. Maybe our hop-hops are genetic relatives of these beings in the ice mountains."

"It is very important," Nacoo emphasized, "that we find out if they came from another planet and settled here or if they evolved here?"

"How could they have evolved here?" Kebeck asked. "They are living in the ice mountains."

"But," Nacoo pointed out, "They are living in valleys with hot springs that enable plants to grow. Each of these developed areas has fields and greenhouses. And their towns are complex with mines and factories. They did not just land here from another planet. They have been here for a long time."

"So either they are aliens who have chosen to come live in our mountains, or they are native animals who have evolved into sophisticated beings." Kebeck scratched his head. "We need to know more."

"And how do we do that?" Solang asked.

"I am not sure. I just know that we need to know more about them. Those buildings show intelligence, dexterity and communication skills."

Kebeck pulled a slantboard over and plopped down. "So, do we fly over in a space ship, introduce ourselves and ask a few questions, or dig a bit more before we meet?"

"Ask a few questions? How can we communicate without knowing their language?" Solang demanded.

Kebeck picked up two photos of two different Ume towns. "The level of development and the style of these buildings in these different villages seems to be about the same. That leads me to assume that they have a method of communicating between the developed areas. These towns did not develop in total isolation from each other. Any ideas?"

Nacoo looked at the photos. "They could have strung lines for communication, like we used to have ages ago. Otherwise, they would have to bounce radio waves off a satellite in the sky. If they had a satellite, we would have noticed it. They probably have cables that cross the ice mountains and connect all the areas."

"There are no lines visible on the photos. If they have lines connecting the towns, then they are buried under a lot of snow."

Solang perked up. "We could send a team to find one of the cables and connect to it."

Both Kebeck and Nacoo frowned and stared at her.

"Why not?" Solang inquired.

Kebeck turned toward Nacoo and motioned for her to answer. Nacoo closed her eyes and shook her head. "Would you like to volunteer to put on four or five layers of clothes, put an electric heat system on your back, and climb around in those mountains looking for a cable hidden under the ice? A cable that is probably the size your finger?"

Solang's shoulders fell. "Good point. Anyone have a better idea?"

"Look." Nacoo showed them a photo of a tower in the center of a town. "This has to be a communications facility. All the developed valleys have one of these towers. I think that they may have placed relays on some of the tall mountains that enable them to send radio signals back and forth. We could place a receiver on a mountaintop near one of the little towns so that we can pick up the electromagnetic waves from the town's tower. That would allow us to monitor their computer communication and televisions and radio and phones or whatever they use for communication."

Solang shook her head. "We don't know for sure if they use electronic waves or some other communication mode with those towers."

Nacoo stabbed a finger at the photo. "But they look just like our communication towers, only smaller."

"It is odd," Kebeck pondered, "that their communication towers look like a miniature version of our designs."

"And if this does enable us to listen to their transmissions, it would help me decipher their language. It's worth trying." Solang added.

Kebeck sat up. "Can we do it? Can we put a receiver near one of these towns?"

"I think so. We can parachute it down from a ship. The problem with a parachute is getting the receiver to land in the right place. No way do we want it to land in a populated area. That would blow the whole spying thing."

"And," Nacoo added. "If it landed near a town, they would probably take it apart to see what it was. That is what I would do if a machine came floating down out of the sky."

"But how do we get the receiver up to the top of an ice mountain?" Nacoo asked.

Kebeck got up, looked at the other two, then paced back and forth as Solang and Nacoo watched in silence. After a few times across the room, his hands shot up. "I have an idea! Our Forest Department has developed a small radio-controlled contraption that can fly low over the trees to photograph and monitor growth patterns. They call it a flying camera. We could borrow one and put a radio receiver on it and connect it to our satellite system. We could sneak it in at night. Maybe a ship can drop it near the right place. Then an operator can guide it to a mountaintop near the town. If their transmission system is similar to ours that might give us access to their oral and written communication."

Nacoo studied Kebeck for a second. "That is what we shall do. I will arrange it."

Solang's face lit up. "If we can hear their language, I can probably determine if they are the ones who were talking in the forest. Fantastic!" She turned to Nacoo. "When can we drop the receiver? Tonight?"

"Maybe, but probably not. It might take a day or two to get everything coordinated and put together. I will see what can be done."

Kebeck caught Solang's eye. "What if they speak a language different from the one we recorded in the woods?"

"Then we have two problems instead of one. Either way, I can start working trying to translate their language once I have enough recordings."

Nacoo wiped a hand over her green head. "I hope the languages match. I do not relish the prospect of dealing with two different alien groups on our planet.

48

EARTH

Jane was still walking on a cloud when she got home. *I talked to aliens… People from another planet! And I can't tell anyone. But I have to tell someone. Should I tell Ava? Would she believe me? This is so amazing. They're real. I feel like I'm in a movie. But I'm not. They're real!*

A strident voice interrupted her thoughts and brought her back down to earth. "Jane, please come in my office." *Definitely not telling my mom.*

As she put her coat away, Jane's thoughts turned to her own problems. *Is mom going to tell me that she's sending me away to Alberta. She rarely calls me into her office. But I just met little fuzzy space people. I have to stay here and help them.* "I'm coming." Jane kicked off her shoes and headed to the office her mother had set up in the little room off the living room. As she entered the office, she could clearly see that her mother was in a bad mood. "What are you wearing, and why are you such a mess?

Jane looked down at her clothes. Her heavy faded fleece-lined jeans were covered with bits of dry leaves and dirt. "I was in the woods. It's cold. So I dug these old jeans out of the back of the closet and… " She looked down again,. "I tripped on a root and fell. They just need to be washed."

"I thought I told you to throw those things in the trash?"

"I just use them for going into the woods to do my tree research. Nobody sees me in them."

Her mother stood up and shook her head in disgust. "I see them, and those heavy pants and big jacket make you look like a chubby hobo."

"When I'm sitting on the ground doing tree… "

She was cut short with her mother saying, "That's another thing we need to talk about… your tree research. Jane, you're a high school student and you're very smart, but you're not a trained scientist. From listening to you talk, one would think that you were involved in vital research that could change the world." Now her mother was waving her hands for emphasis. "I've put up with this nonsense long enough. You've got to accept the fact that you're just playing at doing research. You can't think you're doing anything of significance. Maybe someday, when you finish university…"

Jane straightened up. "I know more about trees, dendrology, especially birch trees, than almost anybody on the planet. Finding out how their mycorrhizal fungal threads communicate is important. We don't know what applications might evolve from studying their synapses."

Her mother's face fell. "How did you learn about… what was it? Some kinds of threads communicating?"

"Mom, I read. I'm active in scientific blogs and I'm in touch with several renowned research scientists by email. I have three different experiments going right now."

Now, her mother had her hands on her hips in a stance that was usually accompanied by yelling. "Why have you never told me about this?"

"I tried, but you said you didn't want to hear about trees."

"Oh." Her mother looked down at her desk and shuffled some papers around. "I'm sorry. I should have listened." She picked up the envelope from Alberta, then put it back down. "So, you're talking to real scientists about this tree thing?"

"I've been corresponding with five different dendrology experts. One at Queens University at Belfast, two in Wisconsin, a very nice fellow at Iowa State and one woman at Harvard. I can show you the emails."

Her mother stepped back and cocked her head to one side.

"Oh, I don't think that's necessary. You've never been one to lie, and it sounds very science, well, umm… very complicated." She looked down at the envelope on the desk, then back at Jane. "I'm impressed. I didn't realize that you were doing all this. I thought you went to the woods to get away from people."

The phone on the desk rang, startling them both. Jane wandered over to the window on the far side of the room while her mother held a brief conversation with Mr. Fitzgerald.

Her mother hung up and waved her back over to the desk. "Jane, I'm thinking of going away for the weekend. Do you think you could stay with your friend, Ava, on Saturday night?"

Jane was astonished that after years of pleading to have a sleep over, her mother was finally going to allow her to spend a night at a friend's house. *This is not real. This has to be a dream. Aliens and a night away at Ava's.* Jane could feel her mother glaring at her "Yes… I'm sure."

"Well, go up to your room and change out of that ratty outfit. And call Ava to see if her mother will let you stay over. Call her right now. I need a quick answer. Walter will be here any minute. And please put those pants in the trash."

Jane stumbled up the stairs, her mind too busy to properly guide her feet. *When I talk to Ava, should I tell her about the little aliens? No. Not now and not on the phone. This is not something you tell someone on the phone. And, I want to see her face.*

"Hello Ava. I'm calling to see if you parental units might agree to allow me to stay at your house tomorrow night? I have, believe it or not, finally, after all these years, been given permission for a Saturday night sleep over."

There was silence then, "Who is this and what have you done with Jane?"

"What?" Jane paused in confusion. "Oh, you're kidding. Funny. Now please ascertain if your mother is agreeable with this so that I can confirm it with my mother."

"Sure. I'll be right back to you. Hang on."

Jane was thinking about what to do about the little aliens when Ava came back on the line. "As my mother said, 'We would be delighted to have her.'"

"Thank you. I hate to be abrupt, but there seems to be some urgency in getting this confirmed. I will call you later." Jane hung up and started to head out her bedroom door when she remembered. *I had better change before I go down. If I'm still in this outfit when Walter gets here she will go crazy.* Jane pulled out a white blouse and navy skirt and changed. She picked up the old pants and jacket and took a step toward her trash can. *No.* She smiled, then rolled the clothes into a ball and stuffed them into the back of her closet. Then, she headed down the stairs. When she got to the living room, she noticed that the door to her mother's office was closed. She could hear her mother's and Walter's voice, but couldn't make out what they were saying. *He's already here. He must have called from his car.* She looked around. *There's what I need.* She grabbed an empty antique vase off of a cabinet and pressed it up against the door with her ear against the other end.

Walter said, "Did you talk to her about the school in Alberta?"

Her mother was quiet, then she said, "I umm, I didn't. I will, but not today. The timing has to be right."

"You know it's the best thing for her. She'll be happier with others who are more, you know, like her."

"You're probably right, but let's just go away on our weekend and deal with this on Monday. All right?"

"Sure. Now give me a kiss."

Jane put the vase back on the cabinet and stomped her feet to make some noise, then knocked on the office door.

CHAPTER

49

ICE MOUNTAINS

Mera stood at the window and looked up at the ice mountains. Steam floated up from the hot springs. The wind was blowing from the west and as the steam rose over the eastern mountains, it turned into snow. It would be a lovely day if it weren't for the scary things she was reading on the Ume national news site.

Everyone had an opinion about what to do now that the Palalans knew of their existence. A few refused to believe that the day had finally arrived. The Palalan ships had been spotted flying over almost every town. That wasn't a coincidence. It was suggested that we threaten them with a non-existent WMD. Some people wanted to send representatives by plane to their capitol city. Others wanted to just wait to see what the Palalans do next. Yesterday, she had received a message from her father. It had been relayed to her through government channels. She knew it was meant to cheer her up, but she could tell by the tone of her father's words that his mission on Earth was not going well.

A ring tone on her computer brought her out of her reverie. Her friend Chalao appeared on the screen. "Hi Chalao, what's up?"

Chalao's fur was going in all directions and her ears were standing straight up. "I'm going crazy here. My parents are totally upset and they won't let me go out of the house. My father keeps pacing back and forth in the front room and my mom keeps cooking stuff. This has been going on ever since they heard about the Palalan ships. I told them to just go on like normal We just have to wait and see what the government does about the Palalan situation. But they're bouncing off the walls. Do you know anything? I thought since your father is on that Earth mission… Well, I hoped you might know something. Anything? Did I tell you that they're driving me crazy?"

"Yes. You said that. I don't know what I can do. I don't know anything except what's on the news. But, you could ask them if you can come over to my house and stay with me for a while. Emphasize that I'm alone. Play it up that I shouldn't be by myself at a time like this. Really, I'm fine, but it would be nice to see you. I can't help thinking that whatever happens in these next few days could change our lives forever. We've lived our whole lives waiting for this to happen, not knowing how it would go. Maybe they'll just accept us as neighbors or maybe they'll kill us all. Whatever. What can I do? What can you or your parents do? Nothing. Nothing but wait. Just gather up some of that food your mother's cooking and get over here. For now, I'm alive, worried and hungry."

50

EARTH

Jane stood on the front porch and waved as her mother got in Walter's black Mercedes. She had to work at not smiling. She didn't want her mother to realize how happy she was to see her gone, to have two days without her. And there was no way she wanted her mom to know how excited she was about the little people in the woods. All morning she felt a smile trying to break through when she thought back to her conversation with the little fuzzy aliens. But, thinking about being sent away to a special school in Alberta scared away any hint of a smile. Getting to sleep last night had been almost impossible. She alternated between worrying about being sent off to Alberta and buzzing with excitement over the aliens. *Aliens, little fuzzy aliens, are hiding in my woods and in a few minutes I will be talking to them.* She wanted to dance around and scream with joy, but the neighbors might see her, so she calmly walked into the house, closed the door and jumped up and down yelling, "Yes! Yes! Yes!" After her third leap she began to feel a bit silly and calmed down. *What time is it?* Her watch read 9:30. Jane went to the kitchen and opened the fridge *Lettuce, because they were gathering grass when we met. They might like cheese. And bread, everybody likes bread.* Jane chopped the bread, cheese and lettuce up into tiny pieces, packed it in plastic bags and headed out the door.

It took her no time to get to the designated meeting spot in the woods. Except for a few birds twittering, the woods were silent. There was no sign of the little visitors, so Jane sat on a tree root and waited. Out of the corner of her eye she was two little fuzzy aliens creep out from behind a linden tree. She sat very still and waited for them to speak. The two aliens came around in front of her and stood motionless for a minute.

"I am Senoa-lo and this is Leela-lo. I am the leader of our mission and Leela-lo is our communication expert. She is here to help if my English is not sufficient for this meeting. I have been told that you have offered to help us with our food situation."

Jane reached for the plastic bag that was laying beside her as she said, "My name is Jane."

Both the aliens put their hands under their vests and drew out little silver rods.

Jane paused. "I'm just going to open this bag to show you some of the food I brought for you. I suppose those things you are holding are weapons. I'm not going to harm you. I'm elated to see you and I just want to help.

Senoa-lo nugged Lela. "What is 'elated'?"

"It is 'happy'."

Senoa-lo put her weapon back in her vest pocket and motioned for Leela-lo to do the same. "Jane, please show us the food you have brought."

Jane took out a paper napkin and spread it on the ground. Then she placed some lettuce, cheese and bread on the napkin.

"What are these foods? I think the green one is a plant that grows on the soil, but the other two I do not know." Senoa- lo asked.

"You are right about the green one; it is called lettuce. The white one is bread. It is made from a plant from the soil, mixed with eggs and milk and cooked. The yellow one is cheese and it is made from… " Jane stopped and thought for a second. "It is made from the liquid called milk that an animal, a cow, produces to feed its young."

Senoa-lo looked puzzled. "I know that when humans and many earth animals produce young, they secrete a liquid from pockets on their bodies to feed their young ones. I did not know that his liquid, milk, is used to make food? Do not the young ones need the milk to survive?"

Mentally Jane went 'yuck,' but worked at keeping the yuck from showing on her face. "We never use human milk to make cheese. We only use the milk from cows or goats and they produce enough for the young and to use for cheese and other dairy products."

Leela-lo spoke up. "From my studies, I have read that this milk is very nutritious. It would probably be a good food for our Ume bodies."

"What kind of food do you eat on your planet?"

"We only eat plants. We do not eat animals or things that come from animals."

"You are vegans." Jane exclaimed. "I hope I didn't insult you by offering you the other foods."

"No. We are explorers and we like to try new things."

"Would you like to try these foods?" Jane asked.

Senoa-lo stepped up to take a piece of the lettuce, but Leela-lo stopped her. "I should try these foods first, in case there is a problem with them. You are our leader and we need you."

Senoa-lo pushed Leela-lo's hand aside. "I don't need a poison taster. We can both try them."

Jane sat and watched as they tried the lettuce, cheese and bread.

Senoa-lo took a second piece of the bread. "I especially like the bread. You said it contains something called eggs. What are they?"

This is going to be weird. Another mental 'yuck' went through Jane's brain as she explained where eggs came from.

Senoa-lo scratched her head. "These undeveloped embryos, are they a common food on Earth?

Jane nodded. *I'd never really thought about what eggs really are.*

Senoa-lo continued. "So the young undeveloped bodies of these animals are released from the mother's body in a protective case. Interesting. I suppose that makes it easy to store them for later use as food." Senoa-lo paused. "Much is interesting about your planet, but right now we need to talk about other things. We need to discuss our need for food and security."

"And I have some questions," Jane added.

Senoa-lo motioned toward the big tree roots. "Let us sit and talk."

As soon as they were all seated Jane blurted out, "Why are you here?"

Even though Senoa-lo had prepared herself for that question, she took a second before answering. Senoa-lo had thought about lying and telling the young Earth human that they were just here as part of a scientific study. She had planned to tell her that their unit was just one of several groups sent to several planets to just observe for the sake of science. But, after a discussion with Leela-lo, their Earth psychology expert, she had decided to tell the truth. Not the whole truth, but parts of the truth. Leela-lo said that they should definitely avoid mentioning the term 'weapon of mass destruction.'

Senoa-lo was about to say, 'We are on a mission to save our people,' when she changed her mind. *This human is young and seems to be idealistic. I don't feel that we should trust her with the truth.* So instead she said, "We are here to research the energy systems that humans employ to run advanced machinery. Our planet needs new sources of energy."

Leela-lo was surprised by Senoa-lo's reply, but kept a straight face.

Jane thought for a second. "How do you plan to do your research and stay hidden?"

"All we need is a connection to your internet. We have set up a connection but it's very weak and slow. Thus far we have found some ingenious inventions for using new types of energy."

Jane shifted her seat on the roots. "So you are just here to use the internet for research. Meanwhile, you need food. I can help you with the food."

"That would be very helpful and appreciated.

Jane studied the little furry creatures. "Can I ask? Is your fur sufficient for extreme cold or will you need shelter when this area becomes very cold?"

Senoa-lo looked puzzled. She turned to Leela-lo. "What is fur?"

Leela-lo smiled and said, "Chaleko."

Senoa-lo ran a hand across her fake fur vest. "A warm place to stay would be nice. But, it is more important that we have access to the internet."

Jane smiled. "I might be able to find you a shelter with WiFi... reliable fast WiFi."

Again, Senoa-lo looked puzzled.

Jane quickly spoke up. "Internet."

"Oh. Why would you do that for us?" Senoa-lo asked.

Jane was thrown by the question. "Well, I guess I've been taught that whenever possible I should help people who need help."

Senoa-lo smiled. "So have we been taught in our society. From our research and observation of your planet, I know that not all humans believe such. In fact, we have observed that most on this planet expect some type of payment for any service they do for others. We are fortunate to have met you."

Jane nodded. "Thank you."

"And thank you," Leela-lo said.

Jane grinned. "I am very excited to actually be talking to people from another planet. I want to know so many things about you. Like... like how is it that you speak English?

Senoa-lo stood up. "That is complicated. We will have much time for learning about each other. I should go now."

"Of course. I am honoured to have met you. I hope I can help you with your research. I thought it over last night, and I don't think you're a threat to Canada or our planet. So I'm not going to tell the military or any government agency that you're here. That would not end well. But if you want, I'll do what I can to keep you safe from harm and fed while you're here." She paused again and smiled. "I assume you have a spaceship hidden somewhere around here. I'd really like to see it."

Leela-lo rubbed the fur behind her ear. "The problem… "

Senoa-lo interrupted, "That's not possible."

"I understand." Jane nodded. "You just met me and there needs to be trust before you would feel comfortable showing anyone what is probably your only way of getting home. That's reasonable."

"But to get back to our main problem… food," Senoa-lo nibbled at the chunk of cheese she had in her hand. "We appreciate your offer and we would like to have whatever foodstuff you can bring us."

"How many people are here with you? Jane asked Senoa-lo paused and looked at Leela-lo.

"I'm just asking so I'll know how much food you need."

"We have two more back at our camp."

"And if we don't return to camp soon, they're going to come looking for us," Leela-lo added.

Jane stood up. "Would you like me to come tomorrow at ten with more food?"

"Thank you. That would be good." The two Ume got up, and stood like statues, waiting for Jane to leave.

Jane was perplexed for a second. Then she realized what they were doing, so she turned and pranced off toward home.

51

EARTH

Jane's mind was buzzing like a hornet's nest. She had little aliens from space living near her. Her mother was away for two days, leaving her free to do whatever she wanted. And then there was the possibility of being shipped off to a boarding school lurking in the background. It was all too much. *I need to sit down with a piece of paper and figure out how to deal with all this. And I need Ava's thoughts on the situation. But there's the rub. I told the aliens that I would keep their existence a secret. Now that I think about it, I don't know if I can. I need to talk to someone I can trust. Meeting the first aliens ever is too big, too earth shattering, to handle by myself. I'll go crazy if I don't talk to someone about them. Should I believe these little creatures? Are they what they seem? Should I help them or contact NASA? Ava is the only person I can trust with this. Certainly not my mother. I have to tell Ava.*

Jane was just closing the door when the phone rang. "Phenomenal timing, Ava. I was just going to call you. Might you be able to come over here now? My mind is a jumble and I think you will be quite excited by what I have to tell you."

"So tell me."

"No, not on the phone. That would not be prudent. Can you come soon?"

"All right. Be right over."

"I'll put the kettle on for tea. Or, on second thought, if you have anything alcoholic that you might be able to sneak out with… this bit of news might require strong drink.

"Right. And I also have news that could shake up your world. Be there in a jiffy."

CHAPTER

52

EARTH

Jane opened the door the minute Ava's feet touched the porch. Ava strolled in and slowly pulled a small bottle of rum out of her backpack. "You want some of this now or after we tell each other our news?"

Jane took the bottle and set it on the coffee table. "Later. I've been thinking and you should tell your news first. Shall we sit?"

"Definitely. You should be sitting for this."

Ava sat on the couch and Jane sat on the fancy old chair that faced it.

"Well," Ava started, "Mr. Fitzgerald is not what he says he is."

Jane's shoulder's drooped. "Oh no. Mother is going to be hurt and disappointed. I don't like him, but he makes her happy."

"I did some research. He is not British. He spent 6 years in England in high school and university. Then moved back here to Canada. So his accent is not real. And he's not rich. He taught high school in Toronto and just retired last year."

Jane looked relieved. 'But he's not a criminal or gangster?

"No, he's just a big liar."

"She hates liars. She is going to be so hurt. I wish I didn't have to tell her."

Ava leaned forward. "You don't have to tell her."

Jane leaned in. "Yes I do. I couldn't live with not telling her. And she would be so upset if she found out that I knew and didn't tell her."

"She's going to be upset anyway when you tell her. She's happy now. Maybe she'll never find out the truth. And remember, this is the woman who is thinking of sending you off to a boarding school. Maybe you don't owe her the truth."

"Well… "

"I know it's a difficult situation. But when you tell her about her lover boy, she'll dump him and probably any idea of sending you away. I know she'll be unhappy and you don't want that, but if you keep his secret and keep her happy you could end up in Alberta." Jane paused. "Or you could blackmail Mr. Fitzgerald into insisting that you not go to Alberta and everyone would be happy. Problem solved." Ava leaned back and grinned.

Jane stared off into space for a moment. "Not really. I have to tell her. I couldn't live with it any other way. That's just who I am."

"Yeah, I thought so. Should we have a bit of that rum now?"

Jane started to reach for the bottle. Then pulled her hand back. "Not until after I've told you my news."

"I can't imagine that you've got anything to top my jaw-dropping discovery."

Jane gritted her teeth and took a breath. "Well, I'm going to tell you something that will sound unreal and you're going to have to allow yourself to ignore how incredible it sounds and just believe me. I can prove it to you later. I just can't show you any evidence right this minute. But it is real."

"Wow."

"And I need to ask you to promise not to tell anyone about this. And I mean no one. Not your mom. No one. I need a serious, grown- up, swear-on-your-life promise. Can you do that?"

Ava was beginning to be scared. *What could be so important?*

Jane glared at Ava. "I need an answer before I can proceed."

"Does this concern anyone's death?"

"No." She thought for a second. "But revealing this secret could possibly lead to someone's death. Maybe… "

"I'm intrigued. And I'm relieved. I thought for a second that I might be helping you bury a body."

"No. It's a good secret."

"I'm in."

Jane got up and headed toward the kitchen.

Ava called after her. "Where are you going?"

Jane yelled back. "I'm getting glasses for the rum."

Jane rustled around in the kitchen for a few minutes then reappeared with a tray carrying glasses, a bowl of ice, a coke and sliced limes.

"You're making us Cuba Libres? How do you know about Cuba Libres?"

"I do read, you know." Jane mixed up two drinks and sat them on coasters on the coffee table.

"Now you truly and seriously promise to keep what I am about to tell you secret from everyone?"

Jane sat up straight and raised her right hand like she had seen people do in courtroom scenes. "I swear."

"All right. No screaming or yelling." Jane paused and looked down at the floor. "There are little aliens in the woods and I have talked to them."

Ava licked her lips. "You mean small people from other countries… right? Illegal foreigners from Mexico or South America?"

Jane looked up into Ava's eyes. "No. I mean small furry creatures from another planet."

Ava sat very still. She examined Jane from top to bottom. She looked down at the glasses on the table and watched a bead of water slide down one of the glasses. She spoke, one word at a time. "Jane, I appreciate a prank and for a second you almost had me believing that you're talking to little green spacemen, but really."

Jane perked up. "Yes, really. Do you not think that there are other people, intelligent creatures on some of the billions of planets out there?"

"Well yes. There are probably other sentient beings on some of those planets. But… "

"I'm not pulling a prank on you. That's not my style. You know that. I rarely joke and when I do, I'm not very good at it. This is for real."

Ava reached for one of the glasses, took a big swig and started coughing. When she caught her breath, she said, "You mix a strong drink."

"Sorry. It's my first time."

"So… you really met and talked to some people from another planet?"

Jane grinned. "I did."

A ringing phone startled them both. Jane jumped up and ran for the phone in the kitchen.

As Ava sat mulling over things she could hear excitement in Jane's voice, but she couldn't make out the words. Jane rushed back into the room.

"Hoop has lost Ted!"

"You're talking about Hoop's autistic brother? That's too bad. But back to the aliens in the woods. When did you… ?"

"No. I can't talk about them right now. They're safe for the moment. We've got to help Hoop. Ted is out in the woods, probably lost and terrified. Anything could happen to him. Hoop said his parents went to do some shopping and have a meal out. They left Hoop in charge. Hoop went into Ted's room to tell him lunch was ready and he was gone. Hoop said Ted's never done anything like this before. He's never been out of the house without Hoop or one of his parents."

"So has he called his parents or the police?"

"No. Hoop'll get into big trouble over this. He wants me to help search before he gets anyone else involved. Ted's only been gone thirty minutes or less. They live on Village Avenue and their house backs on the woods. He said the back door was half open and he found Ted's footprints in the mud leading into the bush. I've got to go help him. Poor Ted."

"Want me to come with you?"

"No. You'll just slow me down. Especially in those shoes."

Ava looked down at her feet. She was wearing open-backed clogs.

"I'm going to run over to the pool and work my way back toward Hoop's house while Hoop goes from his house toward the pool. Ted couldn't have gone far." Jane grabbed a pair of tennis shoes out of the closet and jammed her feet into them. "Just stay here. I'll be right back. If we don't find him in the next hour, I'm going to insist that Hoop call his parents and the police."

Still trying to get her mind around the concept of aliens in the woods, Ava muttered, "Good luck," as Jane slammed the door behind her.

53

EARTH

Jane hit the sidewalk running and was at the pool in no time. The gate to the pool was locked. Jane shook it just to make sure. There was no one around. The pool was closed and locked up for the day. She climbed up the side of the fence so that she could see the water. *No one in the water. Good. So he didn't sneak off for a swim.* She glanced right and left as she trotted toward Hoop's house, rig-zagging to cover a bigger area. *I hope he's all right. Maybe I should just call the police now, instead of waiting an hour.* Jane paused and did a 360° turn, searching for any sign of Ted. *I'd feel so guilty if anything happened to him because I didn't call the police right away. But, that's Hoop's decision, not mine. I must quit thinking and use all my energies to search.* Then, she heard a noise, a whistle. She stopped dead and listened. It wasn't really a whistle, it was more like a shrill yell. The sound was coming from the base of a big tree to her left. She moved closer. A little furry head appeared from behind the tree. It was Senoa-lo. She came hopping toward Jane waving her hands. Jane ran over to the little Ume and keeled down. Senoa-lo kept waving her hands in exasperation as she told Jane about a young human male who had grabbed Leela-lo.

"We were walking back toward our camp and as we rounded a tree, we came upon a young male of your species sitting on the ground looking up at the sky. Leela-lo squealed in surprise and the young one quickly reached out and caught her. I didn't know what to do. If I spoke to him, he would know we are unusual and Leela-lo could end up in a lab being studied. So I hid and waited to see what he would do. Please help."

Jane's first question was: "What does the boy look like?"

"A young human male with fur on his head and wearing clothing," Senoa-lo fired back. "I do not know your people well enough to describe him better. He picked up Leela-lo and will not let her go. Come with me and talk to him." Senoa-lo hopped twenty more feet into the woods with Jane following. There, in a little clearing, sat Ted, gently but firmly holding Leela-lo in his hands. Jane waved Senoa-lo back and slowly approached Ted.

"Hi Ted."

His head jerked up and his shoulders tensed.

"Ted, you remember me. I'm Hoop's friend.

His shoulders relaxed. "You're Jane. You know about trees." Then his eyes went back down to the little Ume he was holding.

"Did you know that the white tree beside you is a birch tree?"

Ted glanced at the birch, then his eyes went back to Leela- lo.

"People used to use their white bark to make canoes.

Ted stared at the birch tree. "Interesting. I will have to look on my computer to see how it was done."

"Ted, the little animal you're holding does not seem happy. Can you please not hold it so tight?"

Ted loosened his grip.

"Ted, may I hold the little animal?"

"No, it's mine. I found it."

Jane pulled out her phone and held it where Ted could see it. "I'm going to call your brother Hoop now. Hoop wants to see you. He's worried about you."

Ted hugged Leela-lo closer to his body. "Don't call Hoop. He is going to be mad with me. I'm not allowed to go out alone. But I like to sneak out here and sit so I can watch the clouds. Don't call Hoop."

"Then I must call your parents."

"No, not mom and dad! They will be very unhappy that I sneaked out." Ted shook his head back and forth violently. Jane could see that Ted was getting upset.

"Ted, I'll make you a deal. I will not call Hoop or your parents if you will let the little animal go."

"But he's nice and quiet and has soft fur. He can be my pet."

Jane held up the phone. Ted sighed and released Leela-lo. Leela-lo took two steps away from him, then took off hopping away as fast as she could. Jane watched as she disappeared into the woods.

Jan held her hand out to Ted. "Let's go home now. Hoop has your lunch ready." Ted wouldn't take her hand, but he got up and walked with her toward his house. Before they got ten feet, they saw Hoop coming toward them.

Ted scrunched his head down and jammed his hands in his pockets when he saw Hoop running toward him. Hoop stopped three feet in front of his brother and gently reached out to touch his arm. "Are you all right?"

Ted swayed from side to side as he lowered his eyes to the ground. "I am not hurt."

Hoop stepped back and words poured out of him. "Where have you been? Why did you go out alone? I thought you were afraid of the woods. Do you know how worried I've been?"

Jane caught Hoop's attention and signalled him to slow down. "Ted needs to go eat his lunch."

Ted's shoulders lifted and he started walking toward home. "Yes, we should eat lunch."

Jane and Hoop fell in behind him and Ted led them to the house.

Once home, Hoop insisted that Jane eat with them. "We're just having chicken salad sandwiches, but mom's chicken salad is very good."

Jane called Ava and told her that they had found Ted. "Can you hang out there for another half an hour? I need to be here a bit longer."

Ava said she would stay. "I always have a book with me. Did you see any more little fuzzy aliens while you were in the bush?"

Jane hesitated and moved further away from the boys. "I did and as my friend I would appreciate it if you would not doubt what I have told you. This is real and serious. Should I have kept them a secret from you?"

There was silence on the line. "No. You're right. I should believe you, I do believe you. I'll be here when you're done at Hoop's."

"Thank you. Bye for now."

Jane walked back into the kitchen and picked up her sandwich. She took a bite. *Hoop's mom does make an outstanding chicken salad.*

54

UME ON EARTH

Senoa-lo and Leela-lo were huffing and puffing as they staggered through the door into the Ume camp. They had run all the way. It was a grim twosome that turned to face them as they stood catching their breath. Senoa-lo looked around and said, "What?"

Jolocko-lo broke the silence. "We were worried because you took so long. And," he took a big breath,. "as we feared, they know about us."

The words tumbled out of Senoa-lo. "Who knows? About what? The Palalans? Other Earth beings? Who knows about whom? Explain."

Jolocko-lo stepped closer to Senoa-lo. "We got a message from our government that the Palalans have been flying interstellar vessels over our cities. And, our people intercepted Palalan officials discussing our cities in the ice mountains.

"Oh no, we're too late." Senoa-lo staggered over to sit on a box. She sat staring at the ground.

Toboo-lo put a hand on one of her slumped shoulders. "What do we do?"

Senoa-lo slowly raised her head. "Leela-lo, what are our instructions from headquarters?"

"They didn't say what we should do. They just told us about the flights and about overhearing the Palalans discussing what they might do about us."

"And what actions are the Palalans considering? What's being proposed?"

"We don't know. We just know they are having a meeting to talk about us."

Jolocko-lo studied Leela-lo. "You look like you've been in a fight. Why is your fur in such a mess? Did the Jane human try to hurt you?"

"No." Leela-lo ran her hands through her fur, putting it back in place. "She is our friend."

Jolocko-lo looked over at Senoa-lo. "So why did you come running in here out of breath?"

"First, I must tell you that the Earth person, Jane, is truly our friend and I feel that she can be trusted."

Jolocko-lo picked a leaf off of Leela-lo's fur. "Let us not be too quick to trust a human. Their history shows them to be violent, self-centred and deceptive."

Leela-lo smiled. "I would assume that many of them are, but not all. Their history also speaks of humans who are generous and caring. The one I have met, Jane, is intelligent and seems to be protective of all living things. But," she took a big breath, "I think it unwise to take the chance of meeting other humans at this time. I just had a frightening experience with that."

Jolocko-lo "What happened?"

As soon as Senoa-lo and Leela-lo were finished telling the story of Leela-lo's capture and release, Jolocko-lo stepped forward and said, "See, we are not safe here. These woods have too many humans walking around."

Toboo-lo agreed and Leela-lo nodded her head.

"And where shall we go? Senoa-lo asked.

"We can scout around for a safer place. Most of the houses beside the woods have storage buildings behind them. We might sneak into one of those." Jolocko-lo said.

"Would that not be dangerous? A human home owner might discover us in one of those." Leela-lo asked. "Wouldn't it be better to ask Jane about a safe place for us?"

Jolocko-lo moved over to face Leela-lo, hands on his hips. "Jane, Jane, Jane! Is she all you can talk about? We are independent, strong people. You meet one hostile earth being and now Jane is the centre of our lives?"

"Jolocko-lo, settle down. We have been fortunate that the first human we have met is nice and willing to keep us secret. Remember, the second one we met wanted to keep Leela-lo as a pet. Jane wants to help us, and as the leader of this mission, I say we accept her help. Does anyone have an intelligent, reasonable objection to that?"

Jolocko-lo stepped away from Leela-lo and mumbled, "Like we don't have enough problems. The Palalans have discovered our towns in the ice mountains and we don't have a WMD."

Senoa-lo glared at him. "Maybe some food would help your attitude." She took a package of cheese and bread out of her vest. "Try these. They are good."

Toboo-lo examined the items, sniffing and turning them over. "These are foods? What are they made from?"

Senoa-lo paused. "It's complicated. I'll explain later. Just try them. Jane says they are nutritional and I like the taste."

In minutes, all the food was gone and even Jolocko-lo admitted that he liked the cheese and the bread.

"Tomorrow, when I meet with Jane, we will see if she can help us with finding a safer place and, of course, more food. By tomorrow, we should know more about what is happening on our planet. Meanwhile," she hesitated and looked each of them in the face, "we must continue working on our mission."

55

PALALA

It was a bright sunny morning. The big jungle leaves were still dripping from the heavy rain that had come in the night. Kebeck closed up his computer, grabbed a Lunga fruit off a shelf, and started out the door to meet with Solang and Nacoo. *These beings in the ice mountains are fascinating. I'm so glad to be on the committee studying them.* His mind was turning over the possibility of the creatures they found in the ice mountains being aliens and wondering about which galaxy they might have come from.

A whiff of someone's odor brought him back to reality. *I smell my friend Sheme coming toward me. What to do?* He looked around for some place to hide. There were only small bushes and tall slender trees along the path. There wasn't anything nearby big enough to conceal him. He had been avoiding her for some time. He had been putting off one of life's big decisions, whether to have a son with Sheme. Kebeck had a grown daughter and raising her had been a delightful experience. The female he had shared the experience with had been a good partner. The twenty years they had lived together had been full of joy, but they found that they had little in common after she went off to university. After the child raising time, his parenting partner had gone back to her own house. And, he had to admit that he had been glad to have his solitude again.

Sheme had also had a daughter with a partner; now she wanted to have a male child, as was her right. Some people were not happy with the law that only allowed females to have a maximum of one male and one female offspring. But they adhered to the law because it was the custom and a law that had been democratically established hundreds of years ago. Kebeck didn't know if he was ready to share his life with a female and a son at this time. It is a big commitment. He remembered many times of needing all four hands to keep up with his children.

Suddenly, Sheme was standing in front of him, with her hands out in greeting. "How are you?"

Kebeck puts his hands out. "Life goes well. How does your life flow?"

"My work flows as a strong pure river, but my mind wants more. Have you thought about my query?"

"I apologize for not contacting you sooner." *Sheme is known as one who quickly dispenses with courtesy and says what is on her mind.* "My work has dominated my life lately. You asked a question that deserves an answer." *What to do? What to do?.* "So, I propose this… " *I will stall. I must think.* "I want to meditate and think so that I can determine what the best answer should be. You are an admirable person and I am sure life with you would be very pleasant. It is the aspect of raising a child that I need to think on. I want to sit in cool water and consider how I wish to spend the next twenty years. But I cannot take the time for contemplation at this time. My work dictates my time at present."

Sheme kicked at a rock on the lane. "What work? You study humans on your computer."

Kebeck stepped closer to her. "This is not a secret, but not something that should be shared with others. I tell you because of our close relationship." Kebeck looked around to see if anyone was nearby. "There are alien beings living in the ice mountains."

"Impossible."

"No. I am working with a language expert and people from the Foreign Planets Department to determine who they are and why they are here."

"Really?"

"It was quite a surprise to find them here on our planet.

So you understand why my life is dominated by this. I can think of nothing else at this time. I apologize that I cannot talk with you more. I have to go to a meeting now."

"Kebeck, I accept your apology. I must admit that I was feeling rejected, but now I understand. I look forward to seeing you after this is resolved. I see that you are walking toward the government buildings, so I will not keep you longer."

Kebeck wished her clear water and continued on. *Oh, I have some thinking to do.* As he came within sight of the Foreign Planets Department, his mind went back to the beings in the ice mountains. *Now that I know that these creatures really have nothing to do with me and that note, I am finding these meetings about them to be very interesting.*

Solang and Nacoo were sitting on slantboards, studying photos when Kebeck entered the office. They both rose and greeted him with open hands and broad smiles. *Would I feel differently about having another child if one of these two asked me?*

Solang spoke first. "I am making progress now that I am receiving recordings of their conversations in the towns. These are definitely the beings that were heard talking in our forest. The spy recorder we planted is working well. It is an odd thing that most of their words are totally foreign, but quite a few words seem to be Palalan. And, speaking of communication, we now know that they have small flying machines that enable them to travel between their cities."

"And now that we have more detail photos of the cities," Nacoo added, "we see that they have steel plants and all sorts of manufacturing. I think that they have been established on our planet for a very long time. We see that many of the buildings and other structures are somewhat similar to ours. They are not identical, but I see a resemblance. This leads me to believe that they have borrowed some building designs from us. And using that as evidence, I suspect that they have been aware of us for quite a while. Since we do not know what types of technology they have, we cannot know for sure if they have been watching us, but I suspect that they have. How else can you explain these similarities and the fact that they use some of our words in their communications?"

"Maybe… " Kebeck suggested. "Maybe they have been watching us the same way we watch earth?"

"Could be." Nacoo sat back on her slantboard. "When we first became aware of these cities in the ice mountains, there was a rush to know more and do something about these beings. But now that we have been able to study their buildings more closely, we are certain that they have been on our planet for a long time. And during that time, they have caused us no problems. So, I no longer feel that something needs to be done immediately. I think that we need to slow down and study them further. We have no reason to think that they are a threat to us. What is your opinion on this?" She looked at Kebeck.

Kebeck studied the photos in his hands. "I agree with you. From the photos you sent me, I see nothing that looks like a weapon. We have looked at photos of three of their cities and I don't see anything that in any way looks like a military base. I don't see them as a menace."

"I ask you, Solang, to continue working on the language and contact us both if you make any progress. I want to wait until we have a better understanding of the language before we try to communicate with them. And, I will send both of you more photos as they become available. I suggest that we meet again at this hour in four days to talk further. Now I think Kebeck and I should let you get back to your tapes and we can continue our work via our computers." Nacoo held out her hands. "I wish you both clear water."

As soon as Kebeck walked out of the building, his mind went back to his conversation with Sheme about having a son together. *Maybe I should think on this in sections. First, I should determine if I would like to spend the next twenty years as a parent. Is this what I want to do with my time? There is no reason to parent now. My age is one hundred and twenty five. I probably have many years in which to do this, if I do it at all. Then, that decided, I should think on whether Sheme is the person I desire as a mate. Maybe I should spend more time with Nacoo and get to know her better. I need a plan.* Kebeck eased into the clear water of the river and started swimming toward his home. The current was flowing in his direction, so he was able to float much of the way. *My plan is to soak myself in a meditation spring tomorrow morning and determine whether I want to parent in the near future. And I will contact Nacoo to ask if she would like to join me in playing a waterball game. I need to play. Life has been too serious lately.*

CHAPTER

56

EARTH

As soon as Jane finished her sandwiches with Hoop and Ted, she rushed back to her house. Ava jumped off the couch when she heard Jane coming through the door and said, "Well?"

"We found Ted. He's fine. He was just sitting in a clearing near his house." *Better not to mention him grabbing one of the aliens.* "No harm done. All is copacetic."

"Good. I'm glad. Now back to your aliens… "

"Just let me get something to drink and… just where are the Cuba Libras?"

"I tossed them out. Booze is overrated and I want to be alert for this. Sit down and I'll get you a glass of plain coke."

"Yeah, I'd rather have that." Jane plopped onto the couch, took off her tennis shoes and put her feet up.

Ava returned, handed her the drink and sat in the fancy little chair facing the couch. "Now please tell me about the aliens."

After spending an hour telling Ava all about the aliens, they gathered Jane's things and went to Ava's house. This was going to be Jane's first ever sleep-over.

Later that night, at Ava's house, when Jane was trying to sleep, Ava kept asking her questions about the aliens. "How old are they? What do they eat? Why are they here? Are they male and female or are there more than two sexes? Do they carry weapons?"

"I've told you everything I know. I have repeated every word they said to me over and over. Ava, go to sleep. It's called a sleep-over because you are supposed to sleep. You'll meet them in the morning."

"I can't sleep. I'm sure you can't sleep either."

Jane rolled over to face her. "But I *can* sleep. Or I could if you would cease your endless chatter. This is a sleep-over and I want to sleep. So here is my suggestion. Go sit at your desk and write out all your questions, but do it quietly. Tomorrow we can ask them."

"Great. Good idea. And, by the way, this is not your normal sleep-over. We should be talking about boys, and clothes and makeup. But, I'm excited. I'm going to meet aliens! This is way better than boys, clothes and makeup."

Jane rolled her eyes.

"I'll shut up now and write my questions."

"Good. And after you've listed all your questions, number them in order of importance. I don't want them to feel that we're interrogating them. They might just run away if we throw too many questions at them. Remember, they're shy and scared."

"Right. I'll try to phrase the questions so they're part of a casual conversation. We don't want them to feel like they're at the inquisition."

"Fine." Jane rolled over to face the wall. "Good night. Go write."

"But first, one more question. This one is for you."

Jane sat up. "What?"

"You seem quite comfortable with the idea of meeting aliens from another planet. Why? How is that?"

Jane thought for a second. "When I was small, my mother read to me, of course. One book she read was about talking anthropomorphized ants and spiders. They were cute likable characters with houses and lives like humans. That book was one of my favorites. I was so young that I didn't know fact from fiction; I thought the ants and other bugs in our backyard were like the ones in the book. So, well, I refused to walk in the grass. I didn't want to step on them. It was quite a problem for a while. Mom said that when we went outside, I'd throw a fit if she tried to put me down anywhere except on asphalt or cement. She and the doctors thought it was part of my Asperger's. Of course, I got older and realized that the book was fantasy.

But I think that was the beginning of my feeling that the whole planet and the universe is one big connected thing. And as I learned more about incidents like dolphins coming to people to get them untangled from nets and communication between trees I've felt more certain that everything is connected. After I studied more science and astronomy, I began to see even more how it is all related.

Even now, I walk carefully through grass, trying to avoid stepping on bugs. Because of various scientific studies, we now know that many plants and animals communicate with each other. So I'm quite comfortable with the idea of communicating with anyone; spiders, plants or furry animals from far away, it's all the same to me.. Of course with the universe being so immense, I think that there had to be other sentient beings out there. So when I found the aliens, I wasn't that surprised. I was just happy that I was lucky enough to meet some aliens. And it's marvelous that they speak our language. Communication would have been so difficult otherwise."

"Yeah. How is it that they speak English?"

"I have no idea. That can be your first question tomorrow. I am so tired. Please let me sleep. Goodnight."

CHAPTER

57

UME

Mera stepped around the muddy puddles in the path as she rushed home. It was the rainy season when clouds released their water as they scraped over the ice mountains. As usual she came straight home from school and sat down at her computer to see if there was news about her father's mission to earth. Today, at school, a friend asked if she was worried about her father. She had replied, "I don't worry. Of course I am concerned. My father says worry is a waste of energy and time and I agree. We're only here on our planet for three hundred years. Way too short a time to waste any of it worrying. I try to spend my energy and time on things I can control. My father wants me to be happy and contribute something to our people. I also want that. He and I both agree that getting a good education is important in achieving this. So for now, my job is learning everything I can in school. I can't do that if I waste time worrying."

My friend had just looked at me like I was crazy. I guess that was a bit of a lecture, when all she probably wanted was a quick answer. I think she just asked that so that she would appear to be a considerate person. Or, maybe she really is a thoughtful person. Here I am pondering her sincerity when maybe I should just take what she says as what she means. I guess I really am worrying about my dad. Either that or all this stuff with the Palalans is making me crazy.

Mera punched more computer keys and opened up a message from Zenbaco, one of the earth WMD mission coordinators. One of his jobs was to keep the families of the people on the earth mission up to date. It read: "Our team on earth has made contact with a human who is willing to help them with food and security. Things have settled down in Palala. Our listening device in the Foreign Planets Department has heard their committee say that they are in no hurry to contact us and wish to study us further before doing anything. They have discussed options for communicating with us. And they have planted spy machines near two of our town, Risus and Colme, to listen to us for the purpose of learning our language. They are not aware of the fact that some of us can speak their language and some know English and other earth languages. Thus, people in those towns have been asked to only speak Ume as long as the spy machines are there. The Palalans working in the Foreign Planets

Department have not informed the general public in Palala of our existence. So only a few know of our existence."

Mera reread the message again and again. It didn't say anything about weapons. She was glad that her father and his team were safe and had a new food source. But even though she wasn't supposed to worry, she had to admit, at least to herself, that she was concerned about what action the Palalans might take against her people. She had been raised in a peaceful society and she would prefer peace with the Palalans. But she hated the fact that her people are powerless. *There must be a way to gain some advantage over the Palalans before they learn how helpless we are.*

58

UME ON EARTH

Jolocko-lo was the first one up. He was nibbling on a cookie when Senoa-lo opened her eyes. "I thought you said weren't going to eat those."

"The thought of eating food made from the embryo of one animal combined with bovine natal liquid intended for their bovine young disgusts me, but these do taste good. And I need to eat something in order to survive."

Senoa-lo reached for a cookie. "Yes, survival is what all this is about. Our survival and the survival of our people. It was good to hear that the Palalan Foreign Planets committee is going to take their time studying us before recommending any action. It is to our advantage. I remember when they first became aware of how easy it was to observe earth through earth television, radio and internet waves. The committee took many years to observe and study earth before they shared this knowledge with the general public. Our people were watching earth long before the technology was introduced to the general Palalan public. It is fortunate that their committees always move slowly when introduced to anything new. It buys us time."

Jolocko-lo stopped chewing. "But now that they are aware of us, our people in our mountain towns are scared and nervous. That is unfortunate. I don't like to think of my little girl back home being scared."

"I wouldn't be concerned about Mera. She's strong and intelligent. For now, all our people have to do is to act normal and avoid speaking Palalan or any earth language." Senoa-lo smiled. "I find it amusing that the Palalans planted spy monitors on the edge of two of our cities and they think we're not aware of them. But I shouldn't be surprised. They're a trusting people, who rarely lie. We've been spying on them for many lifetimes and they never suspected anything."

Leela-lo stepped between the two and put out an open hand. "Thanks to your chatter, we're all up. Where are the cookies?"

After a breakfast of cookies and water, Senoa-lo got everyone's attention. "When we meet with Jane this morning, I will introduce you all. Then I will say that Jolocko-lo and Toboo-lo need to leave to gather food. You two walk away. Then hide behind something so you can stay hidden and listen."

"Why?" Toboo-lo asked.

"In case something goes wrong, we need someone to survive and carry on. But, we want to give the appearance of being open and relaxed with her."

"Good idea," Jolocko-lo nodded.

Senoa-lo continued her plan, "We can talk about our Ume people but we should not mention WMDs. I plan to tell her that we are here only to gain technical knowledge from the internet. We can let her know that we can view earth TVs and computer screens from our planet. But we needed to come to earth get on the internet for technical research."

"You want us to lie about our weapon research?" Leela-lo asked.

"Think of it more like avoiding the truth," Senoa-lo replied. "If Jane asks something that you shouldn't answer, don't answer and ask her a question about earth instead. That will be the signal for me to guide the conversation in a different direction."

"And this is why Senoa-lo is our leader." Toboo-lo added.

CHAPTER

59

EARTH

Jane woke up just as the birds were announcing the sunrise and lay there with her eyes shut thinking. A weird feeling crept over her. She felt like she was being watched. She opened her eyes to see Ava sitting at her desk, staring at her. "What?"

"I was just waiting for you to wake up. I have my questions ready," Ava replied.

And thus it continued all morning. Dealing with Ava was like babysitting a five year old. She couldn't sit still and she couldn't shut up. Jane was beginning to wonder if telling Ava had been a good idea. As they walked through the woods, on their way to meet the Ume, Jane stopped and took Ava's elbow. "You have to settle down. If we mess this up, it could mean the death of these little people. You can't see them as cute little creatures. You have to respect them as adults here on a mission that is important to them and their society. I don't have all the details yet, but I want you to take them seriously. So can you dim that big smile down a bit and get the bounce out of your step? You're going to scare them."

Ava put her hands to her cheeks trying to wipe the smile off her face, but there was still a gleam in her eyes. "Right, I can fake it and act like an adult. Will do."

"And let's do this Ava… You don't say a word until I signal you by pulling on my ear."

"Which ear?" Ava asked.

Jane glared at her. "Either ear."

Soon they were sitting on the ground in the agreed upon meeting spot. The air was chilly, but not cold. There were still a few leaves on the trees but most were lying on the ground making a carpet of reds and gold. Jane picked up an oak leaf and was studying how the veins branched off from the midrib when Senoa-lo appeared. Ava's eyes were gleaming, but she managed to sit still and only say, "Nice to meet you" when she was introduced. Then Leela-lo, Jolocko-lo and Toboo-lo joined them.

Senoa-lo pointed toward the three. "I will now introduce you to Leela-lo, who is our language and communication specialist and she has studied earth psychology. This is Toboo-lo, who is our expert in chemistry and plants. And, this is Jolocko-lo, our physicist and computer expert."

Ava's smile could not have been any bigger.

"Is this everyone?" Jane asked.

"Yes. Jolocko-lo and Toboo-lo need to go gather food while we talk."

With that the two turned and left.

Jane started the conversation. "I'm sorry about Ted grabbing Leela-lo." She turned to face Leela-lo. "I'm sure you were terrified. Were you injured? Are you all right?"

"I was not hurt. I was just scared."

"Good." Jane sighed and turned to look at Senoa-lo. "I think I have a secure place for you to stay while you're here. My neighbor lives alone and is in a wheel chair. She never goes in her back yard because it's too difficult for her. She has a shed that backs onto the woods that is almost empty. I asked her to let me keep some of my tree research equipment in the shed and she has agreed. So if I move you into the shed, you'll have a warm place for the winter and I will have an excuse for going to the shed regularly."

Ava's face said, "When did you do all that?" But she sat quietly, with big eyes and waited for Jane to give her the signal to start her questions.

Jane ignored her and went on. "I'll put a battery operated camping heater and some blankets in it. You'll be cozy."

"Can we access the internet from the shed? Leela-lo asked.

"Yep. The WiFi in our house is in the office on the north side, close to the shed. You should get good reception."

Toboo-lo nudged Jolocko-lo as they lay hidden under a pile of leaves, watching and listening. Jolocko-lo smiled.

Senoa-lo was silent for a moment. "That does sound better and safer than where we are camped now. The weather wasn't supposed to be a problem. The space ship was scheduled to land in a warm place called Florida. There, we would've had plenty of green plants to eat." Senoa-lo picked up a red leaf. "We can't eat these. I thank you for your help."

Jane felt awkward and wanted to ask about how they could have ended up so far from their destination, but she pressed on. "Senoa-lo, we would like to know more about you and your purpose for being here. Can I ask some questions?"

Senoa-lo glanced over at Leela-lo. "Of course, it is only fair that you know something about the people you are providing food and shelter for. What would you like to know?"

Out of the corner of her eye, Jane could see that Ava was fidgeting about and clearly anxious for Jane to let her join the conversation.

"We're curious about where you come from and why you're here."

Jane almost had her hand up to her ear when Ava blurted out, "Where's your planet and what's life like there?"

Senoa-lo nodded at Leela-lo and she spoke up. "We are from the planet we call Ume. It is also called Palala by some."

Senoa-lo jumped in, "You call this planet Earth, do you not?"

"Yes," Ava replied. "Where is your planet?"

Leela-lo paused. "It is in the Tarc galaxy, not far from here. From what I see on the internet, your astronomy experts are not yet aware of our galaxy. It is located behind the central plane of your Milky Way, and thus extremely difficult to discern. It is possible for one galaxy to mask another located beyond it, but I can show you where it is located if we had a map of galaxies."

Ava sat up straight and grinned at Jane. "An undiscovered galaxy. Wow! If you could locate it on a telescope and publish a paper about it, they might name it the Jane Galaxy. Wouldn't that be something?"

"Ava, we can't do anything that would expose our friends to the public. So, forget it."

Jane turned back toward Senoa-lo. "You've come a long way. Why earth? You mentioned a mission for your people."

"Yes, we will get back to that, but Ava asked about our life on our planet A large part of our planet has icy mountains. In some of the valleys between those mountains there are hot springs that flow with enough warm water to grow plants. In these valleys, millions of years ago, our people evolved. We have factories and airplanes and computers. Our society is a democracy. We are much like earth people, but with some different customs."

Jane was thoughtful. "We would like to hear about your customs. I understand that it is not your custom to eat meat. When I offered ham to Senoa-lo yesterday, she seemed to be upset that we eat animals. I get the impression that you usually don't eat anything that comes from animals."

"That is correct. The concept of eating your eggs and milk is very odd to us. But the bread and cookies are very good." Leela-lo added. "And I have researched their benefits. The animal products are nutritious and we need that right now. We've been eating a lot of grass and leaves lately."

Ava yawned. "I'm sorry. I didn't get much sleep last night. *I was thinking about possible reasons for you to be here on our planet.* "Why are you here on earth, I mean?"

"For research. We need your internet." Senoa-lo said. "I'll explain. We have developed a method of collecting information from other planets through their electromagnetic waves. We can see and hear anything on a radio, television, or cell phone, but we can not access the internet. We have watched earth for a long time. I learned English by watching your television. Our people watch earth for education and amusement. Earth watching is popular on our world."

"Oh wow!" Ava exclaimed. "That's how you learned English, from TV, from earth TV."

"And from watching your people who are in front of the televisions, computers and cell hones." Leela-lo added.

Ava's eyes grew big. "So if I'm sitting in front of my TV or computer… you can watch and hear me?"

"Yes."

"But only when the TV is turned on… right?"

"No, not right. The device does not have to be functioning. It only has to be connected to electricity," Leela-lo replied.

Jane and Ava looked at each other with a glazed look in their eyes. One could almost hear the thoughts running through their heads.

Senoa-lo saw that this news had shook up their world. "We mean no harm. Some of our people have become very fond of the earth people they watch."

"So some of the people on your planet sort of follow specific people here on earth like we would watch a TV series? Is that what you're saying?" Ava asked.

Leela-lo smiled. "Yes. I watched a young male living in New York when I was younger. It was interesting, but his life became sad. So I quit watching him. Also, my life became too busy and… "

Senoa-lo interrupted. "I understand that knowing this could make you feel uncomfortable. I apologize for that." *I didn't realize that being watched would upset them so. But since no one on earth knew of it, as we saw it, there was no damage done.*

Ava came out of her stupor. "Now, I'm going to have to be fully dressed in front of my TV and computer and cell phone."

Jane let out a big breath. "So, we're being watched. How long has this been going on?"

Senoa-lo turned toward Leela-lo. "I don't remember. Leela-lo, this is your area of expertise. When did we first start watching earth?"

"It started when the earth invented their radios and TVs."

Ava turned toward Jane. "It seems that after spying on us for years, they just dropped by to borrow our internet for a little research. No biggie. That's what neighbors from another galaxy, do."

Jane was still concerned. In so many sci-fi stories, the aliens came to earth to conquer or destroy. So, of course, a part of her had been worried that these cute fuzzy creatures could be up to no good. *But that was sci-fi; this is reality. I'm so relieved to find this it is just a research mission.*

Ava scrunched up her nose. "Why didn't you just contact one of the earth governments and do the research out in the open? Why hide here in the woods?"

Jane glared at her as if to say: "Are you stupid?"

Leela-lo explained. "You can understand that from what we have seen of aliens in your movies, we have concerns that we might be killed by your government. And if they captured us, we would possibly end up in a lab being prodded or dissected."

"You're probably right. That would be awful. So… " Ava inquired, "what kind of research are you doing?"

Leela-lo looked at Senoa-lo. Senoa-lo piped up, "We are doing research on different types of weapons invented by humans."

Ava looked concerned. "Are you here to build a weapon?"

"No. We are just a research committee. It's interesting to see what types of different things have been invented on various planets."

"Then of course we'll help you."

Jane reached beside her and moved a basket of food to the center of the circle and pulled back the red checked napkin. "Let's celebrate with some goodies. I brought cake and dried fruit and nuts."

Jolocko-lo and Toboo-lo lay hidden in the leaves and watched the others as they ate. Jolocko-lo's mouth watered as he watched. Toboo-lo rolled over on his back and tried to send Senoa-lo telepathic messages about bringing some of the cake back to camp for him. He knew telepathy didn't work, but it was better than watching them eat.

Jane glanced at her phone. "We have to go. I would like to come with a wagon and move you to my neightbor's shed tomorrow afternoon. Can you have your equipment packed and ready to go on Monday or Tuesday?"

Senoa-lo put down the piece of walnut she was chewing on. "Tell us a time and we will be ready."

Jane made a face. "My situation is complicated at the moment."

Ava interrupted, "Email."

Jane and the others turned to look at Ava.

"You're on the internet. Go to Google and get an email address. Then Jane can contact you about the move. Can you do that?"

Senoa-lo nodded. "Yes, we are familiar with that system."

Jane pulled a pen and notebook out of a pocket and scribbled her email address. She ripped off the page and handed it to Senoa-lo.

Ava took out her cell phone and looked at it. "We've really should to go now. My mom insists that we go to the mall with her."

Jane stood up. "Senoa-lo, please email me tonight."

CHAPTER

60

EARTH

The weekend passed quickly for Jane and Ava. Sunday afternoon Jane and Ava lay across Jane's bed rehashing their conversation with the Ume. Ava leaned on her elbow. "So interesting that they say they have no religion, but they say that water is sacred."

"I think water should be thought of as sacrosanct. It forms 60% of our bodies. Without it, we die. Water does not get the respect it deserves. We pollute it and abuse it."

"I guess it does make some sense to worship something that you can feel and use, something that is essential to life, like the sun. Egyptians used to worship the sun." Ava glanced over at the photo of Jane and her mother that sat on the dresser. "Speaking of which, the sun will set soon and your mother will be coming home. When do you expect her?"

"Any time now."

"Then I'm out of here. Knowing you, you'll have to tell her about her man. And I don't want to be here for that."

"Yikes, I almost forgot about that." *How could I forget about him? Aliens, all I can think about are our little aliens.* Jane helped Ava gather her stuff, then stood in the front window, watching her leave. *I have to tell mom the truth about Mr. Fitzgerald. She's going to be hurt, but it's the right thing to do.*

When she turned and went through the house checking that everything was clean and neat. She threw together a green salad and reheated some pesto chicken from two days ago. She certainly wasn't hungry, but she managed to eat a few bites of salad. Then she sat down with a book, dreading her mother's arrival. She found that she kept reading the same page over and over. She'd read a paragraph, then think about the aliens, then start the next page only to realize it made no sense because she had lost her place. Reading was impossible.

Finally, just at seven, she heard a car in the driveway. *Should I be sitting here reading or standing at the door when she comes in? Should I tell her tonight or wait?* Jane was still on the couch when her mother swept through the door. Jane got up and gave her an awkward hug, offered her food and took her suitcase upstairs for her. When Jane came back down, her mother was in the kitchen nibbling on the salad. *I'd better have the conversation now, while she's relaxed. Conversations around the kitchen table are supposed to better than in a more formal setting. And I'll go crazy if I don't get it over with. I'll sit down, that will make the situation more relaxed. Here goes.*

She looked at her mom's right shoulder instead of her face as she began. "Mom, I need to tell you about something."

Her mother's shoulders slumped. "What happened? I'm away a few hours and you get into trouble." Her voice got louder. "What did you do?"

Jane looked down at the floor.

Her mom grabbed Jane's arm. "Look at me!"

Jane looked at her mom's lips. "I didn't do anything except some research on my computer."

"Research about what? Don't tell me it's about trees. I don't want to hear about trees tonight. I'm tired. Unless a tree is about to fall on the house, I don't want to hear about it."

Jane moved her eyes from her mom's lips to her right eyebrow. *I guess I have to jump right into it* "It's about Mr. Fitzgerald."

"What about him? You hardly speak to him. We just had a lovely weekend in Toronto. How can you know anything about him?"

Jane took a breath. *Better just blurt it out and get it over with.* "He's not British, he's Canadian. He spent 6 years in England in high school and university. So his accent is not real. And I don't think he's rich. He taught high school in Toronto and just retired last year."

Jane's mother sank back in her chair, she dropped her fork onto the plate and stared into space for a minute or two. "You found all that on the internet?"

"Yes." *I'm definitely not going to tell her that Ava found it and then showed it to me. I'll just get Ava in trouble.*

Her mother sat up, looking like a mad dog preparing to attack and yelled at her. "Why were you snooping on Mr. Fitzgerald? He's not your business. Who do you think you are?"

Jane slid her chair back a couple of inches, stared directly at her mother's nose and said, "I'm your daughter. I was concerned about you. I love you and I don't want to see you deceived or hurt."

Her mother deflated like a balloon. She sat for a minute staring at her plate, then pushed her chair back and got up. "I'm going to bed. I can't talk about this now." She reached out her hand and gently touched Jane's cheek. "You're sure about this?"

Jane nodded.

"We'll talk tomorrow, after work." Then she turned and trudged up the stairs.

EARTH

The next morning as Jane rushed off to school and her mom rushed off to work, they hardly spoke. Jane could think of nothing to say that could make her mom feel better better, so she decided to say nothing about Mr. Fitzgerald. *I'll leave it to her to decide when to broach the subject. Life is weird. I'm so down about my mom falling for a man who's deceiving her. And at the same time, I'm thrilled about meeting and talking to aliens. Why does my life always have to be so complicated?*

School was school. Her good teachers were a delight to listen to and the others, the ones just putting in their time, were a waste of her time. When she arrived at the table for lunch, fortunately, Hoop was there all alone. As soon as she was seated, she noticed that Hoop looked around like a spy checking out the area. Then he moved closer to her. "Saturday, when you found Ted in the woods, did he have an animal in his lap?"

Now, Jane glanced around before she spoke. "He had caught a small rabbit but I persuaded him to let it go."

"Ted usually doesn't talk much, unless it's about weather or video games. But he was very chatty yesterday. He told me that he caught a rabbit and that it was an unusual rabbit because it had small ears. He was on the computer for quite a while Googling types of rabbits. He was upset when he couldn't find one exactly like the one he caught."

"I didn't notice the ears. It was just a little bunny. There are long-eared rabbits, and I guess there are short-eared rabbits. I know very little about leporidae."

"About what?"

"Rabbits."

"Oh." He glanced around again. "This is going to sound completely crazy, but he said the rabbit said, 'Damn,' when he caught it."

Jane paused and thought through several options before replying to Hoop. "A talking rabbit? Does Ted get fantasy and reality confused very often?

"No. That's what disturbs me about this. He's into his own head a lot, but he's never done anything like this before. I'm sure the rabbit just made a noise when it was caught. I'm just surprised that he said it spoke. I explained that it was impossible for rabbits to talk, but he insisted over and over that it said 'Damn'." Hoop sighed. "It's just that I could see that he's been making progress and now this seems to be a setback. Mom and Dad and I so want him to be able to be independent some day. We're doing everything we can to move him toward that goal."

Jane started to lay her hand on Hoop's arm, then she remembered who he was and where they were. "Has he ever mentioned talking animals before?"

"No. He's always had a firm grasp on reality."

"Then maybe you should just view this as a one time thing. He heard a noise that sounded like a word. If he starts telling you about conversations with the neighbor's poodle, then, it's time to worry."

Hoop peeked over at the door to the cafeteria. "You're right. The rabbit made a noise and he thought it sounded like a word. Not worth worrying about. Thanks for getting him to release the rabbit. Him having a rabbit would have been difficult to explain to my parents, since we weren't even supposed to have been out of the house." Hoop slid back to his tray and picked up his fork. "Here comes Bruce. Thanks for your help."

Bruce and two other guys joined them and soon the conversation turned to football. Luckily, Jane had taken a few minutes that morning to read up on the weekend's games and she was able to hold up her part of the conversation. *I don't get why they so enjoy talking about football, but it feels good to be included as part of a group. Are they keeping abreast of the teams because they really like the game or are they like me and only keep up on it so that they will have something to talk about with the group? I suppose I'd have to really know someone well before they would tell me the truth of it.*

CHAPTER

62

PALALA

All three moons were shining on the leaves of the barapa bushes, as Kebeck and Nacoo walked down the gravel path toward the town.

"I never thought I'd be saying this," Kebeck admitted. "But finding that note in the spaceship turned out to be a good thing. I met you."

Nacoo's neck turned pink. "You flatter me. It is logical that we would eventually meet because you are on the earth committee and I am head of the Foreign Planets Department."

"Probably. But at this moment I am trying to be romantic."

Nacoo studied him. "You mean romantic as in earth movies, in which people become emotionally attached to others for no logical reason, yes?"

"Yes. Do you not feel some attachment to me?"

"Of course I do, but for logical reasons. We share many interests. We both enjoy waterball, you are attentive when I talk, and you are intelligent in a way that enables you to absorb and explore new ideas. And, I almost forgot, your body is well- proportioned." She hesitated. "I know body shape and appearance are not important. And to judge someone by their appearance is considered bad. But a slim shape indicates that one sees exercise as important and that they are willing to take the time to keep a healthy body."

Now, Kebeck's neck turned pink. "Thank you. I suppose you are correct in saying our relationship is based on real characteristics and shared beliefs." He stopped walking and looked her over. "I like that your eyes seem to open wider when we discuss new science discoveries. I also like that you are attentive to one's mood when broaching a topic of discussion."

"Explain more."

"An example: my friend Sheme. She will enter a room and immediately throw a question at you followed by a demand for a quick answer. She is not subtle. She does not take the time to sense the mood of the one's she talks to. Life around her moves too quickly. I do care for her, but she is abrupt and impatient. I like time to think before I put my ideas into words."

"It is natural that one prefers to be around people with similar ways of thinking." Nacoo stretched her upper arms toward the sky. "I have enjoyed the time we have spent together these last few days, especially today. But now my body tells me that I need exercise. So I will leave you now. I want to do a long swim before I go to my home."

As Kebeck watched Nacoo disappear down the lane, he realized that their discussion had solidified his decision about his future, about Sheme, and about how he wanted to live his life. *I cannot have a child with Sheme. We are too different. I have to tell her.*

CHAPTER

63

EARTH

After school, Jane came home, finished her homework, straightened the house and made some grilled butter carrots and a tomato garlic pasta dish to go with the honey mustard pork she had pulled out of the freezer. She thought about going to the woods to check on the aliens, but decided that she should be home when her mom arrived. *I'm dreading talking with mom. I'm sure she is hurt and she's probably still angry.*

At five-twenty, her mom walked through the door. Jane froze. She had been washing a pan when she heard the door open. She rinsed her hands, dried them and slowly entered the living room. Her mom was sitting in there in a little antique chair, leaning down, with her head in her hands. "Mom."

Her mother looked up. She looked ten years older that she had looked on Saturday. "I didn't sleep much last night. Jane, are you sure of your facts?"

"Yes. The only thing I can't be certain of is whether he's rich. I can't look at his bank account. But his birthplace, education and job are lies. So I doubt that he's got anything except a house and his teacher's pension."

Her mom looked down at the floor. "It's been a fairy tale, a lovely fairy tale. I don't want it to end. He didn't need to lie. I would have been happy with a retired teacher from Toronto. I hate lies and liars."

Jane started rubbing her fingernails. "Does the fairy tale have to end?"

"How can I see him without telling him I know?"

"Well, you used to tell me to act like everything was all right and then it probably will be all right."

"I don't think I can do that. It hurts to be lied to."

"Maybe he was doing it to make you feel good."

"He was lying to me to make himself look good." She glared at Jane.

"Maybe he thought you deserved better than a retired teacher. Maybe he didn't think he was good enough for you. So, he sweetened the package with a few lies."

"He didn't have to do that."

"Well, he thought he did. And, as my therapist, used to say, 'there is only one question: what are you going to do about it?'"

"I don't know." She looked up at Jane. "Now, you're the therapist and I'm the patient?"

"Works for me." Jane flopped down on the couch. "What are the options? Option one: Tell him you know and break up. Option two: tell him you know and keep dating. Number two only works if he can handle admitting to his lies. He might just disappear. But there is option three. Act like you know nothing of his lies and enjoy his company, hoping that he will eventually admit to who he really is. You could live the fairy tale for a while longer."

She stared at the floor for a moment more, then got up and stood tall. "I've got to think about this."

"When's your next date?"

"Tomorrow. He is supposed to pick me up after work and we're planning to go to Port Dalhouse and picnic on the hillside as the sun sets into the lake. I must admit that he's very romantic."

"Are you going to go? Or are you going to call and cancel and tell him you know?"

"No, I guess I'll try option three while I do a bit more thinking. I'll see how it goes tomorrow. He must honestly care for me, or he wouldn't be working so hard to impress me. I don't want to give up on him. I like him." With that said, she took her purse and headed up stairs.

As soon as Jane heard her mother's door close, she rushed into the kitchen and called Ava. "Can you talk?"

"Sure. Nobody home but me and my math book. This book does not like me. I do a problem, I look in the back... wrong. I try it another way... still wrong. I know I'm distracted by the fact that I talked to aliens. That was so unreal yesterday. But, I have to get this math done. Help... "

"Want me to come over?"

"Of course. But first, did you talk to your mom? And how are the little fuzzes?"

"Mom and I talked. I had my qualms about how it would go. Fortunately, there was no yelling and she was relatively logical about it. About your dastardly math, I see no reason for my mother to object to me going over to help you with it. But first, I must visit Ms. White and see about getting her shed key, then we can attack the math and talk further about mom and the other thing." Jane hesitated. "Please be discrete and say nothing aloud about the other things… "the fuzzes." Don't even say that word, "fuzzes." I suggest that in further conversations we refer to them as 'our friends.' You have a little brother living in your house. From what I hear they are curious and troublesome. Please be cautious."

"What part of 'no one's home' did you not understand?'"

"Children can be very sneaky, especially the males. You can not be too careful. We'll talk when I get there."

64

PALALA

Nacoo pulled herself out of the water and plopped down on the grass beside Kebeck. "What is wrong with you today? We won! Usually you are reviewing every detail of every play after a waterball game, *even* when we lose. It was a good game, against a very competent team." She tapped his upper arm. "You should be smiling."

"I apologize. I do not mean for my sad thoughts to cast a shadow over our game. It was an exciting game and you were amazing. Few people can leap up out of the water like you did today. I promise that I will be back to normal tomorrow."

"Would you like to tell me what troubles you?"

"I appreciate your concern. My troubles are just a passing shadow, so I will not bother you with it. All will be well in a few hours. So, I must go now and deal with my problem so that it can float away, like a cloud in the wind." Kebeck rose, touched his lower palms to Nacoo's lower palms, and trudged down a path toward Sheme's house.

I don't like to disappoint people. I want everyone to be happy. I know Sheme will not like what I have to tell her. But I could not be happy sharing parenting with her. Our child would feel it and thus have problems. We are not a good match. There is nothing wrong with her. We are just different. Our waters flow in different directions. She is going to hate me. I hope I can make her understand.

Kebeck stopped walking and looked around. He realized that he had been walking the wrong way. He had branched off toward his house. *I've got to quit daydreaming and watch where I'm going.* He turned and broke into a jog. *I might as well get there quickly and get it over with.*

PALALA

Sheme was standing in her doorway when Kebeck reached her house. Her face lit up as he approached the door. Kebeck slowed to a walk and stopped several feet in front of her. He signaled her a greeting and looked down at his feet. *How to start this?*

Sheme backed up and motioned him into the house. Neither said a word. He stepped up to a shelf and picked up a piece of fruit. "Oh, you have hajas. How fortunate. May I have this one? Mine will not be ripe for six to eight days."

Sheme scowled at him. "You are not here to discuss fruit, but take it and enjoy it. Tell me, how does your work with the ice mountain aliens go."

"I will wait for mine to ripen." Kebeck put the haja back on the shelf. "I did not come here to talk about the aliens, but since you asked… We have learned enough to make us assume that no urgent action is needed. They are very interesting and seem to be harmless."

"So, Let us talk about why you did come. Now that you have had time for thought and contemplation… tell me what you think."

"About?"

"About us, of course."

"I think… " He paused and straightened his shoulders. "I think that us parenting a child is not a good idea."

Kebeck saw her neck starting to change color. If she were in an earth cartoon, steam would have come out her ears.

"Why? Just tell me why?"

"Because we are too different."

"Of course we are different. That is one factor in a good parenting pair that is good for the child."

"I mean we are so dissimilar that out lifestyles would clash. We would not be happy."

She slammed her hand down on her bed platform. "I would be happy. Well, I thought I would be happy. We are good together."

"We are good together at games and when we have worked together. But, you and I move at different speeds. There would be much conflict. It would not work."

"But I chose you." Sheme's neck was bright with anger.

Kebeck looked toward the door. "It pains me to see you unhappy, but I cannot do what you want. Please forgive me for causing you distress. I… I do not know what else I can say to make it better. I should go now."

Before he could get to the door, she put a hand out to stop him. "You have hurt me and I will not forget it." She pulled her hand back and he rushed out the door.

CHAPTER

66

EARTH

The temperature had dropped during the night and Jane had to dig out her heavy coat before she headed out to school. It looked to be a normal day at school for everyone except Jane and Ava. They were excited, but they hid it well. Only when they were alone did they dare mention the aliens. "Why can't I go with you to move the 'you know who?'" Ava asked for the third time.

"I just think people are less likely to notice me in the woods. I go there all the time. Two people are more noticeable than one. And you will talk, and thus draw attention to us."

"I can be quiet."

"No you can't. Especially when you're excited."

"How can I not be excited by meeting aliens?"

Jane glared at her. "You just said the 'A' word."

"Oh. Sorry."

"And that is why I am doing this alone. You can come with me to the shed later in the week." She started toward the door, then stopped. "Ava, we have to be very careful to keep their existence secret. If anyone finds out about our friends, they could spend the rest of their lives in a lab. Their lives are in our hands. This is a serious situation. I suggest that from now on, we should never use the 'A' word. The consequences of someone overhearing us would be dire."

"Point conceded. Just call me when you get back home from visiting our friends." Ava huffed, then put her head down and shuffled off toward home.

67

EARTH

Jane dashed home and changed clothes.. She was fortunate that her mother was reluctant to throw anything out that might be reused. So... she was able to find her old wagon in the shed and a big box in the basement. She had been in contact with Senoa-lo by email and the Ume were packed up and ready to go when she arrived at five o'clock to take them to their new camp. It only took minutes to load up the Ume and their equipment into the big box. Jane closed the box and secured the top with a piece of tape. As she put the tape roll in her pocket, she heard voices. She froze, hoping whoever it was would go away. The voices continued to come toward her. She could see figures through the trees. *Oh, no. It's the three stooges… George, Anthony and Bart. They're so stupid. I wonder how those idiots have managed to stay in school. Their only purpose in life seems to be torturing me… and a few others. Oh, they're coming this way.* Jane's mind raced and her stomach flipped about. *How can I get rid of them?*

Jane leaned down and whispered, "Don't make a sound. There are people near us." Jane's hands came together and she started to rub her nails with her thumb. She looked down at what she was doing and took a breath and put her hands by her sides.

The three guys walked up to Jane, looked at the box and looked at Jane. Bart put his hand out to touch the box.

"I wouldn't do that," Jane glared at him.

Bart smirked, but dropped his hand to his side. "Lots of things you wouldn't do."

George laughed.

"What's in the box?"

"Snakes."

"Yeah… right. Let's see your snakes."

"Not a good idea."

"Cause they're going to bite me?" Bart snickered.

"They could bite. They've probably thawed up a bit since I put them in the box with a warm blanket."

Anthony, the smartest of the group, stepped forward. "What's really in the box?"

"If you must know… I found two Mississauga rattlers in the bush. They were half frozen, so I went home and got this box, barbecue tongs and a blanket. I'm taking them home to spend the winter in my old aquarium."

Bart put his hand on the box. "I don't believe you."

Jane moved his hand off the box. "If you're planning on opening this box, tell me first so I can get out of the way. Snake bite is an ugly way to die. I know I'm not strong enough to drag you out of the park, so you'll have to depend on your pals to get you to a hospital in thirty minutes. Think they can carry you? I doubt it and I'm sure that they won't be willing to suck out the poison for you."

Bart glanced at his buddies.

Anthony motioned to Bart. "Just open the box. There's no snakes in there."

Bart stepped back. "You open it."

George rubbed his chin, where a little fuzz was beginning to grow. "You know she's crazy enough that she might just have snakes in there."

Anthony studied Jane for a second. "So if you do have rattlers in the box, how are you going to move them to an aquarium without getting bit?"

"Uh, well, I'm going to put the box in our freezer for a few minutes, and then transfer them."

Bart smiled. "We want to come watch. I'd like to see that."

"Yeah, we'd like to see that." Anthony's eyes lit up.

Jane relaxed. "I'll have to ask my mom if you can come over. You guys have a phone handy? I'll call her. She's very fussy about who I have over."

"Your mom?" Bart questioned.

She turned to face Bart. "I think you've met my mom."

"Yeah, she yelled at me." Bart turned to the other two.

"I'm not going near her mom. She's worse that any snake."

"What? Did she bite you?" Anthony sneered.

"Worse. She yelled stuff about my body and my brains and then called my parents. All I did was walk across her yard." He turned to face Jane. "Your mom's a regular witch."

"So I had better hurry home before the witch comes looking for me. She doesn't like it when I'm late."

Anthony started to walk away. "Let's go. Sean's working at his parent's 7/11. He'll probably give us free chips or ice cream."

"Good idea. Much better than wasting time with plain Jane and her mystery box. Probably nothing good in it, anyway." Bart followed Anthony and George trailed behind them.

Jane picked up the wagon handle and started home. She dared not look over toward the boys as they disappeared through the woods and she dared not say a word to the Ume yet. After ten minutes of trudging through the bush, she stopped and opened the box a crack. "Are you all right?"

Senoa-lo said, "We're fine. I must compliment you on fast and creative thinking. We were quite alarmed and frightened by what we heard. On our planet, telling things that are not true is rarely done, either by us or the Palalans. I have read and watched much of earth fiction. I admire people who can think fast enough to devise a reasonable lie. Your display of creative lying was impressive and saved us. Thank you."

"Very impressive," Jolocko-lo piped up. "But, it's stuffy in here. Maybe we should get going?"

"He's right." Jane closed the box and continued on.

68

UME

Mera had expected life to be different while her father was away on earth, but she never thought she would feel so lonely. She had school to keep her busy and her friends to keep her amused. She had thought that she would feel free and independent without him around, but she didn't. She still had him in her head, reminding her to study hard and do the right thing. As Mera walked past one of the bubbling hot springs that sustained her people, she let her mind wander. *I can't just sit around and worry about our situation with the Palalans. I have to do something.* Mera, like her father Jolocko-lo, was a person of action.

Yesterday, she had received a message on her computer from a friend of a friend. The person had asked her to meet with him at the floating pool near her aunt's house. *I know this person I'm meeting is part of the insurgent group that has been in the news. I don't think father would approve, but I'm going to meet him anyway. Just listening to him can do no harm. Father says everyone should be heard. I'm just going to go to hear what he has to say.* As she sped along, something in the sky caught her attention. She looked up. *The Palalans are doing another fly over with one of their space ships.* She stopped and glared at the thing in the sky. *Just go away. Leave us alone.*

The Palalan ship was gone by the time Mera arrived at the pool. As she put her bag in a locker, she looked around to see if anyone was watching her. It looked like a normal afternoon. No one looked out of place. Everyone was quietly preparing to float and meditate. *I'd better quit looking around or I'll look suspicious.* As she approached the pool, she glanced around one last time before she got in the water. Mera was laying on top of the saline pool trying to relax when she heard her name. She turned her head to her left. A reddish brown male was floating beside her. "I assume that you are Mera."

"I am. Who are you?

"Well, my parents named me Waloo, but I don't like that name. It was the name of a famous inventor. Do I look like someone who lives his life in a lab playing with chemicals? It's just not me. I have watched earth movies and so I have chosen to go by 'Tom'. It is the name of my favorite movie actor."

Mera studied him carefully. "And do your parents and friends now call you 'Tom?'"

"Most of the time. Occasionally they slip up."

"And you are disturbing my peaceful float because?"

He smiled. "Because I was told that you are one of us. A friend told me that you also tire of waiting for the government to do something. You are a person who wants to do something about our situation. Our elders like conjecture and study. By the time they decide on an action, it will have to be a reaction to what the Palalans do. And there will be few or no options."

Mera felt a burning anger brewing inside her. *He's right. I hate feeling helpless and I hate waiting for our government to decide what to do.* "And what is this action you propose?"

"I think it's unwise to talk here. I suggest that you meet with some of us tonight. Be at the Canlom bridge when the sun sinks behind the mountains. We can walk to the meeting from there."

Mera glanced around to see if anyone was near enough to overhear them. When she turned her head back toward Tom, all she saw was his back as he climbed out of the pool and headed toward the showers.

CHAPTER

69

EARTH

Jane managed to get to Mrs. Campbell's shed without attracting any more attention. She rolled the wagon into the shed, turned on the camp lantern she had hung from the ceiling and closed the door. "We're here." She ripped the tape off and opened the box.

Jolocko-lo climbed out first. "That was a rough ride."

Senoa-lo's eyes shot daggers at him as she hit the ground. Then she turned to Jane. "We thank you for all you are doing for us."

Leela-lo asked, "Who were those three young males who wanted to look in the box?"

"Just some boys from my school."

"Please tell us about them. Why do they act in such an aggressive manner?"

"They have problems. Anthony, the smallest, has had a chip on his shoulder ever since he was a little kid. His father was a professional wrestler, a big brawny guy. Anthony was always a bit small for his age. His family is Norwegian; so he is pale with blonde, almost white, hair and eyebrows. His dad died in the ring when Anthony was eight. Anthony doesn't like the fact that he's puny and pale. He wants people to think he is a tough guy, so he acts hard and mean.

George is the one with black hair. He is half-native American, from the Iroquois tribe, and half-Japanese. His problem is that neither side of his extended families will accept him. He has no brothers or sisters because when his parents saw that neither set of grandparents would accept him, they decided not to have more children. A well-meaning first grade teacher made his life more difficult by having a project where each child talked about his heritage. Ever since that day, kids have teased him. They call him racist names. I think he feels very alone.

Bart is the big one. His parents are alcoholics. They stay sober enough to do their jobs, but not sober enough to be good parents. So Bart would rather be anywhere but home. He's really a good guy and he spends a lot of time taking care of his little sister. But, as you can see, he wants people to think he's tough."

Leela-lo looked like she was going to cry. "That's so awful."

Jane agreed. "It is, but it's no excuse for how they treat me and some others at school."

Senoa-lo straightened up and took charge. "No excuse at all, but now we must get to work."

Jane helped the Ume unload the box and then took a slip of paper out of a pocket and handed it to Senoa-lo. "This is the code for our WiFi. It should be good here. This shed backs on our yard. I like to sit in the Adirondack chair beside this shed and work on my computer, so I set up the Wi-Fi to reach here." She lifted the last of the Ume's cartons out of the box. "Do you mind if I stay and visit with you for a few minutes?"

"You are always welcome." Senoa-lo replied.

Jane put her hand to her cheek. "I almost forgot. Mrs. Campbell has a cat. Watch out for him. He's a big orange one. But the good news is that she brings him in every night around nine or ten. And he wears a bell. So you can hear him as he moves."

Toboo-lo stopped unloading a carton and turned. "Why did Mrs. Campbell put a bell on the animal? Is this common?"

"Not really. The cat's name is Cougar and he likes to kill birds and squirrels. Some people put bells on aggressive cats so animals can hear the coming and run away."

Toboo-lo smiled at Jane. "Oh, then we shall, as you say, 'keep an eye out' for Cougar."

Leela-lo stopped unloading her crate and sat on the edge of it. "I know that that is an English adage, but it describes a distasteful image. Could you possibly find a more pleasant way to express yourself."

Jane tilted her head as she sat down on the cement floor. "Interesting. And I agree with you. I never thought of the actual image that evokes. 'Yuck.'"

Jolocko-lo looked up. "But really we should hear him before we see him, so… it would be more appropriate to just keep our ears alert for the sound of his bell."

Leela-lo stepped closer to Jane. "Can we ask you some questions about about other earth things that bewilder us?"

"Sure. And we can eat supper as we talk." Jane took her backpack off and took out three plastic containers. "I brought cheese and crackers and carrots."

Leela-lo picked up one of the crackers and nibbled the edge. "Very good. I am reluctant to inquire about the ingredients. But my scientific curiosity demands that I ask."

Jane thought for a minute. "They just contain flour, salt, nuts, and oil."

"Then I am not eating the embryo of a bird or the fluid produced by the mammary glands of mammals when I eat a cracker. Good. I prefer food that does not come from animals."

Jolocko-lo broke off a piece of cheese. "This comes from the mammary glands of a mammal. And it tastes wonderful. Get over yourself, Leela-lo. We are on a different world and things are done differently."

"Speaking of which," Leela-lo interrupted, "you mentioned supper. Why do you earth people have three daily occasions during which you eat instead of just eating whenever you are hungry? Why do you make consuming food into a special ceremony where people gather and eat as a group?

Jane was puzzled. "I never thought about it. I'll have to do some research to see how that custom evolved. I'll have to get back to you on that one." Her eyes turned to Senoa-lo. "I assume that I also get to ask questions."

Senoa-lo nodded.

"What do you eat on your planet?"

"Plants, a great variety of plants. We have never tasted the flesh of an animal."

Leela-lo made a face. "And I prefer not to. It puzzles me that some animals you keep as pampered pets and other animals, very intelligent animals, like pigs and octopus, you eat."

Jane was beginning to feel uncomfortable. "Some animals are more useful and easier to tame than others. I think cats were domesticated because they would eat the mice that were eating people's grains. And dogs were domesticated long, long ago. They were used to do many types of work. They pulled wagons and guarded people's houses and livestock. They're easier to train than most animals." She smiled. "And we feel a kinship with them. Zebras could never be domesticated so people hunted them for food, whereas, they tamed horses and used them for farm work and transportation. Our people have been eating animals since time began. It seems natural to us."

Jane went on, "There are vegetarians and vegans among us. Most are people who view animals as sentient and intelligent and thus want no part in killing them. I guess we meat eaters have chosen to ignore the intelligence and feelings of certain animals. We have chosen to distance ourselves from the reality of how food animals spend their lives and how they're killed. Pigs are the second smartest animal on the planet. They're much smarter than dogs. Yet, I'm looking forward to some sausage for supper and I could never eat a dog." Jane hung her head. "Now I feel guilty, but I'm still going to eat the sausage."

Senoa-lo stepped forward and put a hand on Jane's knee. "We do not mean to upset you."

Jane straightened up. "No problem. I am used to living with conflicting ideas. Life is a complicated blend of feelings and logic. In general, I lean more toward logic. But now that I think about it, there is no logic to eating pigs and not eating dogs. I must admit that in this case feelings wins over logic." She leaned her head back and closed her eyes. "Let's leave that topic for now. What other questions do you have for me?"

Leela-lo stepped forward. "Why do earth people wear clothes? Of course you wear them when it's cold, but your people always have parts of their bodies covered. And they seem to regard being nude as something very undesirable. Why?"

"I think we can blame religion for that. All the major religions present nudity as being wrong. Really, when I think about it, I don't know why. It went from being a religious rule to being the custom among most people. And in most countries, public nudity is against the law."

"Speaking of clothes, please tell us about fashion." Leela- lo asked. "I don't understand how fashion works."

Jane took a big breath. "Not my forte. Now I wish Ava were here." She paused again. "Fashion is when people, who are influential in the society, make and display to the public, clothes that they consider pretty. Because these individuals consider the clothes to be pretty, people buy those clothes or similar ones. This makes a profit for the clothing manufactures and gives people the opportunity to wear something different."

"I don't understand the word 'pretty.' It says in the dictionary... 'pleasing to the eye.' I don't get it." Leela-lo declared. "What I find pleasant to look at can be different from what someone else deems to be delightful to view. Is there a person or a committee who sets the standard of what is pretty?"

"Well, that's a good question. I've never given it much thought." *Do they ever ask difficult questions.* "It's one of those things that has always been a part of my life. I'm going to have to do some research and some thinking before I can explain it."

"As I understand it, fashion changes every year. What happens to people's old clothes?" Leela-lo asked.

"Old clothes are given away or thrown away. Most people don't buy a whole set of new clothes every year. Most people just buy a few things every year."

Leela-lo tilted her head. "You mentioned that gives them the chance to wear something different. Why not just wear practical clothes that are appropriate for the weather or job. I have looked at some fashion magazines. There is great emphasis on one's appearance, especially for females. The shape of one's face and body seems to be very important to most humans."

"It is. And I am ashamed of that aspect of our society. I… "

Senoa-lo interrupted. "Then we shall say no more on this topic for now." She could see that Jane was becoming flustered and uncomfortable. "We have taken enough of Jane's time today."

"Yes, I should go." Jane took a small padlock out of her bag and handed it to Senoa-lo. "With this, you can lock yourself in when you want, or, if you all go out, lock it on the outside. Just turn it to 3333 to unlock it." Jane demonstrated how to lock and unlock the padlock. As she rose off the floor she studied the aliens. "I promise to think about your questions and come back with better answers next time." Jane turned and left, closing the sliding door behind her.

CHAPTER

70

EARTH

Jane had finished her homework and was just finishing cleaning up the kitchen when she heard her mother come in. She cautiously peered into the living room. Her mom was perched on the edge of the couch, staring into space. "Hi, how are you?" *I shouldn't mention Mr. Fitzpatrick. I'll wait for her to bring up the elephant in the room.* "Want me to make you a cup of tea?"

"No. I think I'd rather have a glass of wine. There's an open bottle of white in the fridge. Would you mind?"

Jane opened the kitchen cabinet. *Should I get a crystal glass or a plain one? I don't think we're we celebrating.* Jane glanced around the corner at her mom. *Better to use the good stuff. She deserves the good stuff.*

Jane handed her the glass and sat in the antique chair facing her mom. *I'll let her speak first.* She looked down at her hands and realized that she was rubbing her nails. Jane pulled her hands apart and grabbed the sides of the chair. She waited. *How long am I supposed to just sit here? Should I say something about Mr. Fitzgerald or maybe talk about something else?*

Her mother glanced up at her then went back to staring at the wall.

No, I'm not going to be the one to mention him. "I finished my homework. Would you like something to eat?

"No. I'm not hungry. More silence.

"Then I'll just go up to my room."

"No, wait." Another big pause. "I should tell you how it went with Walter."

"Only if you want to talk about it." *I didn't know if I wanted to hear about it.*

"He showed up with a wonderful picnic basket full of my favourite foods. We ate on the hillside as the sun went down into the lake. We both said very little until after it got dark. Then he asked if anything was wrong. I lied and said I was not happy about an incident at work, but that I didn't want to talk about the details. We chatted about inconsequential bits of nothing. Then I said I had a headache and had him take me home. Option three didn't work. I have to confront him." She leaned her head down into her hands. Jane moved over beside her and put a hand on her shoulder.

"Can I do anything?

She turned and looked at me. "No. I guess I should arrange to meet him somewhere for coffee and tell him what I know." She squished up her forehead. "Are you sure about this?"

I reached in my pocket and pulled out a folder paper and offered it to her. "This is a copy of the article in the high school paper about him retiring. When I first met him I got the impression that he didn't like kids, but the students really liked him. It seems that he was a good teacher."

"Well, at least there's that. I'm going to bed now. I'll think about this tomorrow." She took her glass of wine and climbed up the stairs.

71

PALALA

When Kebeck arrived at the Foreign Planets office, Nacoo and Solang were engrossed in looking at more photos of the aliens. "Hi, anything new?" They both turned and greeted him. They were both smiling.

"Tell him what you found." Nacoo prodded Solang.

"This is so good. It's almost as good as finding a dictionary that translates alien to Palalan."

"What?"

"Our little spy listening station found a public channel with earth English movies being shown with Ume subtitles." Her grin couldn't have been any bigger. "I am learning so much. Give me a few more days and I should able to speak Ume."

He scrunched up his nose. "What's Ume?

"They refer to themselves as Ume, so I'm going to call their language Ume. They call us Palalans and refer to our language as Palalan."

He nodded. "That sounds logical. So what have you learned about our little neighbors?

"Not very much yet. I am just working on the language. I think we will be able to translate their newscasts in a few days. I have some students working on it with me."

"And you're not going to believe this," Nacoo said. "They seem to like earth gangster movies. So Solang has to translate the gangster slang into regular English so she can understand the Ume subtitles."

"Interesting."

"Speaking of which, I need to get back to my office and get on with it." With that, Solong headed out the door.

Kebeck turned to Nacoo. "It seems that we finally have a breakthrough."

Nacoo shoved a photo into his hands. "It seems that we have two breakthroughs. Look carefully at this photo. What kind of animal is that?"

"It is a hop-hop."

"No. That is a photo of one of the creatures living in the ice mountains."

Kebeck examined the photo, then looked up with eyes as big as bowls. "You mean that they have been hopping around in our jungles for as long as our people can remember? These are the aliens that have built cities in the cold mountains? We've always assumed that they were just cute fuzzy wild animals." Kebeck flopped down on a slantboard.

Nacoo grabbed a bottle and handed him a drink of water. "I just discovered it this morning. They are the same animal, right?"

"That is a hop-hop. I thought they looked somewhat like hop-hops. But they are the same animal."

"These new photos were taken yesterday with a special camera that can enlarge things. It is the first time we have had a good picture of an individual animal in the valleys of the ice mountains. It is a hop-hop."

"Maybe there is an intelligent species of hop-hop that evolved in the mountains and a wild simple-minded species that evolved in our jungles." Kebeck got up and put the bottle back on a shelf.

Nacoo picked up a photo and studied it. "Or maybe they have been acting dumb and spying on us for years."

"You think so?"

"That could explain why Solang has been finding that there are many Palalan words used in their language."

"I suppose that we should now try to find out if the animals in our jungle are intelligent Ume or simple hop-hops."

"So what do you suggest? Should we capture one of our wild jungle hop-hops and see if he will speak?"

Nacoo studied the photo. "Well, if it is wild and unable to talk it will not talk to us and if it is a sophisticated spy… he is not going to talk to us."

They looked at each other, thinking the same thing. Kebeck spoke first. "Fortunately for them, we are a civilized society that does not believe in torture."

"But… " Nacoo said, "we could capture one and see if it might talk. They have got to have noticed our flights over their cities. And they have got to know that we know about them. I say we capture one and perform some harmless basic tests to see if our jungle hop-hops are intelligent spies or just dumb animals that look like the mountain Ume."

Kebeck hesitated. "I agree. I do not want to harm any animal. And I do not like the idea of caging an animal, but we need to know more about our jungle hop-hops. There has to be some scientists who have done studies on the hop-hops?"

"I looked that up before you came in this morning. I found two studies where they were observed in their natural habitat. Their scientific name is marcotels and they are a species unrelated to any other animals on our planet. They eat plants using their upper paws as hands and go into burrows in the ground at night. They are usually found in pairs and only make sounds when close together. And unfortunately we have no recordings.

The paper said they rarely make any noise and when they do, it sounds like rapid mumbling. I think the scientists grew bored with watching them hop about and moved on to studying more interesting animals."

Kebeck's eyebrows went up. "Well… let's do it. Let's capture one."

Nacoo immediately called the Animal Studies Department and arranged for a team to set to work on the task of capturing a hop-hop.

As Kebeck walked back home through the jungle, he met up with his son Prigo. After the usual greeting, his son said, "I am going to a waterball game. Want to come?"

"Not today."

After a few minutes of catching up on friends and family, his son paused and stared at him. "I know that look. You have something on your mind that you are reluctant to discuss. You might as well say what you are thinking. Not talking will leave you tense and me curious."

Kebeck looked down and pushed a rock around with his foot.

"How are you and Sheme getting along? I know that it is none of my business, but when I saw her earlier today she said something unusual."

Kebeck nudged the rock again. "I told her that I did not want to raise a child with her. After much thought, I decided that it would not work. I want to continue to be a friend, but I think it would be unwise to live together and have a child. She was upset. I hope that with some time she will see that we are too dissimilar in many ways. She is loud and abrupt, and I think slowly and like peace. She said something about me? What did she say?"

"I just happened to see her at the computer parts store. I greeted her. When she looked up from the counter and saw me, her neck turned pink. Then she said that she was going to make you regret your decision. I did not know what she was talking about, so I nodded and left the store."

"So she is still quite angry."

"Very. I hope that there is no way that she has power over you. She was seething with the kind of anger that leads one to forget logic."

"Hopefully, she will calm down and see reason soon. But, do not waste your energy and time worrying about it. She is a nice person who needs a bit of time to get over a rejection. Think no more of it. Since she cannot see the logic of what I said, I shall not concern myself. I have other things to think about. Since we are both going in the same direction, I will walk with you."

Prigo stopped and nodded toward a path off to the side of the road. "Let us take this short cut. It is a prettier and cooler way to the river."

"Lead the way."

CHAPTER

72

ICE MOUNTAINS

Viro-lo hesitated before the door to his office to shake the water off his fur. It was a lovely day. The sunlight glittered off the ice mountains. A light rain had fallen in the night and left their valley looking newly washed. He studied the sign beside the door. It read, "Office of Foreign Affairs." *I don't like the title of our department. It should be called, "Office of Foreign Liaison", and one day I'm going to bring it up at a meeting. But not today.*

He opened the door to see Zenbaco staring at his computer. He did not look happy. Zenbaco looked up from his computer. "They know that we've been spying on them. We have to contact anyone who is in the jungle right now and tell them to get out."

"What?" Viro-lo rushed over to Zenbaco's desk. "How did they find that out? How did you find out that they know about us?" Viro-lo stepped back and put his hands on his hips.

"I thought I told you. Some time ago, I had listening devices planted in some of the government offices. Every couple of days I listen to the recordings. But ever since the Palalans started doing the flyovers, I've had some people listening to them all the time."

He crooked his head. "And what did they say that makes an evacuation so urgent?"

"They now realize that we are what they call hop-hops. And they're going to try to capture one of us. Who's working in the jungle today?"

Viro-lo flew over to his desk and started looking through files. She held up a handful of papers. "We have six people there today. Only Cardo-lo and Rako-lo can be reached by radio. The other four are in places where a radio signal can't be used. We are going to have to ask Cardo-lo and Rako-lo to find them and tell them to evacuate."

Zembaco-lo sighed. "It is fortunate that Rako-lo is there. He is a very experienced spy." Zembaco-lo could see that Viro-lo was glaring at him. "I know it we aren't supposed to call him a spy, but that's what he is."

Viro-lo put the papers down on his desk with more than a little force. "We call them observers. We need to know what is happening in Palala and we appreciate that we have an able team of observers with the skills to monitor the Palalans."

"Whatever… let's get on with it. I'll contact Rako-lo and you radio Cardo-lo."

"Right. And I'll contact everyone who is scheduled to go into the jungle. It would be terrible to cross the desert and go into the jungle just to be captured and… " He turned to face Zembaco-lo. "If they seize someone, what do they intend to do with him?"

"Well, they said they were going to question the captive."

Viro-lo flopped into his chair. "I hope that's all they plan to do."

'We'll think about that later. Right now, let's get our people out of the jungle."

Viro-lo leaped out of the chair and went over to the radio set. "I'm on it."

Zembaco-lo paused. "And after we contact everyone, we need to schedule a meeting this afternoon with the department heads to discuss whether to let the public know what's going on with the Palalans. We want to keep the public informed, but it serves no good purpose to scare them."

CHAPTER

73

ICE MOUNTAINS

Mera pulled her scarf closer around her neck as a chilly wind blew some leaves across the bridge. Steam rose from the water making it difficult to see the far end of the bridge. A figure emerged out of the mist and came toward her. It was the fellow who had spoken to her at the pool. "I'm glad you came. Many of our people make noises about the Palalans, but they aren't willing to act."

Mera moved closer to him and studied his face. "You were in a math class with me a few years ago, right?"

"I was. I remembered you as someone who stands up for people. So I thought you might be right for our group."

"That was just something that needed to be done. So I did it."

"And I was very impressed."

Mera would never forget that day. Her teacher was a bully and one day a slower student was stumped on a math problem. The teacher sent him out of the room telling him to, "Get out of my class and come back smarter tomorrow." Mera lost it. She stood up and told the teacher he was a terrible teacher and that he should "Get out of our class and come back a better teacher tomorrow."

"You might remember that I got into major trouble over that."

"So... was it worth it?"

"Definitely. It gave me a reason to talk to the principal about his bullying. If you remember, after that the teacher was a bit nicer to the slower ones. But that was years ago, let's talk about what action you're thinking of concerning the Palalans."

He touched Mera's arm. "Walk with me. I, and others, think we should go to Palala and find out more about what weapons they have. And we need to find out what they are planning."

"There are trained government agents doing just that."

"Of course. The problem is that they are not keeping us, the Ume people informed. I have sources that tell me that our government has microphones hidden in Palalan government offices. But we are not being told what the Palalans are saying. We have the right to know. They are treating us like children and only telling us about selected bits of the situation. We need the truth. We can't trust the government. We must go find out for ourselves."

Mera stopped walking and looked around. "Please keep your voice down. I don't even know your name and you're going to get both of us in trouble with the authorities."

"Sorry. It upsets me that they are keeping things from us. My name is Tom Nage but, as I said, my friends call me 'Tom.' I work on computers for several government offices. I know Viro-lo and Zenbaco-lo. They are in contact with the Ume who are on Earth looking for a WMD. So I know of your father. He strikes me as intelligent and respected. Because of him, I thought you might be someone who thinks as I do."

Mera's jaw dropped. "You can get into big trouble just… "

Tom interrupted, "I know.

"Have you ever been into the jungle?"

"Not yet."

"But you're going and you want me to go with you, don't you?" Mera looked down at her shoes, then back up to Tom's eyes. "If you think that we might find out something that could help our people, I'm not saying I'll go, but I'll think about it."

CHAPTER

74

EARTH

The school cafeteria was extra busy because it was pizza day. Jane was alone at their regular table, lost in thought when Ava sat down. "You're probably thinking about our 'little friends.' Right? But we can't talk about them here."

"Right. Not a word here. I'll call you after school."

Ava nodded. "So on to another topic… I must tell you that I'm so glad that you've figured out how to talk to boys."

"Compared to girls, they're relatively uncomplicated. Sports and jokes."

"Yeah, that usually works. But, I've been thinking about your difficulty with making friends with girls. So since you're so linear, I've got some rules for you. I call them 'social girl rules'."

"Shoot."

"Number one: Compliments. Compliments are a good way to get people to like you. Find something specific that you like about the person or about something they own. But, be very careful to phrase compliments so that they cannot be taken as sarcasm."

"Number two: Don't ever, EVER give another girl the impression you think you are better than she is. And that will be hard to do since you're smarter than most people. Just say something stupid or mundane once in a while."

"Number three: Stress your similarities. Find something you have in common."

"Number four: Ask them about how they feel and really listen to them. And, after you listen, try to avoid giving advice. But, if you have to give advice, give someone else the blame. Like… 'My aunt always says…' or 'My grandfather told me… '"

"So you think that if I follow these rules I can make friends with girls? Are you going to give me a cheat sheet, so I can glance at it while I'm talking?"

"Maybe I should, but knowing you, I'm sure you've got all four rules memorized word for word. Right?"

"Precisely. And I shall endeavor to apply them. Possibly, later today. I'm curious to see if they have any validity. The girls seem to either dislike me or ignore my existence, so I have nothing to lose."

Ava jumped up. "Sorry to preach and run, but I have a school council meeting. I wish they wouldn't schedule these things at lunch."

Jane watched her go just as Hoop approached. He plopped down beside her. "What's up?"

"Oh, I was just thinking about… how humans are such weird creatures. Why do they do the things they do?"

"Like what?"

"Like… " She paused and thought about her conversations with the Ume. "We eat three times a day. Not two or four times a day. Why is that?"

"Never thought about it. I could eat six times a day, but I'd probably get fat. So three works for me." He turned to face her. "Knowing you, you've probably researched it. Right?"

"Of course. According to what I found, there isn't a biological reason to eat three meals a day. It's more sociological. Long ago poor people ate whenever they had food, like other animals. The Romans only ate one meal and that was lunch. The idea of three meals stemmed from the industrial revolution. Workers needed an early meal to sustain them at work, lunch was an important break in the day to fuel up for more work, and the evening meal was a light meal to relax you before sleeping. Regular mealtimes seems to have evolved as evidence of an ordered and civilized life. There's comfort in predictability. And, having a set schedule gives people more opportunities to socialize."

Hoop tilted his head like a curious puppy. "Interesting. You make me… "

"What does she make you do?" said a voice behind Jane's head. Two of Hoop's buddies put their trays on the table.

"She makes me think. You should try it sometime." Hoop stood up. "I've got to go now. The coach said I should come by."

Bruce sat across from her. "What are you thinking about this time?"

'I was thinking about customs."

"Whose customs?"

"Ours. The things we here on earth assume are normal… like wearing clothes."

"Yeah, I don't understand how those people on Mars can run around nude all the time." He took a bite. "What's there to think about? People wear clothes because they don't want others to see them naked. Not a great mystery."

"But why did our society evolve this way?"

Bruce put his fork down. "I'm assuming that you are discounting the talking snake theory."

"And you would be correct."

He took a bite of his pizza and chewed for a minute. "Well…" He took another bite and looked over at Anthony.

"I don't know." Anthony threw his hands up. "From the time I was little, my mom always had me wear clothes and I'd feel real embarrassed running around naked."

Jane got up to leave. "So If you ran around with a bare ass you'd feel embarrassed. That explains it." She left them laughing. *I made them laugh. It feels so good. I'm really glad that I read those books on humour. A simple play on words that sound similar is a relatively easy method of getting a laugh. And it does work better when one uses something the other person has said. I'll have to tell Ava about this. I wonder if humour works equally well with girls. Probably not. Girls are more guarded and fear being the object of the humour.*

75

UME ON EARTH

As the sun rose, the light coming through the cracks woke
Leela-lo. She looked around their garden shed home. "This is…
all right." Jane had put a quilt in one back corner. It made a
cozy bed. She had left a pile of wooden blocks in the other back
corner. With Jolocko-lo's help they now resembled a desk and
two seats. "I guess we had better get to work." She looked over
at Senoa-lo, asleep on the quilt. *I hate to wake her. I'll give her*

a few more minutes. She turned on her computer and glanced over and saw that Jolocko-lo was awake. "We have a message. I'll decode it and then wake her."

Jolocko-lo grunted,"Sure."

A few minutes passed with no one speaking. A storm was coming and they could hear the wind blowing outside.

A yell broke the silence. "No! This is terrible." Leela-lo jumped back from her computer and began pacing back and forth.

Senoa-lo leapt up off the quilt and rushed over. They all stood waiting for an explanation as Leela-lo paced in front of them.

Senoa-lo grabbed her arm and stopped her. "What? What is so terrible?"

"The Palalans have discovered that our people in the jungle are spying on them and they are trying to capture one of us."

"Stand still and tell me exactly what the message said." Senoa-lo let her go.

Leela-lo took a breath. "Our people have a microphone planted in the Palalan Foreign Planets office. The Palalans were heard discussing the photos they have been taking from their space vehicles and they have now come to the conclusion that the people they have been watching in the ice mountains are the same beings as the ones they see in their jungle. They have discovered that we are the hop-hops they have been seeing in their jungle for many many years. And... "

"We knew that this would eventually happen."

"Jolocko-lo, please let her finish. There is more... right?"

"And if that's not bad enough, they have a plan to capture one of our people."

"And what do they plan to do with the unlucky person they seize?" Jolocko-lo asked.

"They said they would not torture us, but they want us to talk."

"Our people have instructions not to talk."

Leela-lo spoke up. "It's possible that they won't find anyone. Our people have all been instructed to leave the jungle immediately."

"So for now, let's assume that all our people are safely out of the jungle." Senoa-lo scratched her head. "There's nothing we can do. So let's have a bite to eat and get back to work." After a brief meal, everyone went back to their computers. Senoa-lo stared at the screen, but found it hard to concentrate. She had been dreaming of her mother when Leela-lo's shout had woke her. In the dream, her mom was lamenting that she hadn't achieved anything in her lifetime, but she was proud of Senoa-lo." The dream made her think. *It's not fair that because my mom didn't see her life of value, I have to achieve great things. I never thought of it before, but she put a lot of pressure on me by not valuing her own contributions to our society.*

76

EARTH

As Jane approached her house, she noticed a strange car parked beside her mother's car. Her mom had said that she was going to be working from home this afternoon, but she hadn't mentioned she might have company. A tall man in a suit walked into sight. He had been behind her house. He stopped and watched her step up on her porch. "We've been looking for you. You're Jane, aren't you?"

She hesitated before answering. *Who is this? Should I answer or is this one of those strangers that I was warned not to talk to.* She put her hand on the doorknob and turned it. It was unlocked. "I don't know you, so I'm going in my house. Go away." She quickly slipped in and turned the lock. She heard voices in the living room and turned to see her mother sitting talking to another suited man.

"Oh good, you're here." Her mother's voice sounded strained and she was sitting on the edge of the antique chair.

Mom's not happy. What's wrong? Who's he? She put her shoulders back and tried to be casual as she crossed the room.

"This is Mr. …" Her mom was interrupted by a loud noise. Someone was rattling the doorknob.

The man on the couch stood up and went toward the door. "I think you have locked my colleague out." He walked over and unlocked the door. The man who had spoken to her in the yard came through the door.

"Mom. Who are these people?"

"They are from the Canadian Security Intelligence Service and they were asking about you."

CHAPTER

77

ICE MOUNTAINS

The sky was just at that point between sunset and darkness when everything looked beautiful and calm. The icy mountains were silhouettes in the distance. Mera arrived at the bridge and looked around for Tom. She saw him and four others approach from the other end of the bridge. *What am I doing? If Dad knew what we are planning, would he be proud of me or would he be angry?*

She had met with the group twice. It had been decided that they would call their group, "The Truth Seekers." She wasn't happy with the name but she only had one vote. After much discussion and some yelling, they had decided to sneak into the jungle and do three things. One group of two was supposed to seek out weaknesses that the Ume could use if they were to attack the Palalans. One pair were supposed to ascertain what weapons the Palalans possessed. The other two, she and Tom, were supposed to spy on the Palalans to find out what their plans were concerning the Ume.

"Are we doing the right thing?" she asked Tom.

His face turned dark. "How can you ask that now? We have to do something. We can't just wait around and hope the government is taking care of us. If you're not sure, then why are you here?

"I… I guess I'm scared. We need to know what the Palalans are planning and we need a weapon." She took a big breath. "You're right. This is what we have to do. Let's do it."

The next day they were on a plane flying them to the desert that separates the ice mountains from the jungle. "Is this the first time you've been in a plane?"

Mera shook her head. "No, I've been in flying machines all my life. I used to go with my dad on business trips."

"You seem very nervous."

"Of course I am. It's not every day that I sneak into a wild jungle to spy on strange huge beings. I've only seen Palalans in photos. I'd be stupid not to be on edge."

The plane let them off, then quickly took off again. Mera looked around at the miles of sand and rocks. She had never seen anything so flat. "What now?

Tom pointed to a line of green on the horizon. "That is our goal. But first we must cover ourselves with sand. That's what my friend said we should do. He said we should just roll around in it."

"When we were planning this, I heard no mention of rolling around in the dirt. Why would we do that?"

"Camouflage. We need to blend in with the desert in case some Palalans are looking out this way."

Mera reached into her vest pocket and pulled out a spiral metal object attached to a thin rope and placed it on the ground.

Tom sighs. "Why are you carrying a mountain climbing disc?"

"Well, as you know, my aunt thinks I'm off mountain climbing for a couple of days. As I was leaving the house, she came out with this caribiner in her hand and said, 'Did you forget this?' So I had to take it. Who knows? It might come in handy if we meet up with some jungle creatures. These sharp points make it a mean weapon."

"Whatever." He shyly took a knife out of his pocket as he knelt down on the ground. "So let's roll. And then we're off to save our people."

CHAPTER

78

EARTH

Jane moved a step closer to her mom and started twiddling with her fingers and rubbing her right thumb nail. She so wanted to look down at the floor, but she made a concerted effort not to. She chose a picture on the wall in front of her and kept her eyes glued to it. It was an art deco painting of a lady in a flowing dress. Not her favourite, but tracing the folds of the dress with her eyes kept her mind occupied.

The two men whispered to each other for a half minute, then turned to her mother. "We need to ask your daughter some questions. Since she is a minor, you can be here for the questioning, but we must ask you to not interfere or answer for her."

Anyone could easily see that her mother was seething like a pot ready to boil over. She responded by pronouncing every word staccato, "Of course, Mr. Clark." Her mom turned to face her. "Jane, I don't know what this is about, but please sit down and answer their questions." Jane took her eyes off the picture long enough to get a chair from the dining room and drag it over to sit beside her mom. Then her eyes went back to the painting.

"Hi Jane, I'm Mr. Evans and this is Mr. Ladinsky." He gestured toward the other man. The other man nodded, but still looked grim as an undertaker. "We're here to ask you about some of your internet activity." He paused. "Please look at me Jane."

Jane moved her eyes from the folds of the skirt to his right ear. *He has hair growing out of his ear.* She looked at his left ear. *Both ears... yuck!* He glanced at his notebook and grunted. *He must not like being examined any more than I do.* From the corner of her eye she thought she saw a hint of a smile on her mother's face.

"All right, Jane, We need to know why have you been searching weapons of mass destruction, military weapons, and poisons? What's with this interest in things that kill lots of people?"

She glanced at his eyes then back to the ear. "Oh, is that all? You want to know about my research." *Think... think...* "Well, I'm doing research for a book."

Her mom spoke up. "You're writing a book?"

Mr. Ladinsky glared at her. "We asked you… "

Mr. Evans interrupted. "It's all right. Now we know that the mother knows nothing about this 'supposed book'."

She didn't like his line about a 'supposed book', but worked at not showing anything on her face. "I'm not writing a book. My friend Ava is writing the book and I'm helping with research. That's all. If you look on her computer, you'll find where she recently read a book on how to write and has taken some on-line courses on writing. And hopefully, you'll see the beginnings of the book. But maybe not. She has been writing and rewriting it so much in her mind. Could be that she's got nothing on paper yet." Jane got flustered. "When I say on paper, I mean nothing written on her computer. Nobody writes on paper." She then noticed that Mr.Evans had been taking notes on a paper notebook as she spoke. *I shouldn't have said that about paper.*

Mr. Evans sat back a bit on the couch and looked at her mother. "You understand that our job is to protect the national security of the country, so of course we have to check out things like this."

Her mother said nothing. She just looked at him.

Jane tried to stay quiet, but… "Do you think that I would use my own computer in my house if I were involved in something nefarious?"

Mr. Evans stood up. "Well, from looking at your grades in school, I can see that you're very smart. So it wouldn't make sense for you to use your own internet. That I will concede. But, there are all kind of crazies out there, so we needed to meet you." He nodded at his partner. "We'll go now. Sorry to have bothered you both. I think you're telling the truth, but we'll drop by and see your friend Ava since we're in the neighbourhood. Just to tie up loose ends. Have a nice day."

As soon as the door closed behind them Jane was heading up the stairs.

"I assume you're off to call Ava."

Jane turned halfway up the stairs. "At least I can warn her that they're coming. Nobody wants to be surprised by government agents at your door.

"Right. Go call her. That was unpleasant."

It was a short phone call. "Agents from the Canadian Security Intelligence Service will be at your door in a minute or two. They're sort of like the FBI or N.S.A. in the films. They'll want to know about the book you're planning to write. I told them that I am doing research on WMD's and weapons for your book.

"Uh?"

"Thought I should let you know. Bye." She hung up. *I hope they haven't tapped our phone. But I didn't say anything incriminating. Just to be safe, I think it best that I not visit our little friends today.*

CHAPTER

79

UME ON EARTH

The Ume were gathered on the quilt having a bit of food before they went to sleep. They could see that the sun was almost down. The cracks in the shed walls were just big enough to light the little building during the day.

"So really, we have nothing." Senoa-lo put down her cookie and buried her face in her hands. "All our research and we still have no idea how to make a WMD that can defend our people."

"Well… there's always poison. I've found many formulas that we could make and put in the Palalan rivers."

"No! We are not going to even consider poisoning water." Leela-lo yelled. "It is sacred. Our bodies are more than fifty percent water. Water is what gives us life. We cannot use it to kill."

Senoa-lo grabbed Leela-lo's arm. "Hush. Someone might hear you. I understand your anger, but we cannot be discovered. Your shouting could be the end of all of us."

Toboo-lo rushed over and peered through a crack. "I don't see anyone out there."

"That's a relief." Senoa-lo sighed. "Now, without yelling, does anyone else have any ideas?"

"If we made bombs and dropped them from our planes, they would be too small to be effective. Unless they were something like atomic bombs. And, we don't have uranium, so we can't make atomic bombs." Jolocko-lo shook his head. "So that's out."

"I think… " Toboo-lo said, "I think we should talk to Jane about our problem."

"Are you mad?" Jolocko-lo growled. "She is a child. That is a ridiculous idea in so many ways."

"Maybe not." Leela-lo interjected. "She is almost an adult and has intelligence far passing that of most earth adults."

Toboo-lo nodded. "She is really smart."

Senoa-lo nodded. "And we're desperate. So at this point, I see talking to her about our problem as a possibility. She sent an email saying she couldn't meet with us today, but she'll be here tomorrow afternoon. Between now and then I suggest that we think on how to approach her about it."

Jolocko-lo glared at the lot of them. "I'm not comfortable with this… If we tell her, we could end up locked away in a government lab for the rest of our lives."

CHAPTER

80

EARTH

Ava was waiting on the sidewalk when Jane approached the school. "After that visit from the Men in Black yesterday, I was afraid to call you."

"That was prudent. We have ten minutes before the bell." Jane looked around. "This seems to be a safe place to talk. How was your visit from the Canadian Security Intelligence Service?"

"First, thanks for the warning. It was freaky to have two super straight, very serious G-men grilling me like I was a Russian spy. Luckily, my dad was home and he insisted on sitting in on the inquisition. They asked about my computer searches and I told them about the spy novel I'm planning to write. It was sort of fun to just make up a plot on the fly. I wove together stuff from a few action and spy movies. When they were done, dad showed them the door, then turned to me and suggested that I spend a bit more time working on the plot for my book"

Jane looked over Ava's shoulder and saw Hoop walking toward them. She envied the way he ambled through life like he belonged to the planet. She was sure he never had doubts about anything. She nodded his way so Ava looked over to see him coming.

"Good morning, Jane. And good morning Ava. From the way you two were scrunched together earnestly chatting, one might think you were plotting a revolution. Are you going to take over the school and order free pizza for everyone?"

Jane didn't know what to say.

Ava piped up. "Curses, he's on to us. This fellow is obviously smarter than he looks. We were just trying to figure out how to charge it to the principal's credit card. Any ideas?"

"No, but I'll think on it. Now, I must go do a bit of last minute cramming for a test. Unfortunately, my parents frown on low grades." He saluted and started toward the school. "Viva la revolution."

They watched him go before either spoke.

Jane leaned her head toward Ava again. "Do you think the G- men were satisfied with your explanation?"

"Yep. I think they bought it." Ava peered intently at Jane. "So why were you doing research on WMDs and poison and all sorts of weapons?"

"I'm not. And I really doubt that my mother has been researching that type of thing. She just looks at recipes, facebook and cats doing funny things. And don't ever mention the cat thing to her. She logs off the minute I enter the room. It seems to be her guilty pleasure."

Ava glanced around. "So, do you think our cute little friends were using your wifi for… nefarious purposes?"

"Could be." *Why are they researching WMDs?* "I'm going to have to have a conversation with them about this." *I hope it wasn't them.* "Is it possible that someone we don't know… some terrorist, has connected to our WiFi? You're the computer brain. Could someone do that?"

"I think that's possible. Someone might have planted a device in or near your house to connect their computer to your WiFi." Ava raised an eyebrow. "What about Mr. Fitzgerald?"

It's not him. It's our little friends. "Anything's possible." The bell rang. Jane stood up. "We had better go."

CHAPTER

81

UME IN THE JUNGLE

The jungle was wetter and hotter than Mera had expected. "A dripping leaf slapped Mera in the face. "Hey, watch it. If you're going to lead, please hold the bush 'til I'm through."

Tom turned to face her. "What?"

"You're pushing limbs aside, then letting them spring back on me."

"Oh, sorry. Are you hurt?"

"No. This place is just a series of unpleasant surprises. It's so hot. Do you know where you're going? And will we be there soon?"

"My GPS says we're almost there."

"Good. I'm tired and hungry. Can we stop for a brief rest at the next clearing?"

"Sure. There's an open area right in front of us."

Mera flopped down as soon as they stepped out of the bush. She was lying on the grass taking a drink when she spied a tree she recognized. "Look a Gabba tree. And there's some fruit lying under it. I'll get us a couple." As she stepped toward the tree, the ground collapsed from under her and she fell into a pit, screaming as she hit bottom.

Tom heard her yell and jumped up. He cautiously approached the lip of the pit and called down to her, "Are you all right?"

"I don't think anything's broken, but that really hurt. You're going to have to help me climb out of here. I think that the fruit was a lure to catch an animal. I wonder what they were trying to catch."

"Us."

"What? What do you mean 'us'?"

"There is a sign on the tree and I'm not good at reading Palalan, but I think it says to stay back from the tree because this is a trap to catch hop-hops."

"Oh!" Mera pulled herself up off the floor of the pit up and looked up at Tom. There were two Palalans standing behind him. *Oh no.*

CHAPTER

82

EARTH

Jane rushed home from school. *I need to talk to the Ume about their internet searches and talk to mom about Mr. Fitzgerald.* When she went to put her key in the lock, she found that the door was unlocked. She cautiously opened the door. Her mom was lying on the couch in the living room. *Mom never lies on the couch. She says it isn't lady-like.*

She put down her backpack. "Hi mom. Why are you home so early.? Are you all right?"

Her mom sat up. "I'm fine. I just decided to take the afternoon off. I wasn't getting much done because I kept thinking about Mr. Fitzgerald. You see, last night I sent him an email saying that I knew he was a retired teacher. And here's what he wrote back today." She held up a piece of paper. "I printed it out so you can read it."

Jane took the paper and sat down. It read:

I'm so sorry that I lied to you. I apologize. I just so wanted you to like me. Passing myself off as rich was a stupid thing to do. I realized that the day after our first date. I knew I couldn't keep up the facade, but I didn't want to take the chance of losing you. I should have seen that you aren't the type of person who needs money to make them happy. You're better than that. I apologize for assuming for one minute that you might like me better if I were wealthy. I wanted to tell you the truth, but I was afraid that you would dump me. So I kept putting it off.

And… I apologize for encouraging you to send Jane away to school. I had two reasons for wanting her gone. You see, over the years I taught many students and I got attached to quite a few of them. I helped them learn and grow and turn into real people and then they went away and grew up and disappeared from my life. I was distant with Jane because I didn't want to get attached to her and then have her disappear.

And you know that I'm divorced. We married too young. We weren't good together. We had a passionate romance that cooled off as we grew to learn that she and I agreed on nothing. Not religion, politics, money, nothing. We had a son and she took him and left. I don't know where they went. I tried to find them, but she was smart enough to make finding him impossible. I was heartbroken and vowed to never again let another child into my life. So I was being selfish when I asked you to send Jane away. I didn't want to get attached only to have her go away.. I'm so sorry."

"Whatever you think of me, just know I love you. I hope you can forgive me and I hope you will give me another chance.

Jane handed the paper back to her mother and sighed. "So mom, do you forgive him or dump him?

"I don't know. How do you feel about him wanting to send you off to a school?"

"I admit that I was upset. Now that I understand where he was coming from, it makes more sense. But you didn't do it. And that's the important thing. Even with pressure from a man you love... You do love him? Right?

Her mom nodded. "Except for his lies, he's a good person and I think I want him in my life. But, I'm not sure. He'd have to come clean and never lie to me again. And he would have to accept you as part of the package. I'm not ready to let you go. Not yet... not until University."

"Thanks mom." Jane stepped over to her mom and pulled her up off the couch and wound her arms around her. A tear ran down Jane's cheek as they hugged.

CHAPTER

83

UME IN THE JUNGLE

Tom turned around to see two big Palalans standing behind him. His first thought was to run, but he quickly realized he couldn't leave Mera. He was tempted to ask them to help get her out of the pit. *I can't let them know that we can talk.* So, he just jumped up and down, pointing to Mera and squealing.

Kebeck reached down and picked him up with his two lower arms. He held him out away from his body as he turned toward his son, Prigo and asked, "Do you know if these little animals bite?"

Prigo shrugged his shoulders. "I do not know. I have never even got close to one. Many times I have seen them hopping around in the bush, but always from a distance. Why did you pick it up?"

Tom decided to keep still and just listen.

Kebeck paused. "I am going to tell you a national secret, but you must swear to tell no one."

"About hop-hops? These little animals? Are they planning to take over the planet?"

Kebeck put Tom on the ground and loosed his grip, but still held on to one arm. "We have discovered several cities in the ice mountains and the creatures there look like hop-hops."

"You are kidding. No one can live there."

"These cities are in valleys around natural hot springs. They have agriculture and industries. We have been doing flyovers with our space ships. We need to know more about these beings. Since they look like hop-hops, it was decided that we should capture some hop-hops to see if they are similar to the mountain creatures."

Prigo was stunned. "Wow. Interesting stuff. So this is top secret?"

"For now it is 'need to know' and since you are helping me capture these two. Now you need to know. So while I hold on to this little one, will you please get the other one out of the pit?"

"No problem." Prigo jumped down into the pit and reached out to Mera.

She looked up at Tom with pleading eyes. Never had she been so scared. She wanted to scream and yell, "Don't touch me." But for the sake of her people she only squealed as he reached out for her. She batted at his hands, but there was no way to avoid his four big hands.

CHAPTER

84

EARTH

After a quick supper, Jane went up to her room to change. She told her mom that she was going into the woods. "Fine. Go see your trees. I'm going to my room to lie down for a bit." Jane went a little way into the forest, then circled back to the shed at her neighbor's house. She felt so relieved now that she no longer had to worry about being sent off to a school in Alberta. For the first time in her life she was finally beginning to feel comfortable at school. She knew that she would never be as relaxed as Hoop or Ava. All her life she had felt like she was being watched and that people were waiting for her to do something wrong. Maybe Ava was right when she said, "People don't really care about you or what you do. They only care about themselves. So as long as you don't step on their toes… no problem."

As Jane approached the shed, she glanced around. Then she tapped on the shed door. Three taps, a pause, then two more taps.

The door opened an inch and Senoa-lo looked out. "Come in." Before Jane could sit down, Toboo-lo was asking questions. "We have been trying to understand humans and we are confused. From what we see and read on the internet, being sexy is a good thing and a bad thing. Does not sexy refer to being open to copulation? It seems that your people want to appear to be ready for procreation, but do not want to actually do it."

Leela-lo jumped in. "And is sexy part of beauty? Is that part of being seen as beautiful?"

Jane didn't know what to say. She froze for a minute, then turned to Senoa-lo. "I am… too young and too inexperienced to be an authority on this topic. I will see if I can find something appropriate for you to read. It's a confusing topic that psychologists have discussed for years. Wow! That certainly wasn't what I came here to discuss."

"We did not mean to make you uncomfortable. We were just curious about your human customs. It is not important. What do you need to discuss?" Senoa-lo asked.

"Well… someone has been using our WiFi to do research on weapons, especially weapons of mass destruction. And some government officials came to our house inquiring about this."

Senoa-lo jumped up. "Do we need to quickly gather our stuff and move to another location?"

"No, that's not necessary. I told them that Ava and I were doing research for a book."

Senoa-lo sighed. "Again, your ability to quickly invent a lie has saved us."

"So it is you? You've been doing the research on weapons of mass destruction?"

Senoa-lo looked down at her feet. "Yes. We need weapons… big weapons."

Jane's demeanor changed from uncomfortable to angry. "You lied to me. You said you were studying energy sources."

Senoa-lo buried her face in her hands. "We had to." Senoa-lo sighed and looked up at Jane. "When we first met, I didn't know if I could trust you. But now I will tell you the truth. Our mission is to research and find out how to make a big weapon, a WMD."

"I don't understand. How can you have the technology to fly to another planet and not have the technology to develop weapons?"

"In the past, we never needed big weapons. Now we do. We fear that our neighbors, the Palalans, will kill us." Senoa-lo ran her hands through her head fur in exasperation. *Now is not the time to admit to her that we don't have space ships and that we stowed away on a Palalan ship.* She stopped pulling on her fur and put her hands down by her side.

"I must explain… Our planet has a hot tropical area near the equator. The Palalans live there. Far north of this is a vast area of ice mountains. In many of valleys of the ice mountains, hot springs allowed our people, the Ume, to evolve. The tropical jungle and mountains are separated by a dry desert. The Palalans are what earth people would call, 'cold-blooded'. You know what that means?"

"They are poikilothermic. Their body temperature tends to fluctuate with and is similar to or slightly higher than the temperature of their environment."

"Right. So they never leave their tropic zone."

"And you live in the cold mountains around the hot springs. Then you must be homeotherm."

"Yes. Being warm-blooded enables us to live in the frozen mountains near the poles."

"So if the Palalans never leave the tropics, how are they a threat to you?"

Senoa-lo took a breath. "Here on earth all of your poikilothermic animals are primitive. Not so on our planet. The Palalans have four hands, two feet and are covered with scales. They are somewhat similar to some of your poikilothermic animals, but, they are very sophisticated and more technically advanced than our people or you humans.

Jane sat spellbound, trying to imagine the scaly four-armed beings Senoa-lo had just described. "Extraordinary."

Senoa-lo patiently waited for Jane to absorb all she had said. Finally Jane looked back down at Senoa-lo. "So they live in the tropics and you live in the frozen mountains. Since they are poikilothermic, how can they travel in the icy areas? And why do you feel threatened by them?"

Leela-lo jumped up. "Because they have recently become aware of our existence and they have the technology to make suits enabling them to travel in cold areas. We have seen them."

Jane looked at Leela-lo, "But from what you say, they have done nothing to make you think they will harm you. Have they?"

"No, but they are much bigger than us."

Jane looked off into the distance. *She's right. Big animals usually dominate smaller ones.* "So?"

"We are afraid of them and we have come to earth to study weapons." *I almost said 'a weapon of mass destruction.* "Our mission is to access the earth internet in order to research weapons. We need a weapon. Now that the Palalans, are aware of us, we feel threatened by them. We don't have time to develop our own weapons. Earth, especially the U.S. makes and sells many weapons. So we came here to research your weapons so that we can send the plans for a big weapon to our scientists at home."

Jane looked puzzled. "How can you get weapons plans off the internet? I would think that those things are encrypted secrets that are only available to corporations and the government."

Senoa-lo nodded toward Jolocko-lo. "We have a computer expert with us, Jolocko-lo, who can access anything on any computer."

"So, you see," Leela-lo explained, "we are just here to do internet research. We will just be sending home information."

"But you want to build a WMD. What have the other people, the Palalans, really done to make you think you need a major weapon?"

"They have done nothing but discover our existence, yet that is enough. For centuries, we have kept our existence secret from the Palalans."

"How? If you are both sophisticated societies, why were they not aware of you long ago?"

"The Palalans could not travel to our mountains because it is too cold for them, but we could go into their jungle. Centuries ago the Palalans were more advanced than our people, but we made up for that by observing their advances and copying their technology. Over the years, we continued to send people into the jungle to observe and report back to our scientists and engineers. Because we are small and furry, they saw us as just another cute jungle animal. Recently, the Palalans have become aware of our cities in the mountains. Now, they know that we are more than harmless dumb animals."

"We are frightened by the Palalans," Leela-lo added. "They are huge, almost as big as you. And it is possible that they might destroy us. I doubt that they were pleased to find that we have been sneaking around stealing their technology for centuries. So you can see that only by having access to the internet here do we have any hope of learning something that could save our people if the Palalans become aggressive."

Jane looked puzzled. "I still don't understand what makes you think that they might want to attack your people? Have they threatened you?"

"Not yet," Jolocko-lo interjected. "But… "

Leela-lo interrupted. "We have studied the history of earth and several other planets. When there is a weak society near a stronger one, the stronger usually conquers the weaker. What reason do we have to think they will not do the same?"

85

PALALA

Prigo climbed out of the pit with Tom held in his left arms and looked at his father, "What are we supposed to do with them?

Kebeck thought for a second. "For now, I think we should take them to my house. It's getting late and soon it will be dark. The Animal Studies Department had been assigned the task of capturing them. I will contact them and see where we should take them tomorrow."

As they walked the path toward Kebeck's house, Prigo examined the little creature in his arms. "So these little guys have built towns in the ice mountains. You are talking about primitive huts with gardens, right?"

"No. They built real cities. They have vehicles and houses and industries. They seem to have a society comparable to ours, just arranged differently."

Prigo stared at the little hop-hop he was carrying. "How could they do all that without speech?"

"Maybe they can speak," his father replied. "Either these two are just primitive cousins of the ice mountain beings or they are spies from the mountains playing the part of dumb creatures. That is what we need to find out."

"Oh."

As soon as they were inside Kebeck's home, Prigo asked. "Where do you plan to keep them for the night?"

"I guess we can just close both doors and just make them a bed for the night. I was hoping you would stay tonight to help me keep an eye on them."

"Of course I will stay." Prigo looked around. "No way can those little guys reach a window. But just to be safe, we can take turns sleeping."

They laid some towels in a corner and put the hop-hops down on the towels. Mera and Tom looked at each other for a second, then Mera sat down and motioned for Tom to do the same.

Mera watched the two Palalans chat as they took fruit off of the shelves and ate. *I hope Tom has sense enough to keep quiet. I can see by his face that he wants to say something to me.* Mera caught Tom's eye and shook her head, "*No.*"

Tom glared at her, then reclined on the towels, keeping an eye on the two Palalans.

Prigo pulled himself up on the sleeping platform. "So the plan is to take these two little hop-hops to the Animal Studies Department in the morning?"

"Probably. I am waiting for their reply."

"And what will they do to these hop-hops to see if they can talk?"

"I do not know." Kebeck paused as he was starting to bite the fruit in his hand. "In general, we do not harm animals. It is not our way. So I guess they will just observe them."

"Really? The Animal Studies people are the ones who are called to kill dangerous animals when they threaten an area. I don't feel good about this."

"They only kill animals if they are a threat to people in the area. They usually just capture dangerous animals and move them to areas away from people. But, you have a point. We just asked the Animal Studies guys to capture one. We did not discuss what we might do to determine if they are primitive or verbal."

Mera carefully examined the two Palalans to see if they were watching her. They seemed to be looking at each other and ignoring her. She slid over beside Tom and nudged him. She had a paper in her hand holding it between them so only he could see it. The paper said, 'Do not talk.' He looked at her, but didn't look down at the paper. Then he shrugged his shoulders.

Mera sighed. *Is he ever dense.*

Mera was still staring at Tom when Kebeck took a knife off the shelf. Kebeck glanced over at the two Ume, then said to his son. "A few jabs with this knife might help us find out if they can talk."

Both the Ume stiffened, their ears stood up, and their eyes became as big as saucers.

Prigo jumped up. "Dad! You would never do such a thing. What is wrong with you?"

Kebeck smiled. "These little guys probably do not realize that we have very good puerperal vision. I have been watching them as we talked. Of course I will not hurt them. But now we know that they understand Palalan. When they heard me threaten to use the knife, they both reacted." He put the knife back on the shelf.

Prigo and Kebeck walked over to the two Ume.

Kebeck held out his hands in the usual Palalan greeting. "I welcome you to my house. Would you like something to eat?"

Keeping his head still, Tom lowered his eyes so he was looking at the feet of the Palalans. *What should I do? I wish I could confer with Mera. If she'd just look at me and give me a signal.*

Mera sat perfectly still, acting like she hadn't heard Kebeck. *What to do? If we keep up this act, will they take us to someone who will hurt us? Will the Palalans ever let us go or just imprison us forever? He saw us react. What would my dad do?*

Mera stood up, looked Kebeck in the face and said, in Palalan "I would like a little piece of that red fruit, if you don't mind."

Prigo stepped closer to the Ume. "You can talk! Hop-hops can talk. That is amazing."

Kebeck took the knife off the shelf and cut the red fruit into small pieces, put it in a bowl and placed it on the towel between the Ume.

Tom looked at Mera, shrugged his shoulders and ate a piece of the fruit. "Thank you. This is very good."

Kebeck sat down on the floor by the Ume and motioned for his son to do the same. "We have a lot to talk about."

86

EARTH

The sun was setting and Jane snuggled down into her coat as she waited for Ava. She didn't usually sit on her back porch at this time of year, but since her mom's room was on the other side of the house, this seemed like the best place for a private talk. Her computer was on the table beside her. *I should check on the Ume, but the WMD thing disturbs me. I'll email them after I talk to Ava.*

"What's up?" Ava's sudden appearance in front of her roused Jane from her scramble of thoughts. "Before you start on whatever we're supposed to talk about and before I forget, I have to tell you that you were successful with making a favourable impression with Alice Thompson. I overheard her tell one of her friends that she thinks you're not as odd as people say. Now that's not exactly a glowing recommendation, but it's a step in a positive direction." Ava plopped down in the chair beside Jane. "I'm curious, which of the social girl rules did you use on her?"

"Number four. We were in line at the cafeteria and I just said, 'How are you?' And she said,'Really?' So I said, 'Yeah, you look a bit down.' So then she dumped a long story on me about her mother's health and I just tried to look concerned and listened. Then she wound it up by patting me on the shoulder and saying, 'Really, you're a nice person.' Then she tromped off to join her usual group."

"Fantastic. And, did you look her in the eye while she talked?"

"Close. I looked at her nose. She didn't seem to notice."

"That's great. Now… "

Jane interrupted. "We have a serious problem that needs our attention, so as much as I appreciate your help with my social life, let's talk about that later."

"Okay." Ava straightened up. "Your mom's not sending you to that school, is she?"

"No."

"Is something happening with Mr. Fitzgerald? Did he dump her?

"No, she's giving him a second chance. They're still entranced with each other. Please, just let me talk."

Ava leaned back in her seat and made a zipped lip motion.

"The Ume told me the real purpose of their visit here."

Ava leaned forward and opened her mouth to speak, but realizing that Jane was glaring at her, reconsidered and just pressed her lips together.

"They are here to research weapons of mass destruction. And, they plan to send instructions about making the WMDs back to their home planet."

"You mean like atomic bombs?" Now, Ava was sitting on the edge of her seat.

"Yes, but fortunately, their planet doesn't have uranium, so that type of weapon isn't a possibility. But, they are desperate to find some kind of big weapon that their people can build. They are terrified of their neighbors, the Palalans." Jane continued to fill Ava in on the details. As she did so, her computer buzzed indicating that she had a message. She glanced at the computer screen. "It's the Ume. I think it would be prudent to see why they are messaging me.

Ava pulled a water bottle out of her backpack and took a drink while Jane scanned the message.

"Oh no." Jane handed Ava her computer and jumped up. "A more immediate problem has superseded the WMD problem. Leela-lo has been stung by a bee and is swelling up. We had better rush over there. Because of her size and alien physiology she could develop anaphylaxis. I'll run inside and get our first aid kit. While I get the kit, please look on the internet on the Mayo Clinic site for treatment suggestions for bee stings."

Jane was back down in minutes. As Jane rushed out the door with the kit, Ava looked up from the computer. "This is serious. This says her throat could swell up and cut off her air. Let's go."

When they got to the shed, Leela-lo was lying in the middle of the floor with all the other Ume surrounding her. Senoa-lo was holding her hand and Leela-lo was gasping for breath. One arm was swollen. "I don't know what to do. We have no flying creatures on our planet. I heard a noise, a buzzing, so I opened the door just a little to see what was outside and it just flew in. We all jumped away from it as it came near us and Jolocko-lo swung at it with some papers. It did not seem to like that. So we backed into the corners. Then it buzzed over to Leela-lo and did something to her arm. Then Jolocko-lo opened the door a bit, thinking to escape outside, and it flew out. Will Leela-lo be all right?"

Jane and Ava squeezed in beside Leela-lo. Jane touched her arm. It was twice it's normal size. "This is bad. If we don't do something, she could die."

Senoa-lo jumped up. "We didn't know that your flying creatures could kill us. I have studied earth for many years and never came across this information. Are all the flying animals lethal or only the buzzing kind?"

Jane reached out a hand to Senoa-lo. "For most earth people, a bee sting is just a painful inconvenience, but for some, if they are not given medication in time, they can die from it. Since she is from another planet, and having different physiology, I have no idea what the sting will do to her. But swelling up and trouble breathing are symptoms that are normal allergic reactions for earth people. So all we can do is try an earth remedy on her."

Jane could see that Leela-lo was having a hard time breathing. "We have to get her medical help now." She turned toward Senoa-lo. "My mom will know what to do; she was a nurse and she keeps lots of basic medications in the house. Senoa-lo, please let me take her to my mom? Otherwise, I think she might die."

Senoa-lo turned to Jolocko-lo. "What should we do?"

Jolocko-lo stood up. "It's better that she is alive and in some science lab than dead. Jane should take her to her mother and not tell about the rest of us. It seems to be Leela-lo's only chance."

Jane gathered Leela-lo in her arms and handed her to Ava. "Tuck her under your coat and take her to our kitchen. I'll run upstairs and get mom and her big med kit." She and Ava rushed toward the house.

CHAPTER

87

EARTH

Jane rushed into the house and started up the stairs. Her mom was standing at the top of the staircase. "Jane, you're too old to be running in the house. Nothing is that important."

Jane stopped dead. "I… umm… we have a medical emergency. An animal… a rabbit was stung by a bee and I think his throat is closing. Please get your med-bag and help me save the little guy."

Her mom just looked at her for a second then relented. "All right, bring it in the kitchen and I'll see what I can do."

Jane and Ava had Leela-lo laid out on the kitchen table on a towel when Jane's mom came in. "That's not a rabbit. What is it?"

Jane's eyes scanned the kitchen and fell on their Maytag dishwasher. "Ava tells me that it's a vaytag. They live in the jungles of South America. I guess someone had one here as a pet and it got away. Anyway, I saw a bee sting him and he's having a bad reaction. Mom, please save the poor little thing."

"Of course. He's a cute little fellow." She rooted through her bag and brought out an injection pen. Leela-lo was struggling to breathe. She adjusted the pen and stuck it in Leela-lo's neck. "Hopefully, that will do it. I don't remember seeing an animal like this one before, but there was a little animal in the zoo that was very similar." Jane's mom stepped back and watched as Leela-lo's breathing improved. "Jane, you really shouldn't pick up strange animals. He could have bit you. And we don't know if he's rabid. Go get that old bird cage out of the basement. He seems to be breathing better now. We can keep it in the cage until it gets better. I want you to call the Humane Society in the morning and see if anyone has reported losing a… ? What did you call it?"

Jane was rubbing her thumbs and lost in thought.

"It's a vaytag, a rare South American vaytag." Ava spoke up. "If you'd like, I can take it home with me and take care of everything. No worries."

"That's very nice of you Ava, but let's keep him here for the rest of tonight so I can keep an eye on his recovery. Tomorrow, we need to find the owner. Someone is probably very worried about their little pet."

Ava nudged Jane. "Get your computer and let's go up to your room and look to see if anyone has put out a notice about a lost vaytag."

Leela-lo woke up lying on a towel in a cage on the floor of Jane's kitchen. *Oh, that was scary.* Her hands went to her throat. It felt raw, but she could breathe normally now. She stood up and looked around. The cage was locked with a simple slide latch. *That will be easy to open. This cage must be designed for primitive animals without hands. Should I open it and find my way back to our camp or wait for Jane to get me out of here?* She sat back down. *I'd better just rest for a while. I almost died. I am so worn out.*

As soon as the door closed in Jane's room, Jane grabbed Ava's shoulders, "What do we do now? My mom's a very smart lady. We need to get Leela-lo out of the house and away from my mom before she figures out that Leela-lo is not a vaytag."

"And that there is no such thing as a 'vaytag'. You're getting really good at inventing plausible lies. I saw you look at the dishwasher before you made up that name. Quick thinking."

"So, tell me, have you thought of further prevarications that will enable us in getting Leela-lo away from my mom and out of the house?"

"Yes. It seems that vaytags are from the high chilly mountains of South America. Vaytags are not accustomed to heat. So we will suggest to your mom that the animal will be more comfortable if the cage is kept on the back porch tonight. Then, late tonight, after midnight, the little vaytag can escape from the cage and run away home."

Jane nodded. "That should work. I will email Senoa-lo that Leela-lo seems to be good now and to expect her late tonight. Earlier, you said you would need to go home for supper. Since we cannot be seen talking to the vaytag, I'll write a note for Leela-lo and you can slip it to her when you go down to leave."

Jane plopped down on her bed. "Fortunately, we have a distraction tonight. Mr. Fitzgerald is coming by to take mom to dinner. It will be their first face to face meeting since the apology letter. I'm sure every iota of my mom's brain is totally occupied with thoughts about this date. A flying saucer could land on the lawn and she wouldn't notice."

88

PALALA

The two Ume and the two Palalans sat in a circle and chatted as they ate. "Oh, that was good. I was so hungry." Tom grumbled between bites. "Wandering around in the jungle, I didn't know which fruits were edible, so I haven't eaten all day."

"I got that impression when you gobbled down that first bowl of Kimas." Kebeck picked up two empty bowls and stacked them beside him. "If your stomach is happy now, I suggest that we satisfy our brains. I would like to know… "

Prigo held up a hand. "Wait. I smell the odor of a female approaching our door."

"Who?"

"I think it is… it is Sheme." He turned to his father. "Are you expecting Sheme?"

"No. She is the last person I would expect. She cannot see these little people. She hates me. She will get me in trouble. I must step outside to greet her." He looked at the two Ume. "Please say nothing while I talk with her. She has excellent hearing. She may have already heard us talking."

Kebeck stepped out the door and closed it behind him. *I must tell her something, but I cannot lie or my throat will turn red and then…* Kebeck quickly bent down and started pulling weeds with all four hands.

He looked up as Sheme approached, then put all the weeds in a pile and stood up. "I wish you clear water, my friend." He brushed his hands together to get the dirt off.

Sheme just looked at him, then looked at his door. "Why is your door closed? You never close your doors. Even though I always tell you that you should keep them closed because all sorts of animals can get in, you always insist on keeping them open."

"Oh well, maybe I have decided that you are right. *I am not lying. I said 'maybe.'* There are appropriate times for closing the doors and keeping animals from running in and out of my house. It is a good thing that I have a friend like you to help me manage my house. And, you might note that I am pulling up weeds, as you had suggested."

Sheme threw her upper hands up in exasperation. "I am not used to having you agree with me about much of anything. You almost made me forget why I am here."

'Yes. That question is also on my mind. I would be courteous and invite you in for a rest and food, but I am expected at a meeting with my son and some others." *Still not lying.*

"Kebeck, I saw you and Prigo holding on to two hop-hops earlier today. I know that you are hiding something from me. Otherwise, your doors would be wide open, as usual. I am saddened that you no longer trust me."

"You were furious when I did not agree to have a child with you. I did not know if our friendship was still valid after that."

"It still stands. You asked why I am here. I came to tell you that I am no longer cross with you. I will find another to share a child with. Our long friendship can withstand a bout of anger. It does not melt away when things get hot. You do have a point about our different attitudes toward certain things."

Kebeck reached out and touched her arm. "I am glad that we remain friends. I would miss you if we could no longer talk and laugh together."

Sheme smiled and glanced toward the little pile of limp plants. "Suddenly, you see the need to weed your yard? That is not you. For years you have touted that 'All plants are good plants.' So, what are you hiding in your house?"

Kebeck pushed the door open. "Come meet my new friends."

CHAPTER

89

UME ON EARTH

Streaks of afternoon sunlight shot through the shed. Dust motes danced in the light. Worry had made everyone unusually quiet. Toboo-lo looked up from his computer. His face was beaming with joy. "Leela-lo is all right. Jane's mom was able to save her."

Senoa-lo let out a sigh. "Fantastic! That's a relief. Did Jane say how she plans to get Leela-lo out of the house and safe from government scientists?"

Jolocko-lo also sighed and put his head in his hands. "That is the next problem."

"But," Toboo-lo announced, "they have a plan and Jane says we should expect her sometime after midnight."

Before they could react, Leela-lo looked up from her computer and said. "There is a private message coming in from home for you, Senoa-lo."

"I hope it's good news." Senoa-lo opened her computer and read the message while everyone else watched. A frown froze on her face. She looked up, her eyes found Jolocko-lo and she paused.

Jolocko-lo stared back at her. "What?"

"Your daughter is missing. They think she went into the Palalan jungle with some rebels."

"She did what? Mera did what?"

"I am sending the report to your computer. They have photos of her and a young male entering the jungle"

Everyone was silent while Jolocko-lo read the report.

"This cannot be right." Jolocko-lo yelled, "She is too smart to do something this stupid." He banged his fist on a carton, almost knocking his computer off, then jumped up and proceeded to pace back and forth.

Senoa-lo and Toobo-lo decided to ignore him for the moment, eyes on their computers, giving him time to settle down. After ten minutes of pacing, he returned to his seat and sat staring into space. Senoa-lo came over and put a hand on his shoulder. "There is nothing you can do."

"Except worry."

"As you said, your daughter is very smart. She will survive this. They are sending two experienced jungle operatives in to look for them. I am not going to say 'Do not worry', but it will hurt less if you concentrate on the work in front of you, instead of letting your imagination wander."

The room grew darker as the sun sank toward the horizon. They turned on the lantern and continued to work.

CHAPTER

90

EARTH

Ava peeked in the living room before entering. Jane's mom was was standing in the middle of the room, with her head tilted to one side, holding a photo of Mr. Fitzgerald.

"Hi Mrs. Thomas, I've got to go home, but before I go I thought I should tell you about what I found on the internet about vaytags. It seems that because they live in high cold mountains, they need to be kept in the cold. Heat is really bad for them. Do you think we should move the cage on the porch for the night?”

“Oh, what did you say Ava? My mind was scattered in a dozen different directions.”

“I was wondering if the vaytag wouldn’t be better off on the porch. They live in cold climates and don’t do well in heat. Do you want me to move the cage to the porch?”

“Of course. He’s out of danger and breathing normally now.” She glanced at the photo of Mr. Fitzgerald, then tucked it away in her purse. “Whatever is best for the little fellow.”

As Ava moved the cage to the porch, she dropped a little note in the cage. The note said, ‘When the moon is high in the sky, it should be about midnight. That would be the best time for you to get out of the cage and go back to the shed.’ Then Ava nodded to Leela-lo and headed home.

Leela-lo sat in her cage on the dark porch watching the moon as it rose in the sky. The hours seemed like days. *When the moon gets a bit higher, I’ll make my escape.* Leela-lo heard the screen door close as someone came out on the porch. Her nose told her it was a human. *I was wondering when Jane would come to check on me. I heard her mother leave with her male friend hours ago.* Leela-lo sniffed the air. *And I smell something good: cheese.*

Jane’s mom had come home, wandered through the house in the dark and stopped in the kitchen to grab a chunk of cheese, a couple of crackers and a drink. Then she strolled out to the back porch to sit in her favourite thinking chair and nibble on the cheese and crackers. Her date with Mr. Fitzgerald had gone well. She had sat patiently listening as he apologized again and again. *Will I ever feel the affection and excitement toward him that I felt last week? He’s not perfect. I’m not either.* She still enjoyed his company, but found that she felt a bit distrustful toward him. *I guess I'll have to give it some time.* She sighed and took a bite of the cheese.

"Jane, I smell cheese. I'd love some cheese. Someone put some dried pellets in here for me. I tried one. They're awful. Cheese would be wonderful."

Mrs. Thomas jumped up out of the chair and looked around. The moon was bright enough that she could plainly see that there was no one there. The only things on the porch were two chairs and the rabbit cage. She moved closer to the cage and peered at the little animal inside it.

"I think it's almost midnight, so if you'll unlatch the cage, I'll head back to our camp. I would open it, but your mom added a twisted wire to the latch before she left for her date. So you can do it easier from your side. That cheese smells so good. Can I take some back for the others?"

"You talk!" Mrs. Thomas exclaimed. "That's not possible."

"Oh no… you're not Jane."

"You talk!"

"And you're not Ava."

Jane was lying on her bed, finishing a paper for her lit class, when she heard a yell from the back porch. *What was that?* Then she heard a second yell. It sounded like, "You talk." It sounded like her mother's voice. She pushed her computer to one side and leapt up. *Oh no.* She rushed down the stairs.

By the time she got to the porch, her mom had turned on the porch light and was on her knees staring at the Ume in the cage. She looked up at Jane. "Did you know that this animal can talk?" She looked at the Ume then back at Jane. "Of course you did. He said your name." She stood up and moved toward Jane. "You have some explaining to do, young lady."

Jane's mind was churning. *If I continue to say it's an earth animal, Leela-lo will still end up in a lab. But what will mom do if I tell her the truth? I wish Ava were here right now. What to do?*

Jane could feel her mother's eyes drilling into her. "Well?" Then her mom looked back at Leela-lo. "You might as well have this last little bit cheese. I've lost my appetite and you say you're hungry." She held the cheese up to the cage bars and Leela-lo slowly took it.

"Thank you."

"You're welcome." Her mom sighed. "Jane, explain to me how it is that I am having a polite exchange with a small furry animal?"

"It's complicated. I… "

"So start at the beginning. Where is he from and what is this about the others?"

Oh no! Leela-lo had mentioned the others. "Mom, I think it prudent that you and I go sit in the living room and then I will explain everything."

"I'm fine here."

"No. You need to be sitting for this. And I need a minute. Can I get you a cup of tea or something?"

"I don't like the sound of this, but I'll do it your way. A glass of wine would be nice. But hurry. My imagination is working overtime."

Jane went into the kitchen and stood with her forehead against the cool refrigerator door. *What should I tell her? I don't want to do anything that would put the little Umes in danger. She's not going to believe that they're talking earth animals. She won't fall for that.* Jane selected a crystal glass and poured the wine. Instead of the half glass her mom had taught her to pour, she almost filled the glass.

She laid out a coaster and set the glass on the table beside her mom. Then she perched on the couch across from her. *I still haven't decided what to say.* "Can I get you anything else?"

"Jane, you're stalling." She took a sip of the wine. "Quit trying to decide what to tell me and just tell me the truth."

"You're not going to believe this… "

"Try me."

"Last week, I was in the woods and heard voices. That's when I found them." Jane looked down at her hands and found that she was rubbing her thumbs together. "Mom, they're from another planet; they're aliens. Not bad aliens, but nice ones, just here to do research."

Her mom took another quick sip of the wine. Then she placed it on the coaster and looked up at the ceiling. "Aliens… ? Aliens from outer space?"

"Is this some kind of joke? Is Ava hiding in the bushes with a microphone?"

"No. They're really aliens. I can bring Leela-lo in here and you can talk to her." Jane jumped up. "Actually, That's a good idea. Wait here."

The wine glass was almost empty when Jane came back with Leela-lo in her arms. She placed Leela-lo on the couch beside her. "Leela-lo, this is my mother, Mrs. Thomas. Mom, meet Leela-lo."

Leela-lo stood up on the couch and bowed. "It is nice to meet you. Again, I thank you for the cheese." Leela-lo straightened up, then looked down at her feet. "I hope I am not upsetting you by standing on your couch, I have read that it is not acceptable behaviour to stand on seats."

Jane's mother turned white. "You are talking. Wow!" Her eyes glazed over for a minute. Then she stared at Leela-lo "Uh, about standing on the couch, that's the general rule. But we make exceptions for visitors from other planets." She grabbed the wine glass and downed the rest of it. "How... ? How is it that you speak perfect English?"

"We have devised methods of watching your televisions and other communication apparatuses from my planet. I have spent many years studying earth. I am flattered that you call my command of the language perfect. It is only sufficient."

"Mom, you're a bit pale. Do you need to go lie down? We can continue this conversation later or tomorrow."

She glanced at the empty wine glass in her hand. "No, I'm all right. Really. This is amazing and thrilling, but quite unexpected. Leela-lo, do you mind answering a few more questions?"

"No problem, but we should contact the others. They're expecting me and they will be worried."

Jane bounced up from the couch. "I'll run up stairs and send them a quick message. Just, please, pause this conversation until I get back. *I need to hear everything.* "All right?"

Mrs. Thomas stood up and headed toward the kitchen. "I'll just get some more wine." She turned back before she got to the door. "Leela-lo, would you like something? Juice, water, or cheese and crackers?"

"Some more cheese and crackers would be very nice."

"No problem." *I'm talking to an alien and serving him snacks. This is unreal, but it feels real. If it's a dream, it's an odd one and I want to see where it goes.*

In minutes they were all back in the living room with wine and cheese and crackers. As Leela-lo munched away on her cheese and crackers, Jane's mom searched her thoughts for her next question. "So Leela-lo... how did you get here? And where is your space ship? But wait, first tell me if you are male or female. Your name sounds feminine. Or do you have two sexes? Or three or four?

"Just two, and I am a female. I will be fifty of your years soon, old enough to vote."

Jane interrupted, "How long do your people usually live?"

"Most live to about three hundred of your earth years."

"About the space ship?" Mrs. Thomas asked.

Leela-lo paused. "That's complicated. We do not have space ships. We… "

Jane looked puzzled. "Then how did you get to Earth?"

Leela-lo glanced down and smiled a guilty smile. "We sneaked on one of the Palalan ships."

Jane rushed her words together. "They were here? Are they here now? Where are they?"

"They're gone. They only came for one night. They were here for Halloween. Your costume holiday enables them to move amidst you for a few hours. They mean no harm to Earth. They come to study you and for the experience."

Jane's mouth dropped open. "Wow! What a great idea. I might have given candy to one of your alien friends. What do they look like?"

"They were in costumes. You could not have seen them. They are about nine times our height, but not as tall as adult humans. They have four hands and two legs. They are covered with green, gray or brown scales."

Jane's mom put her head back and closed her eyes. "There are two different types of aliens visiting earth? Unbelievable."

"You don't believe me?"

"No. I believe you. Well… I think I do. That's just an expression when something is so amazing."

"Oh. I find that your English has many expressions or phrases that do not mean what they seem to mean."

"Leela-lo?" Jane put a hand up. "I'm confused. You say you sneaked on a Palalan ship to get here. So the Palalans didn't know you were on their ship?

"Right. We hid in a storage compartment."

"How are you going to get back to your home planet?"

Leela-lo sighed. "We don't know if we will ever get back. Our mission is of ultimate importance so we came knowing that after we send our people the data they need, we will probably remain here until we die."

Jane's mom was puzzled. "What data could be that important? What knowledge is worth a kamikaze trip to a foreign planet?

Leela-lo was silent. *I have said too much.*

"Why are you here?"

Leela-lo stood up. "I did not mean to be impolite, but I think it would be appropriate for you to continue this discussion with our leader, Senoa-lo."

CHAPTER

91

UME ON EARTH

Senoa-lo and Jolocko-lo sat quietly chatting while Toboo-lo slept in the back of the shed. "He sleeps while we worry," Jolocko-lo said. "I know that my worry changes nothing, but I find it difficult to sleep while my daughter is in danger."

"I understand." Senoa-lo glanced at the door. "I wish Leela-lo would get here so that we can relax." Senoa-lo's computer beeped and both of them rushed over to it.

"It's Jane. She wants me to come to her house and meet her mother."

"Meet her mother? It was Jane's intention to keep our existence a secret from her mother. Something has gone wrong. Is Leela-lo all right? Do you want me to go with you?"

Toboo-lo woke up. "What's happening? Is something wrong?"

"Yes. I just got a message from Jane. She says Leela-lo is unharmed and safe, but she wants me to come to her house and meet her mother."

Toboo-lo rubbed his face, "I should go with you. I think… "

Senoa-lo waved a dismissive hand at him. "You're not awake enough to think anything. Give me a minute. We need a plan. If this is a trap set up by her mother, then if I go alone, there will still be two of you to continue the mission. As our leader, I must think of the worst that can happen and devise a strategy.

Having one of you with me will accomplish nothing. It's not far to the house and it is very late, so most humans are in bed. I will go alone, but I will take my charger. Stay close to your computers. If I don't contact you in thirty minutes, leave here."

Jolocko-lo said, "I'll pack up two computers and some essentials in case we have to flee quickly. If this is a trap and you escape, look for us at the tree where we stayed when we first arrived."

They gathered around Senoa-lo and hugged her before she headed out the door. Senoa-lo picked up her charger. "I hope this is just a friendly meeting with Jane's mother, but we have to be prepared for the worse."

CHAPTER

92

PALALA

Kebeck opened the door and motioned for Sheme to enter his house. She stepped inside, but stopped as soon as she saw the two Ume. "Why have you captured two hop-hops?"

Prigo stood up and greeted Sheme with outstretched hands. "How nice to see you. Can I get you something to eat or drink?"

Sheme continued to stare at the two Ume as she pulled her clay cup out of the satchel hanging on her shoulder. She held it out to Prigo. "Some cool water would be nice."

"Have a seat. We were just starting to talk with our new friends about their home in the ice mountains."

Mera waved and said, "Hello."

"What? Hop-hops can talk? The ceramic cup fell to the floor, making a loud crash. Everyone jumped.

"I am so sorry." Prigo reached down and picked up the largest piece and examined it. "Was it very old?"

"It was my mother's cup." Sheme just stared at the pieces on the floor. "It carried many memories." She took a big breath. "But feel no guilt. I am the one who let it drop."

Tom whispered to Mera, "Why are they so upset about a broken cup?"

Mera whispered back. "Where was your brain when we studied Palalan customs in school? Is there nothing but hair and water on top of your shoulders. Each Palalan has a cup that he uses throughout his life. Many times they are passed down from parent to child and are very old. That one was probably at least three or four hundred years old.

"Oh."

Sheme sighed. "As I was taught, I must find the positive side of this. It was not a pretty cup and thus this gives me the opportunity to design one more to my liking." She smiled. "But that is for another day. Now, I am excited to meet hop-hops who can talk."

"Just let me get you a drink first." Kebeck handed Sheme a cup with relief designs of a river flowing through vines in greens and blues. "This was my grandmother's cup." Prigo brought out a pitcher of cold water and poured some for Sheme.

"Thank you, my friend. Letting me drink from this old family cup is proof that our friendship is still strong. Now, can I meet these creatures who talk?"

They all sat in a circle and introductions were made.

"Please tell us about your people," Kebeck said. "We were amazed that you are able to live in the ice mountains. What planet are you from?"

"Here. This planet you call Palala, we it call Ume. We're not aliens."

Kebeck, Sheme and Pirgo looked confused.

"It's like this," Mera said. "As your people were evolving here in the jungle, we were evolving amid the hot spring valleys in the mountains. Our scientists say you became sophisticated earlier than our people and because of that you were ahead of us technologically."

"But we caught up with you," Tom interrupted. "Being warm- blooded we were able to explore the jungle and observe your advances. We learned much from you."

"You mean you copied our technology?" Sheme's brow became furrowed and her neck was turning red. "So you have been hopping around stealing our ideas and systems for years... for centuries?" Sheme's voice was becoming harsh and loud.

Kebeck put one hand on one of Sheme's arms and with two other hands he removed his cup from her hands."What?" She glared at Kebeck and pushed his hand away.

"You are getting upset and there is no reason to, really."

"You do not mind that they have been stealing from us?"

"Tell me, how did it hurt us that they watched and copied methods of farming, or systems for refining ore into steel or learned how to build computers? They took nothing. They just observed and copied. And from what I saw of their cities, they seemed to have modified and improved some things."

Sheme sighed, "But they didn't ask. They have been sneaking around and spying on us for... forever."

Mera groaned.

The three Palalans eyed her and waited for her to speak.

"We were afraid of you. You are so big and strong, and you have four arms. You don't eat meat now, but centuries ago your ancestors would have probably eaten ours. Your people ate several animals to extinction before you became civilized."

"But, you have no reason to fear us now."

"So you say," replied Mera. "Look how angry she became when she found out that we copied your technology."

"Sheme is just one person. Most people will not react so... rashly."

"Your country is run by a democracy with everyone voting. We don't know how the rest of your people will react when they find out about us?"

Kebeck wanted a minute to think before saying more. He stood up. "Can I get anyone food or drink? We have some very good hava fruit."

Only Tom replied, "I would like to try some of those, please." Kebeck brought over the bowl of fruit and sat back down. "Here is what I suggest. Prigo, Mera, Tom and I spend the night here and in the morning we all go meet with with Nacoo and Solong at the Foreign Planets Office to discuss introducing our Ume friends to the people of Palala."

"What about me?" Sheme asked. "And why is this being handled by the Foreign Planets Office?"

Kebeck took a breath. "Because we thought they were aliens. Sheme, since you met the Ume by accident and because you are not part of the official group selected to deal with the Ume, I am going to have to ask you to go home and keep their existence secret until we make a formal announcement. Will you do that? Please?"

Sheme huffed. "If I must."

CHAPTER

93

EARTH

Jane was standing by the open door when Senoa-lo arrived. "I'm sorry to ask you to come out so late. I thought we could fool my mother, but it didn't work. So I need to ask you to come and meet her. She has some questions."

Senoa-lo slowly entered the room while carefully looking around. She had found Jane and Ava easy to get along with. *But they are immature humans. Would an adult human be different?*

Senoa-lo moved to the center of the room. She stood tall and straight in front of Jane's mom and said, "It is nice to meet you, Mrs. Thomas. I am Senoa-lo. I am the leader of a delegation sent to earth to gain knowledge of certain aspects of earth culture. We mean no harm to you or anyone on your planet. We only seek knowledge and nothing else. *I must be careful to say enough to satisfy this human, but not mention WMDs.* Your daughter has been very helpful. The ship that brought us here was supposed to land in the place you call Florida, but it landed here. I think your homeland is very nice, but it has aspects that has made it difficult for us to live here. We were not prepared for the cold that kills green plants. Jane has supplied us with food and a warm place to stay. I commend you on raising a child that is considerate and intelligent."

Jane's mom smiled. "Thank you. Would you like to have a seat? And would you like something to eat or drink?"

Leela-lo held up half of a cookie. "They have some really good cookies."

Senoa-lo smiled. "A cookie would be pleasant."

Jane said, "I'll get the cookies." Then Jane helped Senoa- lo up on the couch beside Leela-lo and left to get the cookies.

Mrs. Thomas turned her head to one side like a curious puppy. "I asked Leela-lo about your research and she said that I should ask you about that. What are you here to research?"

Senoa-lo took a breath. "First, I would like to tell you about my people and our planet. My people, the Ume, evolved around hot spring valleys in an area of steep icy mountains. We are warm-blooded vegetarians. We have never eaten the flesh of other animals. In the past, we had wars with Ume in other valleys. That was long ago and now all Ume on the planet are united under one peaceful government.

Near the equator of our planet is an area of hot jungles. The Palalans live there. They are cold-blooded, with four hands and scales instead of fur. They are very big, almost as big as an adult human. In the past, they ate other animals, and they had wars. But hat was centuries ago. Now, they only eat plants and they have organized into one democratic government. The Palalan have always been more sophisticated than the Ume. Because we are warm blooded, we are able to survive in their jungle. We have been able to present ourselves as mute unintelligent animals and watch them in order to learn from them. Because they are cold-blooded, they never ventured into our valleys in the ice mountains."

"You say these bigger beings are advanced. Then why haven't they discovered you?" Mrs. Thomas asked. "I don't understand how the Palalans could not know that there were others on their planet? Would they not have explored their planet?"

Senoa-lo took a second. "I have read that on your earth, there are parts of your oceans that you humans have not visited."

"That's because the ocean is very deep in places and we would not survive at those depths."

"Then you can understand that in the past the cold-blooded Palalan did not explore the ice mountains because they could not have survived there. But now that they have invented a heated suit, we have seen them stomping around the edges of our mountains."

Ava smiled. "Maybe we'll find another civilization at the bottom of our ocean. That would be fantastic."

Neither Senoa-lo nor Mrs. Thomas were amused.

Jane had been standing in the doorway listening. "So the Palalans think you are inarticulate harmless furry little jungle animals."

"Yes. For centuries we deceived them. But now that has changed and they have seen our cities and, well, we are scared."

"What have they done to scare you?" Mrs Thomas asked. "Have they killed any of your people or threatened you?"

Jane handed Leela-lo and Senoa-lo cookies on napkins and sat down to eat her own.

"No. We haven't had any direct communication with the Palalan yet. It is not what they have done. They have done nothing but watch us from afar. We fear what they might do. Thus far we only know that they have recently become aware that we are much more than mute dumb animals. They have seen our cities."

Jane looked confused. "So why do you fear them?"

Senoa-lo put down her cookie. "We have researched your history and the history of several other planets. In every case, powerful people conquer and dominate weaker people. You call it *the law of the jungle*. We have no reason to think that they will not conquer and enslave us."

Mrs. Thomas studied Senoa-lo. "You said you came here to do some type of research. Does your research have something to do with your problem with the Palalans?"

Senoa-lo paused and took a breath. *She is not going to like this, but I don't want to lie.* "Yes. We came here to find plans for a weapon that our people can build. We are helpless against the Palalans. It is our only hope."

Jane's cookie fell out of her hand and broke into pieces.

Mrs. Thomas jumped out of her chair and glared at Senoa-lo. Then she turned to Jane. "Did you know about this?"

Jane was down on the floor and picking up the cookie bits.

"I… , no, I didn't know. They just said they were doing research on their computers. I had no idea that they wanted to make a weapon."

Leela-lo stood up on the couch. "You don't understand. The Palalans can easily kill us all. They are very big and we have nothing to defend ourselves with!"

Mrs. Thomas slowly sat back down and stared at the floor. Everyone was silent. Jane took her napkin full of cookie crumbs to the kitchen and came back with a broom and dustpan. Jane's mom stood up. "Here's what we're going to do. It's late. We are all going to bed now. Tomorrow, after work, I want to continue this conversation. Aliens! Four-handed scaly people! Ice mountains! Weapons! This is too much. I need to think."

94

PALALA

Kebeck and his son, Prigo were up before sunrise. The young Umes still seemed to be asleep in the corner. "I have contacted Nacoo and Solang," Kebeck said. "They are to meet me and these two hop-hops at the Foreign Planets Office. I did not mention that they can talk. If I had, they would have drowned me in questions." He paused. "My son, I know that you are supposed to be at work today. Can you change your schedule and accompany me and the hop-hops to this meeting?"

"I thought you only wanted government officials involved with these people from the ice mountains. I am just an engineer."

"I know these two appear to be harmless and friendly. But it is possible that they are not. Since they are so different from us, I cannot tell if they have been telling the truth. I cannot swim to the office with these two. I doubt that with all that fur they would be able to swim. So, we will have to walk. If one or both decide to run away, I would not be able to catch them. And I do not feel comfortable restraining them with ropes. I want to keep a friendly relationship with them. It is possible that they will be key to setting up a relationship with their kind. So will you go with us?"

With a broad smile, Prigo said, "I was hoping that you would ask me to go with you. This is so exciting. Your colleagues at the Foreign Planets Office are going to be so shocked to actually meet hop-hops who can talk."

Tom overheard this and whispered to Mera, "As we walk with the big one to his government office, we could run off in two different directions and at least one of us might get away from him."

Mera considered it for a second. "As far as we know, we still don't have a weapon to threaten them with. So I want to go with them and learn more about their intentions. They have been very nice to us thus far."

Tom frowned. "You're too trusting. They have the might. We have nothing. They could enslave all of us. I want to get back to our people and find out whether your father's group on Earth have sent back plans for a WMD. The earth beings are very violent and have many weapons. For all we know, our people are building some earth weapon as we speak."

Mera whispered, "We came on this mission to the jungle to find out what the Palalans are doing. We weren't learning anything sneaking around in the bushes. So I plan to go with Kebeck to his meeting. I want to hear what they have to say."

"Did you ever consider that they might torture us? And, don't tell them anything unless they ask a direct question. You're way too chatty. And don't tell them anything about weapons.

"I don't think… "

Kebeck interrupted with a loud, "Hey, I see you are awake." He walked over to them. "Want something to eat before we head out to the office?"

There was very little chatter as they ate some fruit and washed up. Tom whispered to Mera, "When I give the signal we run."

Mera stared at him, then shook her head. *No.*

As soon as they were a little distance from the house, Tom caught Mera's attention and motioned toward the bush. Mera glanced to see if either of the Palalans were watching, then shook her head. *No.* Tom made a face and kept walking.

CHAPTER

95

UME ON EARTH

It was quiet in the shed. After returning from Jane's house, they gathered and discussed their situation, then lay down to sleep. But no one was sleeping. Jolocko-lo was still worried about his daughter. No one had heard from her since she had entered the Palalan jungle. But from a bug planted in the Foreign Planets office, the Ume had learned that some Palalans had captured two Ume. When that message was relayed to Jolocko- lo, he couldn't decide how he felt about the news. *If she was one of the ones captured, then I know she is safe and has not been eaten by some jungle animal. But how safe? We have never heard of the Palalans hurting any animal… ever. Well, not in the last century or two. I don't think they would hurt her, but if they see us as an enemy, would they torture her?*

Before laying down, they sent messages home. Senoa-lo sent a message to her associates on their home planet explaining that it had been necessary to have the assistance of some earth beings in order to survive on this part of the planet. *Telling our people at home all the details about Jane's mother will serve no purpose. Better to be vague.* And she informed them that they had not yet discovered an earth WMD that could be built with the resources available on their world.

Jolocko-lo was adamant that because of the war and conflict on earth, they should trust no one on this planet. He was quite angry that Senoa-lo had been willing to meet with Mrs. Thomas. Leela-lo reminded him that they had to eat and thus they had to rely on some of the humans.

"I must impress on you that we must keep working to find a viable WMD," Jolocko-lo reminded them. "The Palalan government is aware of us and they haven't done anything aggressive yet. Nevertheless, we don't know what will happen when they inform the public of our existence. I am concerned for my daughter, but I cannot let that hinder our mission. She would want me to continue to work for the safety of our people."

Leela-lo kept quiet. She was reluctant to mention that poison in the water was a possible weapon. She had been raised to believe that water was sacred. The whole Ume nation revered the hot springs that made life possible. The thought of sullying that hallowed element was unthinkable.

By dawn, Senoa-lo had devised a plan. In the afternoon, she would go alone to meet with Jane and her mother. Jolocko-lo was to stay in the shed and continue his research. Toboo-lo and Leela-lo were going to pack up a computer and some supplies and head off to hide in the woods. If Mrs. Thomas decided to turn them in to the government, at least two of them would still be safe and might be able to continue their work.

The sun was low in the sky as Senoa-lo approached Jane's house.

96

PALALA

It was a long walk to the Foreign Planets Office. It would have been a short swim, but the Palalan didn't think to ask Mera and Tom if they could swim. The two Ume spoke very little. Prigo asked many questions about where and how the Ume lived. But after a few short answers, he gave up.

"We are almost there," Kebeck told the Ume. "When we arrive you will meet Solang and Nacoo. Solang is a language expert. She heard recordings of your people speaking in the bush and was the first to suspect that you could talk. Nacoo is the head of the Foreign Planets Office. I think she is the appropriate official for this situation. We really thought you were from another planet. You are, sort of, well, foreign."

Kebeck opened the door and the four of them trooped into the office. Both Solang and Nacoo came to greet them. Kebeck introduced them to his son, Prigo, Then with the wave of a hand and a little bow said, "Meet Mera and Tom."

Mera stepped forward and held her hands in the usual Palalan greeting. "Hello, I'm Mera."

Solang's eyes grew wide and her chin dropped. "You speak Palalan?"

"Yes, not very well, but I can get by. I'm still in school. I also know some of the Earth English."

"Amazing. How did you learn English?"

"From watching Earth television."

Nacoo shook her head and stared. "This is truly stunning. You can understand that when we saw your cities, we assumed that you were from some other planet. It is unbelievable that we have shared this planet with you for so long without meeting you. I have so many questions. But first we must be good hosts. Would you like a drink or food? You had to walk a distance to get here. Please relax on a slant board. Do you use slant boards? Or do you prefer to sit on the floor? We have cushions." Nacoo was talking so fast that no one had a chance to get a word in.

Kebeck put a hand on her shoulder. "Slow down. I know you are excited, but give them a chance to say something."

Mera smiled. "I would like some fruit and water. And I would really like to try one of your slant boards. We use chairs at home."

Nacoo turned toward Tom.

"Water and fruit would be nice. I am tired. I'll just sit on a cushion on the floor."

When everyone was comfortable and munching the bowls of fruit provided, Tom lifted a cup in a mock toast, "Let the interrogation begin."

Nacoo's smile faded. "We only ask that you tell us about your people in the ice mountains. We mean you no harm. Of course we want to get to know the people who share our planet."

Tom put his cup down with a loud thunk. "You captured us, kept us prisoner overnight and now you want us to reveal everything about our people. I will not be a traitor. I appreciate your food, but I will tell you nothing."

"Why?" Prigo asked. He looked at Nacoo. "I am not part of this official committee, but may I participate?

She nodded. "I see no problem. We are just becoming acquainted with a neighbour."

Prigo continued. "We are just curious about your customs and your lifestyle."

"And why your people have chosen to hide from us for so long?" Nacoo added.

Mera got off her slant board and stood behind Tom. "You don't understand. Compared to you, we are small, very small. When our people first came to explore the jungles, your big four- armed people still killed and ate animals. Little ones like us. You wiped out several species before you became vegetarians. And your technology was more advanced. We learned how to make steel because brave people dared to sneak into the jungle and watch how it was done. Your jungle is dangerous. It contains animals that would eat us, but dare not come near a Palalan. Many courageous people died by coming here to learn things that enabled our people to keep up with yours. Now we can just use our computers to hack your computers. You might have noticed that you don't see as many hop-hops as you used to. And after we got electricity, the jungle animals weren't much of a problem. We were able to defend ourselves with these." Mera reached into her vest and pulled out her charger.

Nacoo was startled. "Where was that? How can you hide it under your fur?"

Tom stood up and removed his vest. "We wear garments that look like our fur so that we can carry supplies and chargers without you Palalans seeing them."

Solang held out a hand. "May I see that? How does it work?"

Mera turned the charger around and handed it to her. "It emits an electrical shock. We can set it to stun or kill."

Solang examined it. "This would be perfect when one comes across one of those big stinging worms on a path."

"A moment ago, you said something about hacking into our computers. Are you saying that you are able to access all our communications?" Nacoo asked.

Mera and Tom looked at each other. *What should they say?*

She had heard that the Foreign Planets office was bugged. How would these Palalans react if they knew that a Ume was listening to everything said in this room.

CHAPTER

97

EARTH

The last bit of light was fading from the sky when Senoa-lo walked up to the door at Jane's house. She glanced up. There was no way she could reach the doorbell. She stepped out into the yard and picked up a rock and threw it at the door. After the third rock bounced off the door she saw that she had Jane's attention. Jane peeked through the glass panel beside the door and waved at her. Then the door opened. "Welcome. I see you've come alone. Come in and have a seat. Mom will be down in a minute." With Jane's help, Senoa-lo climbed up on the couch. She looked around the room. *I'm relieved that there are no Mounties or police here to take me away.* Beside her on the couch she noticed a tray with cheese and crackers. *Nice.*

Mrs. Thomas came down and eased into the chair across from the couch. She put her glass of wine on the little table beside her. "Well, we have a lot to talk about. Before we start, would you like something to drink or some food besides the cheese?'

"No thank you. Cheese is my favorite earth food. This is very nice."

"Senoa-lo, I think you can understand that I find myself in a uniquely awkward position. I am totally thrilled to meet someone from another world and you seem very nice… people. But when I hear you speak of weapons… " She closed her eyes and shook her head. "It scares me. You say that your people feel threatened because the other people, the Palalans, have become aware of you."

Senoa-lo nodded.

"And you are doing research here to try to find some kind of powerful weapon that your people can make on your planet."

"Yes. We hope that we will never have to use the weapon. We just need it so that we can show the Palalans that they should not harm us because we would have a weapon capable of destroying parts of their world."

Jane's mom sighed and let her chin fall."You can understand that I would feel very uncomfortable helping you find a weapon that could kill thousands of beings. I don't want to be part of helping you kill or harm anyone."

Senoa-lo pulled her shoulders back. "Yes, and I assume that you would feel dreadful if you were to hear that the Palalans killed thousands of us because we had no weapons to prevent their attacks."

Mrs. Thomas sighed again.

"I am not asking you to help us with our research. I only ask that you allow your daughter to continue to provide food and a secure shelter for us for a bit longer. And WiFi. We must have WiFi. We don't eat much. We can stay in the shed and you won't even know we're here. Please?"

"One more week. But only if you promise that you will do nothing to harm anyone on earth while you're here. I don't want you experimenting with weapons here. And in a week we will discuss this further."

"Thank you."

This time Jane sighed, It was a sigh of relief. "Mom, I suggest that we let our Ume friends stay in the house instead of that shed behind Ms. Collins's house. They would be more secure here. They can stay in the empty bedroom. I'm afraid someone might notice my visits to the shed and… "

"You're right. They can stay here. I'd feel terrible if someone discovered them and called the police or worse… the military."

Jane's mom stood up and approached Senoa-lo with her hand out.

"Oh, a hand-shake. I have seen these in movies. This seals an agreement." Senoa-lo put her tiny furry four-fingered hand in Mrs. Thomas's and shook.

As Jane helped Senoa-lo off the couch, she said, "That went well. Later tonight, I'll get my wagon and a box and we can bring everyone here." She peeked out the window. "There's no moon tonight, so this is a good time to sneak you all into the house."

CHAPTER

98

PALALA

The silence in the Foreign Planets office was becoming uncomfortable. Nacoo stood up and got herself a cup of water. "Anyone else want water?"

Mera said, "I would like some water please." Nacoo moved toward Mera to ask for her cup when she realized that that was probably a mistake. *Why should I expect these two foreigners from the mountains to carry cups with them.* Just as she was turning to go look for a spare cup, Mera reached into her furry vest and said, "Here is my cup." She held out a pretty little cup, with a handle that looked like a vine.

Nacoo took it and examined it. "Lovely." The tiny ceramic cup was covered with a mass of delicate flowers. "Is this a family cup?"

Mera smiled. "No. It was made for me when I was born. But, like you, we all carry our own cup with us."

"So you have some customs similar to ours?".

Mera nodded. "We have many customs akin to yours. The most important one is that we both revere water. It has always been foremost in our lives. In the old days, many worshipped a water god. Now, very few people believe in gods, but we all hold water to be sacred."

"What kind of national government do you have? Is it similar to ours?" Solang asked.

"Our government is a little different from yours. Every two rotations of the planet, we elect representatives to make our laws. There is one representative for every thousand people. Unlike you, we prefer to let them run things instead of everyone voting on every detail. We observed your system and found it cumbersome to require everyone to be knowledgeable on so many topics. But, like you we have committees to deal with certain topics."

"Are you part of the committee assigned to spy in the jungle?" Prigo asked.

"No," was Mera's quick reply. "I'm still a student.

We... ," she nodded toward Tom. "Some of us think the government isn't doing enough about the Palalans discovering our cities. We decided to come see for ourselves."

Kebeck smiled. "So you two are are not here representing your government. You're just youngsters who sneaked off to see what the neighbors are doing. Do your parents know where you are?"

Tom broke in, "I am an adult and I do not report to my parents. I have an computer science degree and a job."

Kebeck glared at him. "Then shouldn't you be at work instead of sneaking around here?"

"You don't understand. We feel that our existence is threatened by you Palalans. I felt it my duty to do something." Tom's shoulders slouched. "But it seems that I have failed."

Kebeck turned to face Mera. She looked down at the floor. "I'm sure my father is worried."

Nacoo picked up a map of the ice mountains. "Mera, about your father? Which city is he in? We might be able to send him a message to tell him you're safe."

"That would be difficult. He is away on a mission for the Palalan Committee."

Kebeck asked, "What does the Palalan Committee do?"

Mera hesitated. "It is a government committee in charge of… " She looked up at the ceiling. "Spying on your people."

"Observe might be a better word," Tom interjected. "They observe your people and report on new inventions, technology and political changes, and… well, everything Palalans do."

'Why?" Prigo exclaimed.

"So we can keep up with your technology."

Mera held up a hand. "But, don't think that we are just imitators. We have inventions that you never thought of."

"So there is no way to reach him to tell him that you are safe?"

"Safe?" Tom shouted. "How can we be safe here? We are your prisoners. I have watched Earth TV shows. First, you are nice to us then the torture begins and then you will kill us."

Nacoo threw her upper hands up and shook her head. "We do not torture or kill. And you are not prisoners. We just want to talk to you. Maybe you have watched too much Earth TV."

Tom stood up. "I wish to leave now. If you mean us no harm, then can I leave?"

Nacoo stepped in front of him. "Not yet."

"Oh, then we are prisoners!" He dropped back down on the cushion.

Kebeck peered at the two Ume, the turned to Nacoo. "So what are we going to do with these two?"

Nacoo motioned toward the door. "I think that you and I and Solang need to step outside for a brief discussion."

EARTH

The rain drummed against the windows of Jane's old house. Everyone gathered for breakfast. The sky was unusually dark for nine in the morning. Jane and Ava had put stacks of big books in the chairs for the Ume to sit on. Usually, Jane hated rainy Saturdays. But she was smiling because now she had an excuse for spending the Saturday in the house with her alien friends.

Mrs. Thomas sat at the head of the table. "Senoa-lo, I think it would be helpful if we got to know each other a bit better. Do you mind a few more questions?"

Senoa-lo stopped chewing, looked around at her fellow Ume and swallowed. "What would you like to know?"

Leela-lo perked up. "I have questions about you humans. Can I ask… ?"

Jane's mom interrupted, "Of course. Ask anything."

"I have watched earth movies and TV shows." Leela-lo explained. "Why do earth males desire to see young females without clothing, but not old ones? The young males get quite excited about the idea of a nude young female. And I do not see females seeking to see young or old males without clothing."

Jane and Ava giggled. Mrs. Thomas put her fork down and glared at them, then thought for a second. "It's chemistry. Human males have more testosterone in their bodies. It works in their brains to make them seek young healthy mates to produce young. When the female is without clothing, the male can see that she is healthy for childbearing."

A little smile crossed Jane's face. She leaned over and whispered to her mom, "Well done. I didn't know what to say."

"Now a question for you. Do your people have gods or religions?"

"Not really. Centuries ago there were several gods. The most popular were the sun and water gods. Now, we revere and honour water. It is the essence of our lives. We meditate in clear water when we want to feel at one with the planet. We see no reason to think that there is anything beyond reality."

Ava interjected. "Do the other people on your planet, the Palalans, have religions?"

"They also venerate and cherish water. They had no gods for many centuries, but now a few have decided to worship

Earth gods. But we think it is just a passing fad caused by the Palalan spending so much time watching Earth TV. But their respect for water is the most important aspect of their lives. The common greeting when Palalans meet is: 'I wish you clear water.'"

"What a pleasant way to greet people." How do your people greet each other?"

Senoa-lo stood up and held her hands in front of her body with her palms facing Jane's mom. "Like this and like you here on earth, we usually say, 'How are you?' I think that phrase has one meaning for us and a different meaning for humans. On our planet, it asks if you are happy. Here, it seems to be an inquiry about one's health."

"Are you not concerned about the health of your friends?"

"Yes, but their happiness is much more important. Also, we consider ailments of the body to be private. So it would not be polite to ask about your body."

Ava held up a hand. "Speaking of what is polite, would it be impolite to ask your age?"

Senoa-lo smiled. "No, we are proud of our age. In earth years I am about 150 years old."

They all gasped.

Jane's mom said, "You look young."

"I'm approaching middle age."

"Really? So what is the life expectancy of your people?" Jane asked.

"Let me think. Our year is a bit longer than yours. So, about three hundred of your earth years."

Again, they all gasped.

"Wow! Do the Palalans also live so long?" Ava asked.

"No. Their life expectancy is about two hundred earth years."

That made Jane think. *And we're lucky if we live to a hundred.* "It would be fantastic to see what life is like 200 or 300 years from now." Her thoughts were interrupted by the sound of little feet on the stairs. Jolocko-lo stopped at the bottom stair with a broad smile on his face. "Senoa-lo, we have a message from home. Can you come up?"

Senoa-lo turned around and wiggled down off her chair. *Jolocko-lo is smiling. He must have heard good news about his daughter.* "Excuse me. I'm needed upstairs." She and Jolocko-lo rushed up the steps.

100

PALALA

A misty rain cooled the air as Solang, Kebeck, and Nacoo stepped out on to the porch in front of the Foreign Planets Office. "I suggest that we keep these two young hop-hops… "

Solang interrupted Nacoo, "They call themselves Ume."

"As I was saying, I think we should keep them here overnight as guests, then escort them to the edge of the jungle tomorrow morning. I don't want to start our relationship with the Ume on a negative note, but we need to learn more about our neighbors in the ice mountains."

Solang nodded in agreement.

Kebeck stretched his upper arms up over his head, pulling them up to loosen his tense shoulders "We haven't asked them about the note in the spaceship yet."

"We'll get to that later today. But first I think we should just ask casual questions about their way of life. Agreed?"

Kebeck and Solang nodded.

"Now, lets get back to our guests." The three went back into the office.

"Can we get you anything else to eat or drink?" Nacoo asked.

Tom said nothing, but Mera held out her cup. "I'd really like some more of that red juice please."

"It's from a fruit we call Sabon. Do they grow in your country?" Prigo asked.

Kebeck smiled at his son as Prigo and the little Ume discussed different fruits they liked. *He could be a diplomat. He seems to know that it is best to first find common ground before moving to the difficult subjects.*

Nacoo sat down on the floor beside Tom. "Why are you afraid of us?"

Tom huffed. "It's just logic. Big jungle animals eat small animals."

"Do you not think that we Palalans are smarter and more sophisticated than wild animals?"

"Of course." He huffed again. "I know you're not going to eat us. You only eat plants. But you might capture our people and make us your slaves."

Nacoo's shoulders drooped. "Why would we do that? We don't need slaves. More importantly, we strongly believe that it would be wrong to make any sentient being or animal into a slave."

Tom glared at Nacoo. "We don't know what you plan to do with us. But it is logical to study what your people have done in the past and the history of other civilizations to determine what we should expect."

"Tom, how long have your people been sneaking around in our jungle studying us?"

Tom looked down at the floor. *It will do no harm to answer her.* "We first started watching you during your iron age. You taught us how to make metals. We lost some people to the jungle animals and some were eaten by your early people."

"Sorry about that." Nacoo's neck turned pink. "That was thousands of years ago. Of course nothing like that could possibly happen now. I am sure that you are aware of the fact that we quit eating hop-hops and other jungle animals long ago. How can I reassure you that we mean you no harm?"

"You could let us go."

"We plan to do that tomorrow morning. Since some parts of our jungle are still wild, it would be safer if we accompany you to the area where you entered the jungle. Will you be all right getting back home from there?"

Tom nodded. "Someone will be watching for us and will pick us up and take us home."

Kebeck turned to Mera. "You mentioned that your father is on a Palalan committee. If you could tell me where he is, we might be able to send him a message and start some kind of communication with your people."

"That is a great idea," Nacoo added. "It sounds like he is the appropriate person to contact about establishing a relationship between us and your people. It would be advantageous to both our nations if we were able to contact him?"

"That will be difficult." Mera pursed her lips. "He is on a mission on Earth."

All four of the Palalans were astonished. Words tumbled out, interrupting each other. "How did they get there? What kind of mission... ? You have space ships? Where are... ? Do the humans know that they are there?"

101

EARTH

Jane and her mom watched as Senoa-lo hopped up the stairs behind Jolocko-lo. When they got in the bedroom that contained all their equipment, Jolocko-lo grabbed Senoa-lo's arms and jumped with joy. "Leela-lo says Mera is alive and relatively safe."

"Wonderful!" Then her smile turned into a frown. "Relatively safe?"

"Headquarters has been listening to conversations at the Palalan Foreign Planets Office. We have it bugged. Mera was captured in the jungle and is there along with a fellow named Tom. They have not been harmed and the Palalans say they will take them to the edge of the jungle and release them tomorrow."

"She has not been tortured?" Senoa-lo asked.

"No. They have not touched her."

"Then why did they apprehend her?"

"They say they just want to know more about us. The Palalans have been very nice to her and her friend. One of them was concerned that I might be worrying about Mera."

"And," Leela-lo added, "The one who seems to be in charge wants to contact Jolocko-lo about establishing a relationship between us and the Palalans."

"Why me?" Jolocko-lo asked. "How do they know my name?"

"Mera told them that you are part of a committee charged with dealing with the Palalans."

"Oh."

Senoa-lo tilted her head and thought for a second. "I need to hear the tapes of what was said in the Palalan Foreign Planets Office. Then we can decide whether we should communicate with the Palalans. Leela-lo, please have our people send that." She paused. "Does the head of Foreign Planets have the authority to speak for the Palalan people?"

"Yes," Leela-lo said. "A Palalan called Nacoo is the head. She alone can decide how to deal with foreigners. And by their definition, any being that is not a Palalan is a foreigner. If she decides that a topic is questionable, she can put it out on voting day for all Palalans to vote on. Otherwise, she determines what kind of relationship to set up with foreigners. The Palalans have explored other planets four times. Each time, she opted to have no relationship with the beings on those planets. One of the planets had a major war in progress. Two were too primitive to communicate with. And she decided that Earth was too violent for a relationship.

No Palalan is allowed to communicate with an Earth being. But she decided to let the people watch Earth for amusement. It was decided that they could watch Earth for fifty years. During that time a group of scientists was assigned to study Earth and the Palalans who watch it. Their study is also supposed to determine if Earth watching is detrimental to the Palalan people. That study is almost done and the vote on whether to continue watching Earth will be taken in a few years."

"I hope they vote to continue watching," Toboo-lo said. "I really enjoy it. Since our viewing system is reliant on their system, if they disconnect we would be cut off." Toboo-lo slouched down in his seat.

"You'll survive." Senoa-lo glared at him. "Now back to a much bigger problem. Leela-lo, the minute you get the recording of the conversations in the Foreign Planets office, let me know. We will gather and listen."

"I suggest that… " Jolocko-lo offered. "we invite Jane and her mother to listen with us. One of the Palalans wants to contact Jolocko-lo about establishing a relationship between us and the Palalans. After we hear this recording we will have to decide if we should contact them. Since we have become quite antagonistic toward the Palalans, an unbiased party might be of value here."

Senoa-lo was silent while she examined the possible positive and negative aspects of his suggestion. "I will allow it. Mrs. Thomas seems to be an astute thinker and Jane is very intelligent for her age."

"She's smart for any age," Leela-lo added.

"It would do no harm to have them listen with us. Leela-lo would have to translate it into English for them. Can you do that?"

"No problem," said Leela-lo. "I will write it in English as we listen. Then they will be able to hear the Palalan's tone of voice as they read the words."

Two hours later, Jane, her mother and the Ume gathered around the Ume receiver to listen to the recordings of Mera and Tom talking with the Palalans in the Foreign Planets office. When the recordings ended Mrs. Thomas was the first to speak. "I was wondering about your government. Is there a head official that has the final say on things?"

"Yes," Senoa-lo replied. "Our Juku. It means 'decider' in Ume. He is elected by our representatives. When there is a topic that any selected committee is uncertain about, they contact the Juku. Now that we have heard the Palalans, our committee members here and on our planet will have a discussion via radio and decide on a plan. If we have any doubts about our plan, we will contact the Juku for a decision."

"You asked us to listen and give our opinions," Mrs. Thomas said. "I think you should communicate with the Palalans now. A few days ago you mentioned needing a weapon. Hearing that, it seems that you were considering war with the Palalans as an option. Is that still the case?"

"No!" Jane exclaimed. *Since I'm still a student and this is a really serious topic I should probably keep quiet. But I can't.* "My history teacher says that most of the time, war is the result of a lack of communication. Please, talk to the plalans before this goes any further."

And they did.

Senoa sent a message to the Ume government representatives and presented her case for opening talks withe Palalans.

Basically, she said,"We have no weapons, but we don't need them because the Palalans do not see us as any kind of threat." It was decided by a majority vote that she be allowed to contact the palalans. After a few weeks of negotiations, agreements were reached that Ume people are welcome to visit Palala and that, the Palalans are welcome to visit in the Ume valleys.

In a speech broadcast to the Ume, Nacoo said, "The fact that you borrowed, or imitated our method of refining ore into metal and adopted other aspects of our technology did not in any way affect the lives of the Palala people. So who cares? We Palalans are not concerned. Your actions did not harm us or the planet in any way. We wish all creatures happiness and we look forward to getting to know you."

Breaking Down the Wall So dear readers we now cease the, 'they thought... and he said... then she said... and they decided' to round up our tale of aliens and Janes and war and peace by telling you that the Ume and Palalans decided to give peace a chance.

Jane never dated Hoop, but they remained good friends for many years. Hoop went on to play professional football for two years. Then he was injured, but he had been wise with his money so he was able to live a comfortable life on his savings and investments.

Ted grew up to become a famous scientist. He had quirks, but he was also an expert on quarks.

Jane's mom continued dating Mr. Fitzgerald, spending Saturday and Wednesday nights at his house. He wanted to marry her, but she refused. She didn't want to give up the freedom of having her own house, her own schedule and, most importantly, the possibility of having the Ume living with her.

Although she liked Mr. Fitzgerald very much, she didn't trust him the to keep the Umes hidden from the world. She told Jane, "They're as cute as puppies, very intelligent and great conversationalists."

Jane and Ava remained friends for the rest of their lives. Ava married and had three kids and sold real estate. Jane got her doctorate in dendrology and married a botanist. She and her husband both teach at Yale.

Mera and Tom went their separate ways after their jungle adventure. Mera talks to her dad back on Earth by interstellar radio once a week.

Kebeck stayed friends with Sheme. They play on a waterball team. He and Nacoo are talking about parenting a child together.

The three stooges who pestered Jane all through school managed to stay out of prison. Bart actually graduated from high school. George got serious, worked hard and became a doctor. Anthony sold drugs and drove a flashy car for a few years, then disappeared. When they drained the canal for repairs, they found his body and several stolen cars.

Because they were scientists and scientists have to study something, the Ume stranded on Earth decided that they wanted to stay to study Earth customs and research some Earth inventions. They stayed at Jane's house for some time before the Palalans sent a ship to bring them home. And what happened during their stay at Janes's house? Well, that's another story or the next book.

THE END

www.ingramcontent.com/pod-product-compliance
Lightning Source LLC
Chambersburg PA
CBHW031157310726
48969CB00001B/123